"An attractive, extremely readable combination of conventional thriller and 'serious' lit. This ancient town is peopled with colorful characters, and Zack meets many of them in his quest for his missing son-in-law. Many blows and bullets are exchanged, but the real drama here is about what might happen to a depressed man in middle age who has lost his taste for life."

—*The Washington Post*

"Mewshaw is one of the best American novelists, a master of plot and style at the top of his form. *Shelter from the Storm* is a first-class read and a fine accomplishment."

—Robert Stone

"*Shelter from the Storm* . . . is timely, provocative, and powerful. The sights, sounds, and smells of his exotic Central Asian location are palpable, as are the random violence and confused loyalties of its inhabitants. There is something stunning on every page."

—C. J. Box

"The action kicks into high gear and speeds through several brutal hairpin curves to its end. . . . This is the sort of intelligent and morally ambiguous thriller—like those of Craig Nova or Paul Watkins—that offers a welcome change from typical fare."

—*Library Journal*

"A timely, stylish international thriller."

—*Publishers Weekly*

"Shocking, occasionally moving, and always compelling . . . Mewshaw harnesses every ounce of his considerable writing power to bring to life a nightmarish tableau replete with petty barbarism, hopeless schemes, and desperate scrambles for freedom."

—*Booklist*

"I can't understand why Michael Mewshaw isn't one of the most beloved, bestselling writers in America . . . stunning stuff." —*Fort Worth Star-Telegram*

*continued . . .*

Praise for the work of
# MICHAEL MEWSHAW

"A fabulous and unforgettable novel of extraordinary depth."   —Pat Conroy

"Mewshaw has an instinct for subjects in which something human and crucial is at stake. His honesty and his insight . . . are utterly convincing."
—Larry McMurtry

"A poignant piece of invention with very firm and lucid writing. Such solid construction, such fluency, such totally credible characterizations make for memorable work."   —Anthony Burgess

"Mewshaw has a remarkable sense of place."   —Graham Greene

"Mewshaw has inventiveness . . . Once you start reading, you keep on."
—Robert Penn Warren

"*The Toll* is the best novel I have ever read about southern Morocco."
—Paul Bowles

"Rich characterizations and fluid storytelling make for an entertaining and special book by a wonderfully gifted writer."   —Oscar Hijuelos

"A book I have recently admired is *Life for Death* by Michael Mewshaw. [He] tells the tale . . . very movingly and with a fine sense of moral indignation."
—William Styron

"Drama, action, pace, solidly intersecting characters and unflagging interest. The richness of shadow and dimension, which only a gifted novelist can offer."   —George Garrett

"Michael Mewshaw is a writer who knows things, and reading him is sheer luxury. He doesn't slow down for the curves, and there are plenty of them."
—James Salter

"A remarkable evocation of people, a landscape, a way of life and . . . religious experience. I would cheerfully put some money on Mewshaw's future."
—C. P. Snow

BlueHen Books · *New York*

# SHELTER
*from the*
# STORM

*Michael
Mewshaw*

BLUEHEN BOOKS
Published by The Berkley Publishing Group
A division of Penguin Group (USA) Inc.
375 Hudson Street
New York, New York 10014

This is a work of fiction. Names, characters, places, and incidents either are the product of the author's imagination or are used fictitiously, and any resemblance to actual persons, living or dead, business establishments, events, or locales is entirely coincidental.

G. P. Putnam's Sons hardcover edition: March 2003
BlueHen trade paperback edition: March 2004
BlueHen trade paperback ISBN: 0-425-19375-6

The Library of Congress has catalogued
the G. P. Putnam's Sons hardcover edition as follows:

Mewshaw, Michael, date.
Shelter from the storm: a novel / by Michael Mewshaw.
p.  cm.
ISBN 0-399-14988-0 (acid-free paper)
1. Americans—Europe, Eastern—Fiction.   2. Security consultants—Fiction.
3. Europe, Eastern—Fiction.   4. Middle aged men—Fiction.
5. Fathers-in-law—Fiction  6. Kidnapping—Fiction.  I. Title.
PS3563.E87S54      2003                    2002074640
813'.54—dc21

Printed in the United States of America

10  9  8  7  6  5  4  3  2  1

*Again, with love, to Linda*

*And to Gene Scott, who made
straight my paths in Central Asia.*

Can you walk on water? You have done no better than a straw.

Can you fly through the air? You are no better than a gnat.

Conquer your heart—then you may become somebody.

—Khwāja Abdullah Ansāri of Herat (1005–1090)

*Book*
*One*

*T*he wolf boy, the wild child, the strange feral creature appeared early one spring as the iced-over streams started to crack and the blown snow on the steppes was melting. In that place whose history, in its most objective rendering, read like a conflation of myth, magic and madness, and where recent events were so turbulent and improbable that any future, or no future, seemed possible, each sign was seen as an omen of potential catastrophe.

The first villagers to spot him kept their distance and watched warily. These were mountain people. They lived with their livestock in huts—dank, cave-like and carved out of rock. Having just wakened from what amounted to months of winter hibernation, they imagined the boy to be a dream-memory or a lingering shade from the spirit world. It was the custom of their clan to butcher animals on feast days and dress the bloody carcasses in human clothing. Then they wrapped themselves in animal hides and cantered about disguised as beasts. Legend had it that their ancestors descended from a she-wolf that mated with a man in the Heavenly Mountains. To this day when a baby was born heavily downed with hair, the villagers believed a *yeti* had been among them. So while the wild boy worried them, it didn't so much shock as fascinate them to see him lap water from the communal trough. Silent and stock still, they let him drink and attempted to take his measure.

He was naked, down on his hands and knees. Steam rose in ripples from his bare, weather-browned skin. Bony and misshapen, he might have been mistaken for a cripple, with long stringy arms, claw-like hands and prehensile toes. Yet he moved with lupine grace, and there was a wolfish narrowness to his face. When he caught their scent and jerked up his head, he gazed at them through tilted, agate-colored eyes. Then he whirled around, low to the ground, and disappeared downhill, draining out of their lives and leaving them to the laborious process of assimilating what they had witnessed into tribal lore.

Down on the treeless plains, wind was constant, and people studied it as a sailor would the sea or an aviator the sky. Whenever it blew from the mountains, it was glacial and brought killing frosts and blizzards. When it swung around from the opposite direction, it combed across a thousand miles of desert and carried tons of airborne dust. Wind from the west stank of oil wells and chemical plants, insecticide and fertilizer. The villagers preferred the familiar smell out of the east, an aromatic reminder of horses that had endured ever since the armies of their ancestors arrived a millennium before, bearing nothing but weapons—no art, no skills that weren't martial and only a single maniacal idea: that battle, not building; destruction, not creation, was man's fate and final legacy. These warriors rode for days, sleeping in the saddle, soothed by the susurrus of waist-deep grass that parted and closed behind them. They didn't dismount even to eat. They opened slits in the necks of their horses and drank the blood. This left their lips rouged like a whore's. Myth had it that their leader, Genghis Khan, came from the congress of a wolf with a deer.

The men who lived here still rode horses and they spotted the wild child with a pack of pariah dogs. Starting off on all fours, he built speed in a few strides, then raised up and ran on two legs. It didn't seem to them that he was being chased. Yapping like a puppy, he frisked and howled along with the rest of the pack. A mane of lank hair streamed from his head. Dark tufts sprouted from his back, spiked as the bristles that roached up on the spines of the growling mongrels.

The men mounted up and pursued the boy. To them this was like *buzkashi*, a brutal variant of polo played with a hundred and fifty riders to a team and a dead goat in place of a ball. The boy, too, appeared to regard it as a game—a darting, dervishing pageant that men and animals participated in together. The riders later claimed they couldn't catch him. They coursed the steppes and never gained on him. They said that he remained tantalizingly beyond their grasp, a chimera at the edge of the earth. A few admitted that they didn't care to catch him. They were afraid that once they had him in their hands he would change into something else.

Their terror was as nothing, however, compared to the panic that already gripped cities throughout the region. Wracked by food riots, violence between ethnic clans, turf wars between drug lords and Islamic fundamentalists, they also suffered a ferocious backlash from the Russians who had been stranded there after the Soviet Union disintegrated. Everyone was armed, and each night, along with darkness and a slight diminishment in the heat, there came eruptions of gunfire. Sometimes this signaled a bank robbery or revenge killing, sometimes a mafia wedding where guests shot off automatic weapons in drunken exuberance.

When the wolf child stumbled into this petrie dish of urban disasters, the fear was that he carried disease. Typhus, polio, leprosy and plague—illnesses long thought to have been eradicated—spread through the poorest neighborhoods, and new scourges seemed inevitable. Scavengers at the garbage dump claimed they had seen the boy eat meat too rotten and tainted for any human being. Families found him in their gardens stealing apples and cherries, and they drove him off with stones. He was accused of killing chickens and rabbits, snatching lambs and calves. Some said he disemboweled them, gobbled only their internal organs and abandoned the mutilated carcasses. Others argued that he didn't just consume farm animals, carrion and road kill. He dug up graves and devoured the dead.

Too frightened and befuddled to deal with the boy themselves, people did the unexpected. They appealed to ragtag remnants of the army. Normally, the accepted wisdom was to avoid soldiers at all costs, but this was one emergency when military firepower might help them. The terrified populace figured that if the wolf child were flesh and blood, not some ghostly figment of fevered imagination, troops could shoot him down.

The next time he materialized at the garbage dump, a team of soldiers was waiting for him. They harried the boy out onto the salt flats where blinding white crystals had hardened into a crust. It buckled under his weight, and his feet stove through the surface into damp silt. That slowed him down and exhaustion finally stopped him. A swollen pink tongue lolled from his split lips. His rib cage pumped and deflated and pumped again, each anxious in-suck of air pressing his skin tight against the wickerwork of bones.

Although they had him in the crosshairs of their rifles, the soldiers didn't fire. They could see how skinny and sick and scared he was, just a kid of eleven or twelve, with bleeding sores on his elbows and knees. Dirt, whorled and closely woven as a garment, covered his nakedness from head to foot. Cuts on his chest and face had healed over without having been cleaned, and grains of sand tattooed the scar tissue in beaded hieroglyphics. What they had taken for hair tufted down his backbone was actually mud and matted grass.

For all the ungodliness of his appearance, the men believed they knew what he was—a shell-shocked survivor from the battalions of boy soldiers, a member of one of the massed divisions of cannon fodder that had been routinely dispatched to the front lines in the recent war. After a day of religious indoctrination and no military training, the kids were ordered to march across miles of open fields while, following in their footsteps at a careful distance, the regular army kept to the paths that had been cleared by these unwitting minesweepers.

Miraculously, a small number of them came through the carnage and knee-deep gore more or less alive. But they were hollow-eyed and unhinged. Wailing prayers and imprecations, jibbering *suras* from the Koran, they stripped off their uniforms and fled naked.

The soldiers thought the boy was one of them—a mute remnant from the human wave, too wasted to do anything now except kneel in animal resignation waiting for whatever befell him next. If they brought him to the barracks, they hoped that might bring him back to his senses. But he shocked them by resisting help. When they tried to touch him, he bared his broken teeth, hissed and arched his spine. Rearing upright, he lashed at them with his hands, raking their arms and faces, tearing off ribbons of skin and leaving splinters of his filthy fingernails in their flesh. He bit them. He head-butted and bowled over one man and gnashed at his throat. It took four of them to pull him off. Then they beat him unconscious with a canteen.

They trussed him up in chains and tossed him into an armored personnel carrier. On the clattering ride through the countryside and the barely smoother and quieter drive over a road potholed by weather and war, he clanged around on the metal floor. Whenever he started to stand up, the soldiers knocked him flat.

At a military cantonment, they carried the boy into an empty cage in the guard dog kennel and unchained him. Dogs in neighboring pens barked and hurled themselves at the bars, eager to get at him, sample his smell, challenge him, fight him. But as he climbed to his feet and circled the cage, they fell quiet and watched with confusion. One instant he had appeared to be an animal, the next moment something approximating a man.

He struggled to squeeze between the bars, then seemed to remember that he had hands. Squatting on his rump, he fumbled at the gate, fretting with the lock. He rattled and scratched it, but in the end went back to being an animal. He bit the lock, and when that didn't break it, he wheeled in frustration and paced the cage. His fingernails scraped against the concrete floor as if against slate. He swung his head from side to side, sniffing the air, snapping his teeth. His shoulders twitched, shaking off flies. Others promptly replaced them, roosting on his lips and eyelids and open sores. He didn't bother to bat them away.

He began to whine and whimper, then fell to his hands and knees and arched his backbone. An abrupt fit of coughing turned to convulsions and he retched and vomited and fouled himself. What fell out of him at either end wriggled with pinkish-white worms.

A soldier fetched a fire hose and drove the boy into a corner. The high-pressure spray cleaned the mess off the floor and scoured the mud and weeds off the kid. Now he was truly naked, and resembled a sable peeled of its pelt. The man aimed the hose between the boy's legs. To protect himself, he grabbed his genitals and screamed. This gave his captors an idea, something to do during dead stretches of the day. Whenever the kid calmed down, they stirred him up with the hose.

That night they got drunk and dragged one of the camp whores to the kennel, tossed her into the cage and told her to fuck the wild child. When she refused, they hosed them both down. The jolting force of the water ripped the woman's clothes off and flattened her against the kid. He sank his teeth into her naked shoulder. The soldiers got a laugh out of this—until the boy's bite drew blood. They had to rush into the cage and pry the two of them apart.

As the soldiers resumed drinking, there was general agreement that the kid must be truly crazy and hadn't been in the army after all. Otherwise he wouldn't have attacked the woman or spat out the vodka they force-fed him.

Bored, they abandoned the kennel, taking the whore back to the barracks. The boy crept over to the gate and discovered that they had left it unlocked. Within seconds, he was out of the cage and had clambered over the cantonment fence. Racing through fields of brick rubble, he heard the roar of wind and the howl of penned-up guard dogs in his ears.

He advanced in darkness toward the center of town and the Grand Mosque. A minaret of blue ceramic tile inlaid with gold leaf roiled in moonlight so that the elegant calligraphy that encircled its cylinder appeared to revolve. The gilt letters quoting the Koran were of a size and shape that suggested the legendary beasts—griffins, basilisks and horned seahorses—on an antique carousel. High up in this glittering alphabet jungle, a guttural voice gushed from the minaret, beckoning the boy on.

By now he was very sick. He had cankers on his throat, and it tormented him to swallow or breathe. Scrabbling for food in a trash bin, he fainted, and that's where the woman found him.

She was tall, with sun-freckled skin and long reddish-blond hair. She might have been mistaken for a Russian, but she was American, in her mid-thirties. Faint vertical lines crimped her upper lip; crow's-feet at the corners of her eyes deepened as she squinted at the boy. She had seen starving children in the streets before, but none who looked like this—naked, his hands and feet clawing the ground like a dog lost in a dream of running. She had heard the stories. Her neighbors saw it as their obligation to warn her of all rumors of danger. Still, she scooped up the wild child and carried him into her house.

*T*he flight from Frankfurt started its slow descent to Central Asia hours before dawn. As the plane bumped down through layers of buzzing sand, Zack McClintock was tempted to signal the flight attendant to bring him another drink. But he wanted to arrive sober and realized that alcohol wouldn't help him digest the contents of the report that lay open on his lap. Eddie Diez, his business partner and best friend since their days at the Naval Academy, had done an exhaustive job of intelligence gathering, all in the service of a two-word piece of personal advice: "Don't go!" Eddie didn't insult him by dwelling on the dangers or emphasizing Zack's lack of preparation, and of course he didn't mention the missteps that had caused so many problems several years ago in Switzerland. He simply pointed out how unprofessional it was to get involved on his daughter's behalf, particularly when this put Zack at odds with U.S. government policy.

Rather than read Eddie's report again, Zack filled in the landing card and took a crack at the three-page customs form. It demanded that he list the weapons, ammunition and narcotics in his possession. It also insisted he itemize the precious metals, stones and foreign currencies he was carrying. Finally it asked for an invoice of antiques, art, jewelry, manuscripts, film, stamps, seeds and animals, "including raw foodstuffs of animal origin and slaughtered fowl," that he wished to import.

Zack scribbled a zero next to each question except the one about foreign currency. After some hesitation, he declared what he was carrying loose in his pockets—a thousand dollars in cash. Even that low-ball amount left him feeling like a fat target arriving in a country where the average income was two hundred bucks per annum.

With a headset clamped over his ears, Zack screened out the drone of the plane and the hum of his worry and tried to lose himself in music. Channel five of the in-flight entertainment featured classic jazz, a program introduced by a pedantic DJ who praised the genius of Miles, Cannonball and Coltrane. The man reminded him of an engineering class at Annapolis, some dull lecture about distance, speed and method of propulsion. Zack would have switched channels had a muted trumpet not sounded the first distinctive notes of "Stella by Starlight."

This, too, reminded him of the Academy, of evenings after lacrosse practice when he lay on his bunk, pleasantly biding his time until dinner, listening to WMAL in Washington, D.C. Back then, jazz had been his one act of rebelliousness, the lone symbol of protest that he allowed himself. After graduation he meant to go into the Marine Corps, which, in turn, meant going sooner rather than later to Vietnam.

At fifty-five, he still had the raw-boned, rangy build of a midfielder. Although his body had given in grudgingly to gravity and had thickened a bit around the middle, he hadn't lost much from his chest and shoulders. He worked at it. He went to the gym and he watched what he ate. It pleased him that he didn't look like the type of man who did the bulk of his work these days at a desk, someone who hadn't gotten his hands dirty in the field for almost a decade.

In the Virginia suburbs where he lived, plenty of fellows his age were retired on military pensions, and Zack McClintock might have passed for one of them. But contrary to his plans and preference, he hadn't made a career of the Marines. After a second tour of duty in Vietnam, he returned to the States to raise his daughter Adrienne. By then, Eddie Diez had established a small firm, International Assessment, which specialized in risk analysis, corporate security and private investigation, and he was delighted to let Zack buy into the business.

While he couldn't claim that his life had panned out as he would have wished, Zack kept things in balance as a bike rider does—by moving forward. He regarded himself as someone not overly given to regretting the past, musing about the future or unburdening himself in the present. He even joked about his job. He maintained that his most exciting moments came at a computer terminal and he referred to himself as a librarian rather than a gun-for-hire tracking foreign terrorists and chasing politicians who absconded with the national treasury. To anyone who would listen, Zack counted himself lucky. A lot of people were dead and he was alive. That, he said, was the baseline he built on.

The only problem was, as much as he attempted to keep it to himself, he did have a tendency to brood that he couldn't always disguise, and there were moments when his temper got the best of him. After Zack flew home from Geneva in what he conceded was pretty poor shape, Eddie had suggested that he see a counselor. Going against the grain of his instincts, he submitted to a few sessions with a psychologist who sought to persuade him that his foul moods were anger turned inward and that, unconsciously, he felt it was better to be sad than mad. To which Zack snapped, "If you ever made me good and mad, you'd damn well wish I'd stayed sad." In the end, though, he agreed to take a prescription that, despite its side effects, rounded off his rough edges and got him back on his bicycle, diligently pedaling through the ups and downs of middle age.

The ride suddenly became bumpier when Adrienne announced that she was getting married. Given the degree of their closeness, Zack would have cast a cold eye on any man who fell in love with his daughter, but in the case of Paul Fletcher he was convinced that there was more to his misgivings than fatherly possessiveness. Fletcher, a childless divorcé almost twenty years older than Adrienne, had a smarmy, insinuating manner and the oleaginous charm of a toothy telemarketer.

A professor of plant pathology at a university a hundred miles south of Washington, Fletcher no sooner returned from the honeymoon and settled Adrienne into his house than he signed on as a consultant to a non-governmental organization and accepted a six-month posting to Central Asia, where the political situation was too unstable for his wife to accompany him. When Zack objected, Adrienne said, "But, Daddy, I thought you'd be proud of Paul. Professionally, it's a terrific opportunity. He's doing something he loves that'll help people there and here."

"What exactly is he doing?"

"It's secret. He can't tell me."

"I hate the idea of you being left alone while your husband is way the hell and gone in a place like that."

"You left Mom twice to go to Vietnam."

This touched a raw nerve, and he took a moment before saying, "I didn't have a choice. That was a war and I was a soldier."

"But you're the one who chose to be a soldier."

He couldn't very well argue that. Still, he was tempted to and might have if he hadn't cared so deeply about his daughter. For over twenty years she had been the center, the lynchpin, of his life and he couldn't bear to risk alienating and losing her.

Months later, when Adrienne called in tears to tell him that Paul had been kidnapped by Islamic fundamentalists who demanded a million-dollar ransom, the news sliced through Zack like a razor blade. For an instant, his arterial system shut down. All blood and thought drained out of him. When his heart started pumping again, pain sank deep and rooted in soft tissue. He knew what it was to lose somebody you love. His wife, Adrienne's mother, had died while he was in Vietnam.

As Zack would have predicted—it was, after all, his job to know such things or to have sources who did—the United States refused to negotiate for Paul's release. Government policy forbade dealing with terrorists, and the State Department could do little more than register diplomatic objections and decry international lawlessness.

Neither Paul's university nor the NGO that had retained him on a temporary basis showed any readiness to pony up the ransom. Zack couldn't blame them. He shared their doubts that a million bucks would insure his safe return. Although Adrienne begged him to help, there was nothing he could do. Events every day in Somalia, the Sudan and the Caucasus argued against optimism, but he couldn't bring himself to tell his daughter that. He urged her not to give up hope. He urged her to talk to somebody just as Eddie had urged him. Without any mention of his own prescription, he urged her to take something to lift her spirits and let her sleep. Meanwhile, he and Eddie tried, to no avail, to work through back channels.

When a second ransom letter changed the terms of Paul Fletcher's release, Adrienne declared that no pill or therapist could convince her to wait a day longer. If forced to, she would fly there herself to bargain for her husband's life.

"Honey," Zack reasoned with her, "there's no proof that whoever wrote this letter can deliver what they promise. The State Department has people on the ground. They haven't come up with a thing. Not a single lead."

"I don't care. Even if he's dead, I have to know. I won't stop until I find out what happened."

It was then that Zack McClintock decided to leave his desk and go back into the field.

*T*he plane landed in darkness, and he stepped out of the sterile womb of Lufthansa into waves of swirling grit and insects. The sky swarmed with strange constellations; the air thrummed with unintelligible languages. Yet when he drew his first breath, he recognized the smell, the ripeness. Along the perimeter of the runway, men hunkered down on their heels as if struck low by the heat. They reminded him of Vietnam, of all the looming shapes at the periphery of his vision that had either worked for him or against him, or both, back in Saigon.

He boarded a peculiar people mover—a broken-down, driverless bus towed by a tractor. It crossed the macadam crowded with German business-men in suits bagged at the knees and accordion-pleated at the elbows, Ameri-can oil roughies in blue denim and ball caps, and a few French speakers in windbreakers marked *Médecins sans Frontières*. Far from the standard antisep-tic airport, this one allowed no room for the cozy illusion that he hadn't left home. Ragged soldiers armed with Kalashnikovs patrolled the terminal, and a trooper guarding the entrance to the baggage claim area pored through every page of Zack's passport. Furrowing his fierce scimitar eyebrows, barely able to restrain the rage of his incomprehension, he shoved Zack through a metal detector, jerked him back, ordered him to empty his pockets of keys and loose change, then pushed him through again.

Zack didn't take kindly to being manhandled. Waiting for the conveyor belt to cough up his suitcase, he stood apart from the other passengers and at-tempted to get a grip on himself. Exposed wires and rusty pipes sagged from the ceiling; fluorescent bulbs blinked in random semaphore; the stone floor slanted toward a reeking drain. Incoming luggage went through an X-ray ma-chine while passengers went through a second metal detector and ID check. Zack followed the Green Lane—NOTHING TO DECLARE—which dovetailed into the Red Lane, funneling everybody into a holding pen where customs of-ficials insisted that he register his wristwatch as jewelry and made him count out his thousand dollars and show the contents of his shaving kit.

He did as instructed. He couldn't give them an excuse to frisk him and find out what else he was carrying. A plastic vial of his pills caught their attention. An officer sprinkled the two-toned green and cream tablets onto the counter and demanded to know what they were. To any American—for all Zack knew to everybody in the airport—they were easily identifiable. Embarrassed that he depended on these Yuppie chill pills, he had difficulty explaining and felt a dull thudding at his temples.

The man showed him a list of approved prescription drugs. Zack's wasn't on it.

"Fine," Zack said. "Keep the fucking things."

*O*utside on the sidewalk a man, unmistakably American, jawed a stick of gum. As Zack headed toward a cluster of cabs and drivers, the man followed him.

"Mr. McClintock," he called, "the First Secretary sent me. I have a car waiting." He took Zack by the elbow.

Already rankled, Zack said, "Don't go doing that, grabbing my arm."

"Sorry, the First Secretary suggests—"

"The First Secretary of what?"

"The U.S. Embassy."

"We don't have one here."

"We have a consulate." The fellow flashed a diplomatic passport. "The First Secretary suggests a courtesy call."

"Courtesy to me or to him?"

"*Her*. Ms. Pearson's expecting you."

He wasn't surprised. Zack had made no secret of his trip, and since the country required a visa, there was every prospect that the State Department had been alerted. To preserve its neutrality, International Assessment generally avoided official debriefings when entering or exiting a country, but in this case Zack thought it wouldn't hurt to have an update on Eddie's report.

He let the American stow his suitcase in the rear of a Chevy Blazer. The two of them sat up front. The doors swung shut with the metallic *thunk!* of a safe deposit box. Riding high on heavy duty shock absorbers and tall cleated tires, the Chevy was armor-plated, and its tinted bulletproof windows had wavy distortions at their edges.

The road from the airport cut through outskirts that resembled rural areas in the American southwest. Scrawny vegetation sprouted on land that looked like it had been fired in a furnace; streamers of trash and plastic bags fluttered from thorny branches. Discarded hulks of farm machinery—or was it military equipment?—rusted in empty fields. At this hour, there were few people about, but bony cows and goats cropped the grass on traffic islands.

Near the city's center, the streets widened and were broad enough for a tank to heel around and have clear lines of fire in all directions. Blocks of gaunt, gloomy apartment towers appeared to have suffered recent bombardment. Concrete slabs crumbled from façades, cornices had collapsed, and railings and drainpipes drooped from smoke-scorched walls. In monumental parks, busts of Soviet heroes lay shattered beside their pedestals. Statues constructed of sterner stuff had had their heads and arms amputated, and wires jutted out of their extremities like straw from a scarecrow. Massive billboards that once exhorted citizens to exceed the annual quota or gloated that the affairs of the State were in the hands of the proletariat now advertised Hollywood cigarettes, Toshiba computers and Korean appliances.

Bouncing over abandoned railroad tracks that sprouted fibrous weeds between their ties, the driver sped away from the whelming desolation of the modern town and its toppled leaders, and entered a neighborhood of narrow lanes lined by birch trees and colonial cottages. The huddled streets meandered as if replicating the pattern on a prayer rug. Above them, elevated on iron struts, pipes padded with insulation served as a crude diagram of the quarter.

"Were you around when the Red Army evacuated?" Zack asked.

The fellow quit chewing his gum and leaned his head back in a soundless pantomime of laughter. "Evacuated, my ass. Sneaked away is more like it. Nobody ran them out. The people voted for the Russians to stay. They split anyhow."

"I thought there'd been trouble."

"Not much here. The big bang-bang was up-country, near the border."

They came to a compound whose surrounding walls bristled with razor wire and broken bottles. The driver beeped the horn until a uniformed Marine rolled back a gate. They pulled into a courtyard that was canopied with chicken wire to prevent outsiders from lobbing surprises over the walls. Atop each building, a satellite dish had been set out on the roof like a saucer of milk for a cat.

The Marine escorted Zack into a foyer littered with American magazines and newspapers and effervescing with Muzak. It might have been a doctor's waiting room. But as they advanced toward the business end of the building, one enclosed space succeeded another, each lead-lined and sealed off from the chaos outside.

Ms. Pearson waited in a windowless room that had a telex, a fax, a computer and a television tuned to CNN. Stock prices scrolled across the screen. Take away the electronic hardware and the place reminded Zack of a room in Geneva where he had endured a prolonged and memorably unpleasant interrogation.

"Thanks for stopping by." Ms. Pearson didn't stand up, but she presented him her dry, hard hand to shake. It was five o'clock in the a.m. and she was dressed for success, dressed to kill, in high heels, a smartly cut blue skirt and a blazer over a white silk blouse. Turning off the TV with a remote control, she motioned him to a chair.

"You make an American feel welcome and right at home," Zack drawled.

"We don't see many Americans in this neck of the woods." She glanced at a clipboard, then up at him. She had grey eyes, nicely mascaraed. "So we try to touch base with those that pass through."

She cut her eyes back to the clipboard, which he assumed contained information about him. While she studied it, he studied her. Parted down the middle, her hair, dark at the roots, grew out in sun-streaked tresses. She had a smooth pale complexion that suggested she didn't spend much time in the sun. She was forty, maybe a little older, and quite attractive. In the decades since he had been widowed, Zack wouldn't claim that he had become a connoisseur, yet he had learned a little about women, mostly from his daughter. He wondered what career detours had floated Ms. Pearson to this forlorn spot. And why did she imagine that a brisk, all-business manner suited her?

"You've had an interesting career." She spoke like one of those phone company reps who interrupt your dinner and officiously inquire whether you're satisfied with your current long-distance service. "Two tours of Vietnam, a couple of decorations, an honorable discharge, then work in the private sector." She let a pencil point guide her down the page.

"Except strictly speaking—" she experimented with a smile and crossed her legs, "—I suppose almost nothing these days is strictly private sector."

"Call this personal. I'm Paul Fletcher's father-in-law. That must be in your report."

"Yes, and you're here to look for him. Why? Is there something you know that the State Department doesn't?"

Zack crossed his legs, too. Stiff from the long flight, his knee and hip joints cracked. His body had become dry kindling. "Lately the State Department doesn't appear to be doing a lot of heavy lifting."

"Really? Is that what you and your daughter think? I'm disappointed to hear that. We have limited on-site personnel, but we've done our very best."

"Correct me if I'm wrong, but you haven't responded to the latest ransom letter."

"We don't put a whole lot of credence in that letter, Mr. McClintock."

"My daughter and I, you won't be surprised, we take a different view. That's why I'm here—to explore other avenues."

Ms. Pearson frowned. She had a distracting habit of doing this each time he spoke, as if she were lip reading. Or as if she were many moves ahead and impatient for him to catch up. "I don't know how close a watch you keep on events in the former republics of the Soviet Union," she said. "But kidnapping's getting to be a growth industry. In Chechnya, four British communications workers were taken captive and their families gave up on official channels and decided to negotiate for their release." She paused for emphasis, for maximum effect, before spelling out what he had learned from Eddie Diez's memo. "They found their heads in a potato sack on the side of a road. For your own good, I hope you're not carrying ransom money."

"Got it right here in my pocket." Zack grinned and patted his chest. "A million bucks."

Ms. Pearson didn't pretend to be amused. "Then I trust you're armed. Because if the mafia doesn't grab you, the mujahedin will, and you'll be in the same fix as Fletcher—chained to a radiator somewhere reading the Koran for the next few years."

"Is that who you figure has him?" He wanted to get away from her formulaic cautions and establish a few facts. "Some Moslem sect?"

"To tell you the truth, we're not sure anybody has him now. We can't be one hundred percent certain that there actually was a kidnapping."

She laid the words out in a throw-away line and left it for him to bite or not. He bit hard. "What are you implying, Ms. Pearson? That Paul's involved in some sort of scam?"

"I don't mean to upset you or your daughter. But as you know from your own work we have to consider all the possibilities." Her pencil was moving over the clipboard again, like an oscilloscope. "Even good men have weak moments."

"You really think he's demanding a million-dollar ransom and planning to pocket it himself?"

"That's one theory. A potential scenario we've discussed."

"A theory that was shot full of holes by the last letter," Zack pointed out. "It doesn't mention money this time. Just a straight trade. Fly some kid to the States for treatment and Paul goes free."

"As I told you, we're not convinced that letter is legitimate."

"There's an easy way to find out. Medevac the kid and see what the other side does."

"You know we can't do that, Mr. McClintock."

"I don't see how it violates U.S. government policy to make a humanitarian gesture and provide treatment for a child."

"It's not just a question of one kid. Uncle Sam doesn't have pockets deep enough to solve the world's problems. And we don't have the time to persuade people that we didn't cause their troubles in the first place. It's an unfortunate political reality, but countries like this play next to no part in our national interest. The U.S. maintains a presence only to make sure they don't play a part in somebody else's interest."

"Okay, I hear you. My own interest doesn't go beyond Paul Fletcher. So unless you have information that'll help—" He started to stand up.

She waved for him to sit down; she wasn't finished. "The best information, my best advice, is to think this over. Do you have any idea what Fletcher was doing?"

"As I understand it, he was running an agricultural project. Some sort of research funded by his university and an NGO."

"No, he was on sabbatical from the university. He hadn't taught there in a long time. For the past few years, he'd been working wherever his expertise applied and was getting paid by an independent endowment."

Zack skipped a few moves ahead. "Was he on your payroll?"

"Not precisely," Ms. Pearson replied with perfect precision. "The distinction may not matter to you, Mr. McClintock, but it does to us. We outsource a lot of our, let's say, speculative projects. That spreads around the risks as well as the rewards."

Zack waited. She would volunteer more or she wouldn't, and if she did, he wanted to devote as much effort to listening as she did to choosing her words.

"Despite the shortcomings of the Soviet Union," she went on, "they did some remarkable R and D in the 'Stans. You know, we joke about these sinkholes at the ends of the earth. What kind of place is it, we ask, where you can't tear the toilet paper but the money falls apart in your hands? But you shouldn't overlook the brainpower the Russians brought in.

"They did groundbreaking nuclear research in Central Asia. They developed intercontinental ballistic missile systems. They got a jump on us in the space race. Granted, they flubbed their toxic waste management and ruined their water reserves. They dried up half the Aral Sea and reduced millions of acres of arable land to salt. But agriculturally speaking, as lousy as they were at producing and distributing food to the population, they were on the cutting edge when it came to destroying crops."

"Destroying crops? Are you talking about defoliants, Agent Orange, that type of thing?"

"No, they had something much more sophisticated in the works. Before the economy cratered, they built a state-of-the-art lab that was on the brink of producing a pathogen that could attack specific targets, specific foliage, without killing other organisms."

Zack shook his head, confused.

"Think of it as a neutron bomb to use against enemy farms and food supplies," she said. "Then think about the wider applications. What if, for instance, there was a fungus that could wipe out poppies and not damage different crops?"

"The DEA would be a bunch of sad pups."

"Sad?" Now Ms. Pearson was perplexed.

"They'd be out of business."

"Yes, they and a lot of other people. Fletcher came here to direct the program." As she warmed to the subject, she set the clipboard aside and leaned forward. "The hope was if we sprayed this fungus over the Golden Crescent and killed heroin at its source, we wouldn't just be getting drugs off the streets of America. Terrorists on the right and left, fundamentalist sects, they bankroll their operations by smuggling and dealing dope. We'd be cutting them off at the knees."

"Sounds to me like Paul's the one that got cut down. The wrong people found out what he was doing and kidnapped him. What kind of security did he have? Who was working with him? Has anybody been up there to check out the lab?"

"The lab was firebombed," she explained with elaborate patience. "We don't know who did it."

"Sounds like a no-brainer to me," he said. "The same guys that grabbed Paul torched the building. Did you expect them to let the fungus grow on a back burner until you flew in a replacement? Catch them and you catch the kidnappers."

"Please, Mr. McClintock"—she shut her eyes, paused a beat and opened them—"you're jumping to conclusions. Anybody could have blown up the lab. Up-country, there's no infrastructure, no one in charge except armed gangs. Whatever happened, all we've heard are reports from local sources, and they're not reliable."

"Are you telling me you don't have your own people in place?"

"Not now. Naturally after Paul disappeared, we 'coptered out the rest of his staff."

"I take it that means nobody's gone back to check on this kid they're offering to trade."

"We followed up as best we could by satellite phone. Indirectly we made contact with an American woman, a former Peace Corps volunteer."

"Indirectly?" he broke in.

"A source spoke to her and called us. The child is in her care. But the general agreement is she has her own agenda. Or should I say her own problems? She claims the kid grew up in the wild and was raised by dogs or wolves. She wants to take him to the States to have him studied."

Zack sagged in his chair.

"You see what we're up against?" Ms. Pearson asked. "With all due respect to you and your daughter's feelings, we don't see any sense in debriefing a woman who believes she's babysitting a wolf boy. Not with the airport out of commission and bad guys lobbing mortars onto the runway."

"Isn't there a road?"

"What's left of one. Sometimes it's mined. Sometimes soldiers set up roadblocks and shake down traffic. As we evaluate the situation, it's not worth the risk—especially since the consensus is that Fletcher's probably dead. On the other hand, if he's alive, and you find him, we'd like to talk to him."

"I bet you would."

"We'd make it worth your while," she said.

"What if he's dead and I bring back his body? Will you make that worth my while?"

When she didn't answer, Zack pushed to his feet. Ms. Pearson stood up too. She was shorter than he had expected, though no less attractive and no less assertive for her size. "I meant what I said about carrying a weapon. Go to the bazaar and buy some protection. They sell everything from bazookas to satchel charges."

"I'm a peaceful, low-tech guy."

"Look, Mr. McClintock, it's up to you whether you listen, but I at least want to warn you. One thing the collapse of Communism accomplished, it opened up business on an equal opportunity basis. Everybody's out to get rich or get even or just get what you've got. And they're not very particular how they go about it. That's the secular crazies. The religious nuts are a whole other story."

"I've had experience in Moslem countries."

"I've read your sheet, Mr. McClintock. Nothing you did in Algeria or Iran applies here. What we have, Sunnis against Shi'ites, is the easy part. A month back we had a massacre with Wahhabis executing Hazaras, slaughtering them Halal-style." She drew the pencil along the line of her pearl necklace, demonstrating how the Wahhabis slit throats. "They left the bodies in the street and let dogs eat them."

"Thanks for the warning. I'll take care of myself."

Raising her chin, she indicated the clipboard on the arm of her chair. "After what you went through in Switzerland, I certainly hope you will."

"If you don't mind," Zack said, "I'd like to go to my hotel before I fall asleep on my feet."

*B*ut he came out of the U.S. consulate wide awake. The air had the texture of splintered glass. It lodged in his throat along with Ms. Pearson's barbed reminder of a blunder that would haunt him until he died. He felt a stomach-flipping sensation and feared he was out of his depth. From the start he had been aware that Paul might be dead, and he dreaded bringing the news to Adrienne. But he had never suspected his son-in-law might be off on some greedy frolic. He didn't feature breaking it to his daughter that her husband was trying to con the government or his university or them out of a million dollars.

"Back to the airport?" the driver asked as Zack climbed into the Blazer.

"The hotel."

Sunlight seeped through the streets, tinting the pale dust like blood drops dispersing in sour milk. Pedestrians on their way to work spilled off the sidewalk and onto the street. Shepherds and cattle drovers snarled traffic at intersections where ancient buses, listing under the weight of passengers, belched clouds of blue exhaust. Voices, horn-blasts and screeching brakes were muffled by the Blazer's bulletproof windows, but everywhere in Zack's field of vision undulating letters in Cyrillic and Arabic screamed for attention. On mosques and minarets, on boarded-up apartments and dilapidated army barracks, graffiti in Russian and the local dialect overlapped like flowering vines laced through the iron staves of a prison fence.

One word Zack recognized—Change! Change! It flashed on currency kiosks and banks. Everything in the world was changing, and he had to change with it. He had to think, and more than that, think in a fashion that contradicted his deeply ingrained ideas about the former U.S.S.R. How had he, how had the whole country, lived in terror of this pathetic backwater? Was it really possible that Third World squalor had sustained a First World army?

The driver parked flush with the hotel entrance and removed the windshield wipers before unlocking the rear hatch of the Chevy. "We're in a place," he explained, "where the supply of sticky fingers exceeds the availability of spare parts."

"I'll carry my own bag." Zack didn't want to walk in joined at the hip with this gum-jawing American.

"Suit yourself, pal. Hope you're wearing a jockstrap."

*U*nder its thin icing of Islam, the hotel remained unmistakably Russian with stained wood paneling, polished samovars, carpets bolted to the floor by brass rods and potted palms fizzing with flies trapped in cobwebs. Zack might have been entering a mausoleum where some Party leader's embalmed corpse had been laid to rest. A lugubrious young lady with a full set of silver teeth checked him in. She refused to accept a credit card or any currency except dollars and told him the rooms had no telephones, televisions or hot water.

He noticed on the counter, under plate glass, a line of typewritten advice to English-speaking guests: "All transaction is occurring solely in the existence of paper that confirms your present personality."

The woman didn't bother glancing at the passport he handed her. She must have surmised that she knew enough about his personality.

His room smelled of smoke—wood smoke, not cigarettes. The babushka in the hall cheerfully told him that there had been a fire last week. All the rooms smelled that way. She warned him to be careful of soot when he hung his clothes in the closet.

A lone window framed the lurid havoc of the eastern horizon where towering gothic shapes piled up in a succession of cloud cathedrals that accentuated the drama of the sunrise. The sky looked impenetrable, and Zack couldn't conceive of an airplane plowing through it, back to where he belonged. He shut the drapes on the bruised light, but couldn't silence the mournful sound of wind that piped through the window fluting.

After splashing cold water over his face, he dried off with a towel that reeked of smoke. Even the sheets and pillowcases smelled scorched. He stretched out in bed, as if in a desolation of ashes, and couldn't sleep. He felt he was still on the plane, suspended on thermal currents sweeping across Central Asia. His body had arrived, but his soul and what remained of his heart were lost in transit. He tried to count the 'Stans between him and where he came from. A futile exercise. He replayed the conversation with Ms. Pearson and computed the permutations implicit in her warnings. If he found Paul alive, he doubted that she'd let either of them fly to the States without a debriefing. At best, he had to be prepared for an interrogation like the one he underwent in Geneva. At worst . . . He worried what the worst might be.

3

*I*t used to be that each morning when the caterwauling of the *muezzin* roused her from broken sleep, Kathryn Matthews couldn't remember where she was, why she was here, or how she came to be in this predicament. Even after she was out of bed and shakily on her feet, the best explanation she could offer was a quote from the Koran: "Does there not pass over every man a space of time when his life is blank?" Before she gathered the boy off the ground and bundled him into her house, Kathryn's life had been a blank. Or so it seemed to her now.

She disliked women who blamed their bad moods, bad sex and bad decisions on hormonal imbalances, but she felt that something essential about her body chemistry had changed with the child's arrival. Intellectually she understood that it couldn't be that simple or sudden. The precipitant for the change must have been augmenting inside her for months. Looking back, she realized how long she had been joking in letters to friends that she designed her daily itinerary to take her to spots where she was sure to see children.

At a fountain near the People's Sport Palace she watched boys no bigger than minnows submarine through the murky water. Then she paused in the former Karl Marx Garden, now Tamerlane Park, where a lovely little girl and her brother played a game with Ping-Pong paddles and a badminton shuttle-cock. Her favorite was the beautiful, fine-boned girl who swept the tea shop on Cosmonaut Street. Dressed in a magenta *khalat* draped over paisley leggings, the girl resembled a costumed doll caught up in a sad dance with the broom. Kathryn always gave her a piece of hard candy or a coin. The sight of these kids was like a bow drawn across the quavering strings of her heart. She wanted to bring one of them—no, all of them—home with her.

Once she had the boy, however, she didn't need the others. He dominated her life. He became her life—and it was all she could do at first to make sure that he didn't die.

Her house was cramped and spartanly furnished. Beyond a living room that opened off the street, the bedroom and kitchen in back gave onto a court-yard where the previous occupants had cooked and slept during hot weather. These days, the threat of robbery and random shootings often kept her in-doors, and Kathryn virtually lived in the kitchen. She worked at a manual typewriter at one end of the dining table and ate her meals at the opposite end. After she carried the boy in through the courtyard, she cleared the table and placed him atop it as gently as she would an antique bowl.

To her relief, he remained semiconscious as she tended to him. Although she placed no credence in the stories about his shape-changing powers and doubted that he presented any real danger, she didn't want him to wake up and run off, or fight her as she washed his wounds. Tearing strips from an old bed sheet, she bound his hands and feet. Then she wet the rest of the sheet at the water tap and tenderly wiped him clean.

As the cloth turned black and his body turned pale brown, she marveled at the metamorphosis. He had sores on his knees and elbows, and she scrubbed in vain at the grit that had healed inside his cuts. His skin was hot and sand-papery under her hands. He thrashed and bared his discolored teeth, but didn't utter a sound. Isolated clusters of muscles twitched at her touch. Though his limbs had a strange asymmetrical articulation, they felt strong and supple.

There was a coarse mop of hair on his head and the lightest mist between his legs. She found several fat ticks on his scrotum. As she plucked them out, his balls shifted in their sack like live things looking to escape. Then the pink-tipped length of him straightened, sending a shiver through Kathryn's fingers. She stopped dabbing the damp rag at him and leaned back against the refrigerator. It shivered, too, from the generator that supplied power. She could feel its tremor against her shoulders as she watched him soften and sink deeper into unconsciousness.

She covered him with a light quilt so that he resembled a napping child, not an animal tied at the wrists and ankles. Dragging a chair close to the table, she sat and stared at him. She stared at him as she sometimes did at the typewriter when she was at a loss for words or was lost in thought. Periodically she extended a hand, cupping it above his mouth to check whether he was breathing. She pressed a cool palm to his forehead. He was feverish; his eyelids flickered and roiled in REM pattern. Once he gasped. In dreams or pain—she couldn't guess which. Moistening a sponge, she dribbled water between his cracked lips and heard a grating swallow. She was close enough to notice lice scuttling at the roots of hair and to dredge in his smell which, even after the washing, reminded her of moist leaves and clay.

She labored to make up her mind what she felt beyond bewilderment and wonder. That he might be what people claimed—a creature raised in the wild—didn't seem out of the question. That would have been of a piece with the skewed tapestry of life here.

A fly landed on his lips. He snapped at it and grew agitated, squirming on the table, straining against the knotted cloth. One eyelid rolled wide, and the weight of his yellow, canted gaze lay on her like a stone. She couldn't tell whether he was staring at her or at nothing at all. His eyes might have been doorways in the desert, opening onto emptiness in either direction.

Abruptly he began to throw up. There were worms in the vomit. She rolled him onto his side so he wouldn't choke. As he groaned and gagged, the writhing clots kept coming. Then he fell quiet and motionless, as if in a coma, and Kathryn didn't know what to do.

Before Fletcher's disappearance, she might have appealed to him and hoped to convince him that a cry for help wasn't an invitation to sleep with her. Thrown together by circumstances and homesickness, it was natural for them to become acquainted. But Paul was looking for sex, not friendship. Still, she had seen him from time to time and he had been willing to supply medicine from the dispensary at his lab when Kathryn needed it.

After his kidnapping, there was only the Mullah, who was reputed to have healing powers, and Dr. Medvedev, an aging, ill-tempered veterinarian who sometimes treated human patients. She chose Dr. Medvedev. He lived closer, and she had more stomach for his political tirades than the Mullah's harangues about Sharia law. Then, too, she sympathized with Dr. Medvedev's isolation, which he exacerbated by proclaiming fidelity to Communist dogma long after the Soviet Union fell apart.

Since scavengers had chopped down the poles and stolen the copper wire to sell for scrap, the telephone system no longer functioned. Those who could afford to communicated by cell phone. But Kathryn didn't have one and was forced to hurry to Dr. Medvedev's on foot.

He lived in a neighborhood of whitewashed cottages with bright blue window and door surrounds. Populated by Tartars, reputedly the city's cleanest ethnic group, it used to be a prosperous neighborhood. Now it had an air of profound dereliction, and the streets stank of garbage, busted plumbing and the vet's compound. When Kathryn knocked at the door, the animals inside set off a cacophony of barking, crowing, yipping and howling. A woman emerged from a house across the street. Kathryn thought she was a servant coming with a spare key. But the woman held out a *matrushka* doll and pleaded for money. Kathryn could have the doll for two dollars.

It wasn't worth even that. Cheaply made and gaudily painted, one of the models that glutted the market right after independence, this clutch of wooden figurines started with a burly caricature of Marx. Inside it was a miniature Lenin, then a Stalin, a Krushchev, a Brezhnev, a Gorbachev and a Yeltsin, each smaller and more rudimentary than the last. The doll suggested continuity, cause and effect, comic diminishment. Kathryn would have liked to believe in this or any other pattern, but circumstances didn't permit such luxuries.

Dr. Medvedev flung open the door and chased the poor woman back to her cottage. In profile, with his yellow-white hair brushed straight back from his forehead, he resembled a bird of prey, a beaked avenger. His lined face was a map of every hard mile he had traveled, right down to the broken spider veins that might have been blue backcountry roads. Despite the punishment he had absorbed, he was still capable of dishing it out, and Kathryn hastened to say that she was sorry to bother him, but a child was sick. Immediately he unlocked the garage and coaxed an old dented Moskvich to life.

By car, the return trip to her house took less than ten minutes. At the front door, he kicked off his shoes and, lugging a black leather bag, padded toward the kitchen in socks unraveling at the toes. He had no more patience for personal hygiene than for polite small talk. When he threw off the quilt and noticed the sheets knotted around the boy's wrists and ankles, he shot Kathryn a look. He didn't need to speak. His bushy eyebrows conveyed volumes of contempt.

"I was afraid he'd hurt himself," she explained. "And I didn't want him to run away before you got here."

"This child is too sick to stand much less run." The vet untied him and chafed his skin to restore circulation. Gruff as he was in speaking, he conducted his examination with the solicitude of a saint. He palpitated the boy's belly, tested for broken bones and gently lifted his wrist, checking his pulse. The kid lay there looking up at Dr. Medvedev with sticky eyes, as if mesmerized by his ranting.

"I am no intellectual. I don't live in my head or down on my knees kissing asses. I deal with what's in front of me and I'm not afraid to say what I see. This is a hideous example of the independence everybody brags about. Under socialism we at least had hospitals and orphanages and insane asylums. Nobody believed they were perfect, but they would never let a wretch like this wander loose."

"What's wrong with him?" Kathryn asked.

"Everything! He has worms. He has infections. He may have pneumonia. Without clothes, without shoes, without food, how could he not? And look at his mouth." Dr. Medvedev was doing just that, examining his throat, tongue and gums. "It's full of rotten teeth and sores. And this is only what we see with our eyes. Imagine what is inside—the bacteria, the filth."

He turned to the sores on the boy's legs, squeezing and prodding. A maggoty shape oozed to the surface, squirming through gobs of pus. "Give me a spoon."

"What is it?" Kathryn wailed.

"Do you have a wooden spoon?"

"What is it?"

"Guinea worms. Do as I say."

She slapped a long-handled saucepan spoon into his palm, and he accepted it as though it were a sterilized instrument and he a surgeon about to perform an appendectomy. Using his thumb and forefinger as a hemostat, he seized a guinea worm and delicately drew it out. When he had several inches in hand, he spindled them like so much yarn around the spoon and continued tugging and turning, careful not to let the worm break and burrow back into the cut.

The worm must have been a meter long. Once it popped free of the boy's skin, Dr. Medvedev started in on a second, then a third worm. As he painstakingly pulled them out, Kathryn choked back her gorge, baffled by what she saw. She might have been witnessing a reenactment of Greek drama, with the shabby doctor in the role of Clotho, the Fate who spins the thread of destiny and, at the same time, delivers a monologue full of dire foreboding. He carped about democracy, the insolence of crooks in high office, the short-sightedness of citizens who refused to give Communism a second chance. With no countervailing force to oppose it, fascism was bound to revive, and poverty and hunger and repression would increase, all making for more little boys without clothes and food. The free market had no sympathy for such suffering, he said. "Drug dealers, black-marketeers, bloodsuckers—these are the successes, the kings of capitalism."

Once he had finished worming the boy—he never finished hectoring Kathryn— Dr. Medvedev needled an ampoule of antibiotics into his arm.

"Is he going to be all right?" Kathryn asked.

"Am I a prophet? Send for the Mullah. He'll read tea leaves and predict the future."

"But will he get better?"

"Of course not." The question outraged Dr. Medvedev. "Under the current system, that's impossible. You might as well take him out to the courtyard and kill him yourself."

"Don't tell me he's dying."

"It's worse. He'll go on living and consuming precious resources and my energy while normal children lack care and don't have a chance." He gave her back the slimy wooden spoon. "If I were you, I'd put him out of his misery."


*I*nstead, she put him in a corner of the kitchen, atop a folded carpet, and nursed him, babied him. Buying the medicine Dr. Medvedev recommended, she pushed the pills far back on the boy's cankered tongue and made sure he swallowed each one. She cut his hair, clipped the lethally long nails from his fingers and toes, and attempted to get him to wear clothes. But he couldn't stand the feel of anything against his skin—perhaps because it irritated his sores, maybe because he didn't like his freedom of movement constricted. He even kicked away the quilt at night. This troubled her. She feared it might be a neurological symptom of autism, an indication that his body radiated an aura of static electricity. With reluctance, she let him remain naked.

Once he regained his strength, she fashioned a leather harness from a pair of belts and led him on daily walks around the courtyard. Or rather, he dragged her outside and over to the gate. When he couldn't push it open, he pawed at the lock and whined. Kathryn sensed that if she didn't hold the leash tight, he would scamper over the wall. But after a couple of weeks, there came a point when he quit trying to wrench free from her grasp. She couldn't decide whether he was learning to trust her or had simply resigned himself.

By a process of trial and error, she discovered what he would eat— potatoes, turnips, squash, apples, cherries, everything mashed and moistened with water or milk. Despite the stories about his being a carnivore and a carrion eater, he wouldn't touch meat no matter whether she cooked it or let him have it raw. Left to himself, he preferred to crouch down on all fours, lower his face and gobble what she dropped in front of him on the floor. Kathryn began serving his food on a plastic plate and encouraged him to eat with his right hand, as people did in this part of the world. But she never succeeded in that or in teaching him to drink from a glass. It wasn't that he lacked fine motor skills. He just seemed to enjoy lapping water from a shallow bowl.

Once he finished eating, however, he was surprisingly fastidious. He groomed himself like a cat and waited to do his business until he was outdoors.

As a test of his intelligence, she devised a series of experiments. She rearranged the furniture in the room and was delighted how quickly he noticed the change and tugged his carpet back to its accustomed corner. She neglected to feed him and waited to see whether he'd find a way to remind her. He did. He sniffed, then licked the spot on the floor where she usually dropped food.

Then she hauled in a full-length mirror and studied his reaction to his own reflection. He wasn't confused for an instant. When she stood behind him and held up objects, he didn't reach toward their image in the glass. He swiveled around and grabbed what she had in her hand.

This showed, she wanted to believe, that he was oriented in all spheres, aware of his surroundings and eager to impose order and logic on his life. This proved . . . What did it prove she wondered. Was it evidence of intelligence? Or an indication that she was a hovering, controlling educator with her own obsessions about logic and order that she transferred to him?

Kathryn had flown to Central Asia fresh from graduate school. A Ph.D. candidate in English literature, she had finished everything except a dissertation when her husband left her. Afraid that she would make as big a mess of divorce as she had of marriage, she dropped out of the University of Michigan and joined the Peace Corps. Although friends argued this was a melodramatic solution to a mundane problem, Kathryn reasoned that when love dies, it leaves behind a whiff of the tomb, and any sensible person moves as far away from the stench as possible.

For two years she taught English as a second language to Russian speakers who dreamed of moving to America. Then thinking she had stumbled onto a new dissertation topic, she stayed on to study the linguistic transition that paralleled political events. As republics of the former USSR gained independence, some of the new democratic governments—man for man the old communist regimes—outlawed Russian. Where Kathryn lived, a dialect derived from Parsi roots was declared the official language, and western lettering was supposed to replace the Cyrillic alphabet. But more than half the population didn't speak or read the dialect, and even those who did acknowledged that it was a demotic patois, not suitable for modern science and military command. Then, too, Islamic fundamentalists complained that the Koran had been written in Arabic and Allah had provided all the words that man needed. They protested any additions to this divinely inspired vocabulary.

As a practical matter, the majority of people continued to speak Russian, but debate about the matter was passionate and sometimes resulted in pitched battles. Ethnic tribes and clans shot it out along a volatile frontier bordered by half a dozen emerging nations. Geologically, the region lay on a fault line, a landscape of colliding tectonic plates, frequent earthquakes and avalanches. Sociologically, it was a "shatter zone" of anarchic cultures, a mosaic that had been pressed into place by the Soviets and was now violently unmaking itself.

All of this was interesting to Kathryn—when it wasn't absolutely terrifying. It sparked an endless chain reaction of ideas. What it didn't yield was a thesis. At least not one that she felt competent to deal with.

Still, she stayed on, praying that in a place where so much had happened over the complex course of history, significant experiences would befall her. That it was dangerous didn't deter her. She was committed to coming through this a changed person, branded with a lasting impression of Central Asia—a scar or a beauty mark, it didn't matter which.

To her consternation, however, the same things happened over and over again. In the psychological equivalent of low intensity conflict, Kathryn found herself fighting an ongoing skirmish against tedium and its camouflaged twin, anxiety. These mood swings persisted until the boy showed up, restoring a sense of purpose.

Now each morning when she walked into the kitchen, he was awake and, she liked to think, waiting for her. More and more, she became convinced that he was, except in obvious respects, a normal child, not autistic, not retarded or neurologically compromised. True, he was frightened by the sound of airplanes roaring overhead and of gunfire in the neighborhood. But what little boy wouldn't be? While he never broke down and cried, tears swam in his eyes, and he let Kathryn hold him in her arms and cradle his head to her breast, crooning to him.

From Ling/Lang seminars in Ann Arbor she had gleaned a sketchy knowledge of language acquisition. She had read Chomsky—or she had read about him. She had plowed through Bloomfieldian structuralism and Zelig Harris's analysis of sentence transformations. Then in preparation for her posting to Central Asia, the Peace Corps had familiarized her with recent studies, many of them conducted in Romanian and Russian orphanages, of special needs children. She had learned about marasmus, central auditory processing disorders and various syndromes classified under the general label of "primitivisation of the total personality." She understood that the early years of childhood were crucial for emotional attachment and the development of brain circuitry. In the absence of physical contact and mental stimulation, otherwise healthy babies were handicapped in basic skills, especially the ability to speak.

So if gossip about the boy was even half accurate, if he had grown up in the wild, isolated from humans . . . It made Kathryn queasy, it embarrassed her, to speculate along these lines. She recalled campus cranks who studied UFOs or drafted grant proposals to search for Sasquatch. Still, she couldn't evade the question. Was it conceivable that she had found a feral child? If not a classic case, the kind that endured in perfervid imagination and cropped up in legend and literature, was he a close approximation of the phenomenon?

The scientific, not the science fiction, potential fascinated her. For eons, as people hypothesized about the origins of language, the concept of a wild child, a human being in chrysalis state, recurred as a premise from which certain conclusions could be drawn. As early as the Egyptian empire, the Pharaoh Psumtik had decreed that two newborn babies should be sealed in a cave with a deaf-mute caretaker to test whether they would learn to speak. No results of the experiment survived. There was no word whether the children survived. Yet ever since then, researchers had been obsessed by the notion that those stark conditions which no sane person would consider imposing on a human subject might, by sheer accident, occur outside the laboratory. If for whatever reason a baby had been separated from his parents and reared by animals, that would provide a perfect opportunity to cross-check linguistic theories and solve lingering mysteries: Could a baby who grew up mute be taught to talk? Was language learned or innate? Did a universal grammar exist? Was language acquisition a form of imprinting that played out along predictable lines when triggered by outside stimulus? Did kids acquire syntax or simply access it? If the process wasn't completed by a certain age, did the hard-wiring for speech die?

The questions triggered their own responses in Kathryn Matthews, and along with a conviction that she must teach the boy to talk, it came to her that she had to bring him to the States, to a university with facilities where he could be studied at the same time as he received care. And she had to go with him. But to do this she needed the intervention of a benefactor.

Meanwhile, she continued to work with him. Whenever he would allow it, she pressed his calloused palm to her throat as she spoke. She put his fingers on her lips so that he felt how words were formed. She encouraged him to imitate the sounds she made, and his uncanny gift for replicating a broad range of vocalizations, if not specific syllables, convinced Kathryn that nothing physiological prevented him from learning to speak. The realization gave her immense joy. She moved her own hand to his throat as he whistled and warbled. With his pulse beating against her fingertips, a consoling line came to her from the Koran: "God is as close as the vein in a man's neck."

4

*L*ate that day, Zack McClintock spun up out of jet-lagged sleep like a corpse from the bottom of a well. Silver wires, gossamer thin and crazily askew, crisscrossed the room. His eyes hadn't gone bad. A spiderweb of sunlight filtered through the loose weave of the curtains. When he pushed back the drapes, a dun-colored city wheeled in front of him. Modern high rises, rusty scaffolding and construction cranes soared above the huddled glare of the old town's tin-roofed houses. He found relief—more than that, cool blue beauty—at the horizon where snowcapped mountains humped up out of the khaki landscape.

Downstairs, the coffee shop was closed. He bypassed the bar and its morose clientele of men nursing whiskey and nibbling pistachios. Settling in the lobby beside a brass tray balanced on a carved wooden trestle, he ordered tea and bread—*chai* and *khleb*, two of the few Russian words he knew. Usually, as soon as he had something in his stomach, Zack swallowed his pills, but today he thought the tea tasted better without them and so did the bread, a delicious flat, unleavened round loaf.

As he ate, he debated Ms. Pearson's advice about buying a gun. It had been decades since he carried a weapon. In his experience, if you had one, you used it. Or, worse, you got caught packing it and wound up behind bars. Was the First Secretary setting him up?

The question revolved in his mind, a Russian roulette of wrongheaded possibilities. Still, he couldn't dismiss the idea that he'd be smart to check out the bazaar and see what was for sale.

Outside, ramshackle Ladas, Zhigulis and Volgas lined the curb in front of the hotel. "Taxi? Change dollars?" came the chorus from cabbies squatting and rocking on the balls of their feet. They were all eating sunflower seeds, spitting out the shells on the ground between their feet.

Zack crossed the blistered asphalt parking lot to a patch of grass that gleamed a poisonous green, like an over-chlorinated swimming pool. Sun scalded his scalp through his close-cropped grey hair. There were trees ahead, and he hurried toward them even though his instinct—a hangover from Nam—was not to walk under them. He kept to the leafy fringes of the shade, staring in at old men on benches studying chessboards. Milling kids monkeyed around on a beat-up sliding board without steps and swings that consisted of nothing except gallows-like chains. Still, they seemed happy, and Zack was happy to watch them having fun.

Then there was a burst of gunfire and he froze. It took him a second to recognize the *ack-ack* of jackhammers, not automatic rifles. Workers were chipping names and dates off a marble pedestal. On the ground beside it lay a statue like a fallen warrior waiting to be buried.

Beyond the park, a maze of alleys led into the bazaar where Zack meandered through the hiss of grease and a pall of smoke and charred meat at shashlik stalls. In *chai-khanas*, men in turbans and knit skullcaps lounged full length on carpeted daises sipping bowls of tea and tossing the grounds into the dirt. Women were swaddled in iridescent head wraps and close-fitted leggings shot through with gold and silver thread. Their gaudy clothes, like the waterfalls of glistening majolica on public buildings, appeared to be a protest against the surrounding desolation.

Everybody regarded Zack with the blunt curiosity of one species sizing up another, and he stared back at them. People on the street in the States frequently reminded him of a parade of identical thumbs skinned of their prints. But here every face was different—there were Mongols, Koreans, Armenians, Tajiks and Uzbeks—and each exerted its own emotional force field.

In the meat market, carcasses swung from overhead beams like macabre wind chimes swaying in the breeze stirred by casual browsers. Butchers disemboweled goats and sheep, unspooling yards of intestines in pinkish white spirals that trapped insects as effectively as flypaper. The street streamed blood. Zack felt it squelch under the soles of his shoes. It smelled metallic, coppery, not much different from human blood.

As he came around a corner, polished metal replaced the racks of meat. Kalashnikovs, M-16's, old-fashioned Sten guns and rocket-propelled grenade launchers metronomed from tiers of hooks. Much of this arsenal looked to be secondhand and hard-used, most likely salvaged off battlefields or bought from deserters. But some of the sidearms were fresh from the assembly line, which didn't necessarily mean they were made in a factory. Local tribesmen were renowned for producing hand-tooled knockoffs of brand-name rifles and revolvers.

Searching for something small enough to conceal, powerful enough to knock a man down and light enough to carry without causing a hernia, Zack chose a snub-nosed .38. It had a spotless bore and looked like it had never been fired. Since it didn't have a serial number, he assumed it was a Saturday night special from Islamabad or Jalalabad.

He expected a full court press from the shopkeeper. That's how it would have been in the Middle East—an hour of boisterous bargaining, punctuated by histrionic posturing and, in the end, mint tea and smiles. But the Tajik in this shop, a guy with a beard trimmed to the gaunt contours of his face, gave a glowering impression of total indifference. Sunk lazily on a hassock, he said nothing. When Zack trotted out one of his Russian phrases, "*Skolko stoit?*

How much?" the Tajik leaned forward and scratched a finger at the sand, scribbling 500 with a dollar sign behind the zero.

That was an absurdly high price. Zack erased the 5 and wrote in a 1. The man flicked it away and substituted a 4. Gradually, and in silence, they narrowed the gap and agreed on $225. But before Zack paid, he pantomimed that he wanted to test fire the .38.

The somnolent shopkeeper fished a single cartridge from the folds of his clothing, chambered the round and presented the revolver butt first. Zack mimed, How? Where? The man pointed to the sky. Zack gestured for him to go ahead and squeeze off a shot. If this blew the piece to shrapnel, or brought the police running, he preferred to have the gun in the shopkeeper's hand.

Sighing at the senseless palaver, the fellow fired into the air. Though the noise was enormous, nobody in the bazaar appeared to be startled. More important, the .38 remained intact.

From the wad of dollars in his pocket, Zack peeled off two hundreds, a twenty and a five. The shopkeeper lifted each bill to the light like a farmer candling eggs. He rejected a hundred that had been minted before 1990 and the twenty because it was wrinkled and dirty. Nothing could convince him they were valid currency. He demanded immaculate, freshly printed dollars.

Zack complied and bought a box of ammo. He tucked the .38 in at the base of his spine, between the waistband of his jeans and the synthetic fabric of his money belt. Both were well hidden by his shirttails. But as he hiked back to the hotel he didn't feel safe. He couldn't believe it was this easy. At any instant he expected to be arrested. Worse yet, stripped of the cash he had strapped around his stomach.

The immense evening sky added to the queasy suspicion that he was locked in a race against time. He wanted to be indoors before something— fire? volcanic ash?—rained down on him. Such livid color, such incalculable space, threatened to suck away his soul. Over the mountains, a purple mass of clouds floated like a Medusa trailing long tendrils. A thunderstorm looked to be the least it portended. Forks of heat lightning flickered as if Central Asia had arranged a sound and light show for the express purpose of proving how overwhelming the world was and how insignificant Zack McClintock was.

On the hike back to the hotel, he happened upon a sprawling cinderblock structure that served as the central bus station. Although no buses were in sight, the streets were thronged with passengers. Many appeared to have camped out here for days, setting up tents and cooking over braziers. There was nobody at the ticket window, but a teenager in the waiting crowd spoke a bit of English. When Zack asked him about arrivals and departures, the fellow said, "It's hard to pretend. Maybe next week. Maybe never."

The cab drivers outside the hotel were even less encouraging about his prospects of catching a ride up-country. They didn't have enough gas, they claimed. Their jalopies wouldn't make it that far. Anyway, the road was closed. Or if not officially shut down, then far too dangerous.

Zack went inside worrying where to turn next. He hadn't counted on traveling all this distance only to get stuck a couple of hundred miles short of where Fletcher had disappeared.

The hotel staff, including the receptionist with the silver teeth, had assembled in front of a console TV set. The size of an armoire with a postage stamp screen, it showed *Jurassic Park* in a version that had been neither dubbed nor subtitled. Instead, a bellboy provided a glottal translation in rasping voice over. This didn't work too badly when male characters were speaking, but Laura Dern's dialogue suffered.

Zack was tempted to start drinking. Then one glance into the funereal bar persuaded him to eat first. The same solemn men were working at their whiskies in dead earnest, as though this were a job they had to finish before punching out.

An elevator whisked him to the top-floor restaurant. In the States, it would have rotated and bragged about its wraparound vistas. This establishment didn't have windows, however, and what it put on display in place of a view didn't appeal to him any more than the annihilating evening sky.

Obsequious oriental dolls waited on tables, and when they weren't serving food and drink, they danced to recorded music, shimmying in pasties and G-strings. During classical numbers, they struck poses and appeared to mimic masterpieces of art. When the beat turned up-tempo, they kicked into aerobic routines. For a tip, they'd sit on your lap. For the right price they'd probably sit on your face.

Zack chose a table with his back to the entertainment, ordered vegetable tempura and struggled to sort out how he felt. The dancing girls irrationally fed his dissatisfaction, sharpening an awareness of things he no longer had the capacity to appreciate. He couldn't recall how long it had been since he last had a woman. These days, it was as if there were two of him, one self inside the other, a soft nut in a hard shell. He couldn't get out, and very little got in. Maybe it was the medicine, and now that he didn't have it he . . .

Someone sat down beside him. A prostitute, he presumed. He riveted his eyes on his plate. This had the potential to be ugly. He wasn't in the mood to make nice.

"I notice you're not watching the show," a man said.

This was worse. "Not interested."

"Me neither. I'm a Christian."

"Congratulations," Zack said. "I'm here to eat."

"Me too. Pleased to meet you." He shoved a hand over Zack's plate. Maybe he meant to bless the meal. Zack gave him a curt handshake.

The man's face was a pale boiled potato. He wore a white shirt, a black clip-on tie, chinos and Hush Puppies. Zack pegged him as a missionary, a fact the fellow immediately confirmed, launching, unprompted, into a sermon about his evangelical group which operated educational centers in every obscure corner of the defunct Commonwealth of Independent States. "If you're called to spread the word," he explained, "you have to teach folks to read."

His instinct was to change tables. Then he caught himself. It occurred to him that this Christian might be helpful. "Ever been up-country?" Zack asked.

"Many times. The souls there are in terrible straits."

"What's the best way to reach them?"

"Oh, you know, respect their values. Don't judge them or criticize. Resign yourself to a long pilgrimage. No one's ever won over to the grace of God without lots of hard work."

"I mean, what's the best way to travel there?"

"That's not easy either." He fiddled with his tie, leaving damp fingerprints down the length of it. "For years the Communists executed all the religious leaders and persecuted people who practiced their faith. There's an awful spiritual vacuum. Folks who haven't known Christ's love like you and me don't see any reason not to steal and rob and ride roughshod over the weak."

"I suppose you've had to take steps to protect yourself."

"We're peacemakers. We hold with prevention and caution, not fighting. Still, there's no denying the everyday dangers. One of our brethren was killed in a bathtub. Shocked to death."

"Shot?"

"*Shocked*. There's no hot water unless you plug in an immersion coil and warm it up. Brother Albert forgot and sat on the coil and electrocuted himself."

"That's a damn shame." Zack picked off the tempura batter and ate the limp vegetables inside it. "What'll you have, Reverend?"

"I have to be careful of my stomach. A Coke and a bowl of rice," he told a waitress. "Boil it an extra minute, dear."

"Does your group go up-country by car? Do you have your own vehicle?" Zack asked.

"We don't have any call to be there these days. We've closed our mission until things simmer down."

"But say you were headed in that direction, how would you get there?"

He smiled and thanked the waitress for his Coke. "There's one school of thought that it's unsafe to travel in a thin-skinned vehicle. There's another school that going armor-plated you're just inviting trouble. Hoodlums figure if you can afford armor, you must be transporting something that's worth stealing. We've had good luck hiring drivers with local connections."

"Connections to who?"

"The army. The police. Religious factions."

"What about the mafia?"

The missionary smiled beatifically. "I'll confess that there've been occasions when the Children of Light have depended upon the Children of Darkness. We live in a fallen world. You probably know that from your own profession. You must have urgent business if you're heading up-country."

"Yeah, I've got business." Zack sat back and let the man chew on a mouthful of rice for a minute. "Could you recommend a driver who's dependable?"

"There's one that definitely knows the road and knows the ropes."

"I'd be grateful for an introduction."

"Don't misunderstand me. He won't drive you for the love of Jesus."

"I don't expect him to."

"His name's Misha. That's the Russian diminutive of Michael—as in the archangel. But he's no saint and he's not cheap. He's a feisty, suspicious soul. He'll want to know why you're going."

"Tell him . . ." He debated whether to chance the truth. "Tell him an American aid worker has been kidnapped."

"You think Misha doesn't know that? Everybody's heard what happened to Paul Fletcher."

"I'm his father-in-law. My daughter's desperate. I came here to—to do whatever I can." There was a tremulous intensity to his voice that impressed even Zack.

"God love you. What a wonderful father." But then his potato face pinched into a worried expression. "I'll be straight with you, and I want you to be straight with me. Otherwise Misha will make mincemeat of both of us. Tell me the truth. You're not a government agent, are you?"

"I swear I'm on my own."

"I believe you. But I'd better not tell Misha what you're up to. If it won't weigh on your conscience, I'll tell him a little white lie."

· · ·

*I*n the morning, when Zack came down to the lobby to check out, a big bruiser in an Adidas tracksuit loitered behind the counter, flirting with the girl with silver teeth. He didn't look like an athlete—not unless knee breaking had become an Olympic sport. Nuzzling his mineral blue jaw against the girl's neck, he copped a cheap feel. Then he pocketed a few bills that she filched from the cash register.

Though he hoped not, Zack had a sinking sense that this was his driver. "Misha?" he said.

The bozo swaggered around to the front of the reception desk. His new Nikes squeaked on the parquet. At six two, Zack was taller, but Misha outweighed him by a good thirty pounds and must have been younger by the same number of years. His dark hair was cut short except for a curly rattail in back.

"I ride you to mission?" Misha asked in English.

"Yes." This wasn't much of a white lie in Zack's estimation. He was on a mission of sorts.

"Outside is my car. Make your bill. Make your bags. I wait for you."

"What it'll cost?"

"Three hundred."

"Dollars?"

Misha snorted. "I don't do rubles."

"That's a helluva lot."

"Not for an American. Not for such a car I drive. Or alone or with passengers, I don't go this road without pay."

Nothing in his voice, nothing in his meatball demeanor, invited negotiation. Zack counted out three Ben Franklins which Misha pressed flat, smoothing out the wrinkles and verifying the dates they were printed. He licked one bill. Testing whether it was counterfeit? Or was this his notion of money laundering?

"You know what means the eyeball on top of pyramid?" Misha asked.

"It's on every piece of U.S. paper money."

"But why?"

"Beats me."

"I tell you." He grinned triumphantly. "It's a Jew sign. They own America. In secret, they own every country."

Outside amid the squatting cab drivers, Misha preened like an alpha male lording it over the cringing runts of the litter. His teal-green BMW 525 sparkled next to their clapped-out taxis. As soon as he was behind the wheel, he began blowing the horn and kept at it all the way across the city. When pedestrians didn't move out of his way fast enough, he swerved as if to sideswipe them. Even livestock scrambled out of his path and onto the weedy verges. At stop signs and red lights he didn't bother to slow down.

"No problem with cops?" Zack asked.

"Police are poor and must make a living."

"So who runs things?"

Misha laughed. "The mafia."

*I*n a bleak industrial zone of deserted oil refineries, a row of punctured storage tanks resembled an airfield full of wrecked dirigibles. Hunched like buzzards beside the road, men gazed at the cars that sped past, oblivious of the dust they raised. A truck had crashed through the guard rail, reducing it to a curled strand of celery. Judging by the rust, the accident occurred a long time ago.

Farther on, cotton fields shimmered in wavy rays of heat and chemical fertilizer. Mud-caked farmers, almost invisible in rags the same color as the churned earth, mucked out irrigation ditches. But the women hoeing crops were as brilliant as birds of paradise, swagged in gowns of fuchsia, ultramarine and sulphurous yellow.

"House for horses," Misha said as they whipped by a barn. Then he gestured to a yurt. "People all smile."

"That's nice," Zack said. "They're happy."

"Not happy. Dirty." He pinched his nostrils. "They make pee-pee in yurt and all smile." He tapped the steering wheel. "In America how much costs such a car?"

"Fifty thousand dollars," Zack guessed.

"I pay more. From Germany is long and either by Russia or by Iran, you pay bribes. That makes bigger price. In America how much makes one man in one day?"

"Depends."

"Here one man makes one dollar a day."

"Must take a long time to save up for a BMW."

"That's where capitalism is best. No saving. Just making money and spending." He popped a cassette into the tape deck. "Only permitted in past is music nobody likes. Now everything."

In this case, "everything" sounded like shingles grinding through an airplane propeller. Zack didn't object. Not as long as it kept Misha's mouth shut.

Eventually the arable land gave out. The cotton dwindled to dry twigs; irrigation ditches glittered with salt crystals. The asphalt road had been chewed to bits and was lined with the scorched shells of cars. Zack couldn't tell whether mortars or poor maintenance had done the damage. He stayed alert but noticed few signs of life, much less danger. Then, as improbable as a dream apparition, a woman was walking along the road eating a melon. Her head bobbed up and down and swiveled sideways to spit out the seeds. Misha sounded his horn to scare her, but she never broke stride.

When Zack spotted a roadblock ahead, a sharp claw closed in his chest. He reached around to his lower back as though rubbing at lumbar pain. He gripped the gun butt. He had no intention of getting kidnapped or giving up his money belt.

Misha appeared blissfully unconcerned. He stopped, shot the breeze with four bearded men armed with Kalashnikovs, then drove on to a place that looked to Zack like no place he had ever been. They passed a solitary camel, threadbare and spavine as an overstuffed sofa. They zoomed up on an oxcart crammed with peasants and hurtled around it in a rattle of gravel and a rooster tail of dust. A passel of Orthodox priests as long-haired as rock stars piled out of a van for a communal pee. Shaking off the last drops and zipping up, they swayed like a chorus line. It was difficult to sustain any belief that they were in peril or that somebody out here might mean them harm.

On a faraway, wind-shaved hill, he spotted a stone village that might have been a burial cairn. When Misha drew near it, he pulled off the road onto a barren stretch of pebbles beside a tank truck parked at the center of a circle of grease. A grimy man hopped down from the truck's cabin. Using a garden hose and a funnel, he siphoned gasoline from the tank into the BMW. Wind buffeted them and plastered the grease monkey's clothes to his wasted body. He moved with the jittery imprecision of someone high on gas fumes.

"Petrol all the way from Kazakhstan," Misha explained. "We have little gas. Always we ask, How is here different from Dachau?"

Zack waited for the punch line and watched a beetle nudge a dung ball across the oil slick.

"Dachau had gas," Misha said.

He left without paying. In fact, the gas jockey gave *him* money, and as if it weren't already obvious that he was some kind of protection racketeer, Misha proudly spelled it out. "The business I make, I do windows. I don't wash them for pay. I break them for no pay."


*A*fter an hour of plowing through featureless steppes, they entered a different ecosystem—a lush valley with pools of water that lay scattered like blue fragments of fallen sky. Wind combed across swales of grass in tidal rhythms; clumps of poppies gashed the ocean of surging green. Small brown boys herded huge brindle cows, and men on patchwork bikes pedaled along with caged chickens stacked on their rear fenders and sheaves of hay skirted about their legs. The men reminded Zack of hula dancers, a thought that in turn summoned up memories of Hawaii and of a week of R&R he had spent there with his wife Stefanie. The only shadow on the interlude had been Stefanie's worry that something would happen to him when he flew back to Saigon. Instead, something happened to her. But Zack didn't want to think about that. He wanted to remember the good times they had together. The last night in Honolulu when Stefanie told him not to wait for her, she was fine, she liked to keep her eyes open and watch him while . . .

The scene shattered in Zack's face. The side window fell apart and fangs of glass flew into the Beamer. Misha screamed, "Grenade! Grenade!" But Zack knew it wasn't one. Not if he was still alive. A rock had smashed the window.

Wrestling to regain control of the car, Misha stomped the brakes, sending them into a rubber-burning slide. Zack's head slammed into the padded dashboard and stars spun like poppies in his eyes. As Misha ground into reverse gear and roared back up the road, Zack felt blood trickle down his neck, under his shirt collar.

They reached the grass-skirted bike riders and boys tending cows, and Misha flung open the door and jumped out. Zack climbed out too, but had to steady himself against the front fender. His head spun and he bent over to avoid blacking out. Touching a hand to the back of his head, he expected to find his hair matted with blood. But it was slivers of glass, not blood, slithering down his neck. Spangles of broken glass sequined his shirt front. He couldn't shake them off.

Misha charged across the road, his rattail streaming. The men took one look at him, threw down their bikes and vanished into the fields. Squawking chickens beat a blizzard of feathers out of the broken cages. As the young cowherds hot-footed it after the men, grass foamed around them so that they seemed to be swimming. In an instant the sea of green swallowed everybody except one bare-chested, barefooted little fellow. Dumber or more defiant than his friends, he held his ground. Misha smacked him with the flat of his hand, and a knit skullcap sailed off the kid's head. Still, he didn't run. Stolid as an ox, he stood there while Misha boxed his ears.

"Hey," Zack shouted. "Hey, don't!" He hurried over to help the boy. Glass drizzled off him at each step.

Misha beat the kid to his knees, then slung him over his shoulder and lumbered toward the car.

"Put him down," Zack demanded.

Lathered like a dray horse, the big bruiser tried to jostle past him. But Zack blocked his path.

"I have not the intention to argue," Misha said. "Or this boy's family pays for my window or I beat him till he bleeds."

"He didn't do it. He's too little to throw a rock that far. It must have been one of the men."

"Yes, his father or brother. I keep him so he tells me."

He bulled his way by Zack and started to stuff the boy into the back seat of the BMW. The kid flailed his arms and legs and latched onto the doorjamb. Misha punched him until he let go.

"No, don't!" Zack grabbed the Russian's broad back. But it was like grappling at a sheer rock wall. There wasn't a seam or soft spot to hold onto. So he threw a hammer lock around Misha's neck. "Turn him loose."

Finally he had to plant a knee in his spine to pry him off the kid. But Misha whirled around and broke out of his grasp. He seized Zack by the shirt collar and cocked his fist. In mid-swing, he screamed, shook his hand and howled. His bleeding fingers were studded with needles of glass.

Zack backed up. He knew better than to stand toe-to-toe and slug it out with somebody this size. He made a soothing gesture with one hand and groped for the .38 with the other. He didn't want to use it, didn't want to show it, unless he absolutely had to. But he wasn't about to let Misha beat him or the boy. "Calm down," he said. "No harm done."

"My car," he bellowed. "Look what he did."

"Let him go and I'll buy you a new window."

Sucking the stingers from his fingertips, Misha wavered between greed and rage, weighing the satisfaction of punching Zack against the pleasure of getting paid.

"Come on. What's it cost?"

"A hundred dollars."

"You got it." Zack peeled a Ben Franklin off his roll.

Misha glanced at the boy on the ground, a sack of skin and bones in short pants, and then glared at Zack as if tempted to kiss off the hundred bucks and break him in half. Next he snatched the bill and held it up to the sky, checking its date.

Zack stooped down. Under drum-tight skin, the boy's ribs rose and fell, rose and fell. Crudely tied off by a village midwife, his belly button jutted out like a thumb. Peering into his eyes, Zack saw himself reflected in a pair of convex lenses the size of lockets. Then he noticed something else in them— the same focusless rage he occasionally confronted in the mirror as he shaved.

He hauled the kid up onto his bare feet and murmured encouragement to him. He tried to explain, somehow apologize. He would have liked to tell him that he was an American, so that when the boy thought back on the beating he would remember that somebody from another part of the world had believed he was worth saving. Since he knew better than to ask Misha to translate, he ended up giving the boy a friendly squeeze and a smile. But the kid was having none of that. He knocked Zack's hand aside and broke for the fields while Misha hooted with derisive laughter.

*T*hey set off again with sand-laden air soughing through the jagged window frame. Beyond the lush valley, crossing an arid plain, the wind was an exhalation from hell. They didn't talk, and there was no Russian rap to cover the silence. As the evening extravaganza of storm clouds and heat lightning began to boil up, Zack noticed that in the distance a blue dome arched out of the desert. Its magnificence was lost on him. Locked in a loneliness so profound it threatened to crush the breath out of him, he battled against a maelstrom of memories. He couldn't bear to think about his wife. He wanted to concentrate on Adrienne and why he had come here.

After a range of hills and garbage-filled gullies, the BMW passed through sun-bleached ruins that had once been ramparts. For ages they had withstood rain and wind and freezing winters. Then in the nineteenth century the Russians laid siege to the city. Its defenders sallied forth, a surreal rabble uniformed like court jesters, riding two or three men to a horse. They fought with swords and lances and match-lock muskets, and their artillery pieces were drawn by camels. The Russians slaughtered them by the thousands and razed the town walls into a ridge of rotten teeth. Now everything looked equally old to Zack—cubbyhole shops, moldering log cabins, a ceremonial arch that spanned the main street, municipal offices constructed a decade earlier under Communism, mosques and madrasahs, royal tombs and minarets built a millenium ago.

Misha stopped in front of a Quonset hut. It was streaked with verdigris and pigeon shit, and had a rudimentary cross on its roof that resembled a tire tool. "Mission," he said.

"Take me to the hotel."

"They say me mission."

"The mission is closed. You can see that," Zack pointed out.

"They say you reopen."

"I'm staying at the hotel."

He muscled the Beamer into a U-turn. "Not safe."

"The hotel?"

"Nothing safe. You need bodyguard. I make good price."

"I'll think it over."

"Yes, think. Here you must very be careful."

They swung through a gate, up a circular drive to a charmless, poured-concrete structure whose façade was pitted by small arms fire and crazed like a porcelain cup. In spots, rust bled from bullets that had splattered and stuck to

the cement. Two men on a scaffold were scrubbing off Arabic calligraphy that
had been spray-painted over the Intourist sign.

"What's it say?"

"I read Russian," Misha muttered. "No more."

He parked and disappeared into the lobby. A fellow hurried out from behind the counter to welcome Zack and help with his luggage. He spoke excellent English in an ingratiating manner, but his smile didn't quite reach his
eyes, and despite his smooth professional veneer, he had a face that looked
like it had been roughed out of wood with a hatchet.

"The graffiti on the sign, what's it say?" asked Zack.

"It's from the Koran. They scribble it everywhere."

"They?"

"Moslems." Tapping a ring of keys against his leg like a tambourine, he introduced himself as Tomas Vacek.

"But what does it say?"

Self-conscious as a schoolboy obliged to recite a lesson, Tomas started off
in a flat, unfeeling voice, but was soon caught up in rhythmic cadences. "I
swear by this city—and you yourself are resident of this city—by the Begot-
ten and all He begot, that we created man to try him with afflictions." Then he
added, "The elevator's broken. I hope you don't mind climbing stairs."

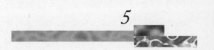

5

*A*fter a day at the front desk, Tomas Vacek liked to take a break before dinner and retreat to his room where Anna was doing dance aerobics to the full
blast accompaniment of a cassette recorder. Though she spoke little English,
she had memorized all the lyrics to a Barry White tape and sang along as he
crooned, "Just the Way You Are."

In his mid-forties, Tomas was often puzzled by Anna who, at the age of
twenty-two, possessed an elfin allure. Wearing a leotard, she appeared childlike and precociously erotic during the strenuous effort of these evening
workouts. Yet strangely, when she stripped and was actually having sex, the
effect was less of sensual abandon than of an athlete counting off repetitions
and perfecting her form.

He wondered whether it wouldn't be more exciting to join her in this trance
of exercise. As she kicked and strutted around the room, they could couple
and move to the music. Better that than the regimented dance they did in bed.

But he limited himself to looking, and while Anna believed he was aroused
by what he saw, Tomas was mulling over the day's events, attempting to force

them into a reassuring shape. Much as she imagined he was waiting for a signal that she reciprocated his desire, he was debating what to do about Misha.

In a hotel with a hundred rooms, Tomas rarely had a dozen paying guests. That number was routinely exceeded by Misha's cronies, who expected to stay for free whenever they blew through town. Tomas didn't dare refuse them. Without their heavy-handed influence, he knew he would never have been made manager when the hotel went private. Still, he needed to convince Misha that his zero-sum business practices would bankrupt the operation and that his demands for favors were destroying Tomas's nerves.

When Anna finished dancing, he undressed her with the delicacy of a doctor unbandaging a patient. At the same time, he continued to fret about his troubles. Soon after the American, McClintock, checked in and went to his room, Misha ordered Tomas to keep an eye on him.

"You have *byk* to do that," Tomas objected.

"Don't call my men goons."

"But why me? And why him?"

"I think he has something to do with Fletcher. Perhaps he came to replace him. That should interest you."

It frightened Tomas far more than it interested him.

The leotard was damp between Anna's legs, and he breathed in her scent as he rolled the Lycra down over her hips. She was short, compact and dark, the hair on her head as curly and black as her bush. The summer sun had burned her complexion a deeper brown, and this prompted suspicion that she belonged to one of the region's despised minorities. Although she could pass for Jewish or Gypsy, she claimed to be Italian and said her father traveled to the Soviet Union in the forties and stayed on to join the socialist struggle. How she ended up in Central Asia, who her mother was, why Anna moved to the city, Tomas never asked.

At the start, he thought she wasn't his type. Usually he preferred tall, elegant women, not sturdy little tumblers and gymnasts. Strolling into the lobby one afternoon with a canvas bag strapped bandolier-style across her shoulder,

Anna had asked to audition as a dancer for the hotel bar. In addition to belly and folk dancing, she was willing to do a striptease and offered him a private demonstration.

Before he touched her, Tomas couldn't imagine whether she would be fleshy or firm. He soon discovered that she was a tantalizing mixture of muscle and plush padding, all her parts enticingly close together. Her breasts were a handspan from her navel, her navel a handspan from her pelvis. Tomas decided to keep Anna for himself and never let her dance, or do anything else, for hotel customers.

Naked, she pranced into the bathroom where an immersion coil was warming the tub. She tested the temperature with her elbow, added a little water from the cold tap, removed the coil and climbed in. Rolling up his shirt sleeves, he scrubbed her back, murmuring in Russian how beautiful she was.

"Not my tits," she protested. "They're too big and saggy."

"There's nothing wrong with your breasts." Not at the moment, there wasn't. Buoyant in bath suds, they appeared high-set, shapely.

"I hate them."

"They have a lovely color and taste."

She giggled and splashed him. "They don't have a taste."

"Sure they do. Every part of your body has its own taste." With a fingertip, he circled her areolae. "They're like a cup of milky tea with cinnamon on top."

"That's silly."

"No. It's a well-known fact that color counts. In ancient Egypt, women painted blue veins on their breasts to attract men."

"You're crazy."

She crossed her arms and covered her chest, but was eager for him to continue. He was glad—no, more like relieved—to accommodate her. Though he infused commonplace remarks with a passion that seldom showed in his eyes, talking calmed Tomas even as it flattered and pleased Anna. The sound of his voice created a crawl space where he could curl up in private and ponder whether it was more likely that McClintock had come to ransom or to replace Fletcher. In either case, the American was in danger and so was Tomas.

He stood up and undressed. With his fierce, scalloped cheekbones and sharp features, he had the kind of face that cuts into some women like a blade. By contrast, his body was smooth and pale, almost fragile, with a faint tracery of veins under translucent skin. Sliding into the tub behind Anna, he wrapped his arms and legs around her and washed her belly and breasts. Hands slippery with soap, he shampooed her springy hair, kneading her scalp and the nape of her neck, whispering all the while that she was his baby. Sweet and sibilant, the words flowed from his flinty face like sugar squeezed from stone.

This was the way his mother used to talk to him, the way she washed him when he was a child. A Czech, she had married a Russian and followed him to Moscow. By the time Tomas was born, her husband was dead, and rather than live alone as a foreigner in that harsh frozen city, they moved back to Prague. There his mother readopted her family name, Vacek, and subsisted on the grudging generosity of relatives. Tomas recalled a succession of temporary accommodations in strange houses, now all confused in his mind with rooms in the hotels he had managed. Dressed in hand-me-downs, sleeping in beds that smelled of other people, surrounded by photographs of unknown families, he grew up with a deepening distaste for the personal debris of domestic life.

In a world of flux and volatility, he craved a fixed point as a child and he found it in his mother. They fit together as snugly as a switchblade in an ivory handle. Inseparable even in sleep, they hugged one another until he dozed off, and he luxuriated in the scent of cologne and cigarette smoke in her hair. Later, as a teenager, he loved it when she pressed his face between her cool palms and cooed what a handsome man, what a heartbreaker, he would grow up to be. Tomas was grateful that she hadn't lived to see what he had become, had never known the hideous little bug that existed beneath the butterfly she imagined.

As he passed his hands over the folds and creases of Anna's body, he regarded events as if through an extended telescope, with him gazing down the wrong end. Everything seemed smaller, emotionally distant. At the same time, detached from him and his musings, his cock pulsed against Anna's spine, like a watch ticking in a locket around a woman's bare throat. It occurred to him that she might have taken such baths with Fletcher. That Fletcher had fucked her was beyond doubt. But the worst of it was that he had promised to bring her to the States. Or so Anna said. Tomas had no way of knowing the truth. Still, he knew how badly she longed to leave. She had told him this from the start. If she didn't make it to America, she wanted to move to Italy and reunite with her father's family.

Tomas believed he had been candid with her. He didn't feel he had deceived her, not in any essential respect. Early on, he admitted he was married to a woman in Prague and that he had a son. He simply didn't add that the boy wasn't by his wife and that he had no desire to get divorced. Clinging to the illusion that he wasn't locked in so long as he stayed loosely connected to a woman in the Czech Republic and haphazardly linked to a child in a corner of this country cut off by ethnic fighting, Tomas was persuaded that a future remained available to him.

Meanwhile, more as a casual topic of conversation than a serious suggestion—just another of the nightly talks that excited them both—he had said that they should move to Rome together. Creating the impression that he had been to Italy before, he described the long journey west, the sights they would see on the way, the delights that awaited them there. He warned her that it would take time to accumulate hard currency, then bribe officials to obtain a visa. She needed to be patient. But soon she began to question the depth of his love and his commitment to the idea of moving. For months she nagged him about departure dates and itineraries. Then, abruptly, she fell silent and after a few weeks of dithering, she ditched him for Paul Fletcher.

The strength of his reaction had stunned Tomas. He had accepted that this spree couldn't last. For a man his age, it was a diversion that brightened the end of the work day. For a girl Anna's age, it was an educational interlude, a brief detour from whatever lay ahead in life. Convinced he held all the cards, he hadn't expected to become dependent on a girl who depended so completely on him. He had always counted on dropping her first. But caught off-guard by her deviousness, embarrassed and infuriated by the betrayal, he faced the stinging truth that he had waited until it was too late.

Now he realized that he had lost the knack of living alone. He had forgotten how to forget, forgotten how to focus on anything other than Anna. He cringed at how cravenly he had yearned to win her back, how willing he had been to forgive, and after Fletcher's disappearance, how pleased he was when she agreed to move in again. Given the degree to which her absence had filled his mind during the day and his dreams at night, it was remarkable once she was physically present how little space she occupied. Her cosmetics—samples of soap, shampoo and scent she had stolen from the hotel—went back onto the window ledge above the bathroom sink, her clothes into a single drawer and onto a couple of hangers in the closet.

*W*hen Anna finished shaving her legs, she swiveled around on his lap. "It's your turn."

"This is my nightmare—to be naked next to a woman with a razor."

She tested his beard. "You're all prickly. You look like a truck driver."

"I wish I was one. They make good money."

"Be still or I'll slice off your nose." She dragged the dull blade through stubble. "Tell me about Italy. Tell me what it'll be like."

With the pretense that they would eventually settle in Rome, he resumed the narrative that had become part of foreplay, an invariable component of the evening's eroticism. He had repeated the story so often that he had the sense of holding up for her admiration one of those globed gadgets that contain a miniature town. Shake it and Rome magically appeared amid motes of golden dust—a cityscape of sunlit campaniles, red tile roofs, a sky of washed blue Murano glass streaked with opalescent clouds as fluted and spiraling as church finials. A river flowed through it, sinuous as a snake, and the shop windows were all full of silk scarves, designer gowns and jewels the size of cut glass decanters.

In fact, Tomas had never been to Rome and had no prospect of ever going there. The city he described was Prague, the place where he grew up and married and had lived until he had gone off to do his military service in Central Asia. After he mustered out of the army, he asked his wife to join him here, but she said no, and he didn't ask a second time.

These days he only vaguely remembered her, but he clearly recalled Prague, block by block, building by building, all its celebrated landmarks top-heavy with plaster cherubs and bronze mythological heroes. Having promised Anna Rome, he believed he was living up to his word as he told her about his hometown, which had been designed by architects imported from Italy. Praising the beauty of Ponte Sant'Angelo, he described Charles Bridge, which had soot-blackened saints instead of white marble statues perched along its balustrades. Leading her on an imaginary tour of Chiesa del Gesù and Santa Maria Maggiore, he based what he said on memories of the floor plan of St. Nicholas Cathedral and the Church of Our Lady of Tyn. He swore that in summer heat flowed over the cobblestones like lava, the streets were dead as church Latin and people withdrew to cool hillside parks. But he didn't let on that he was referring to rare Prague heat spells and the gardens on Letna Hill, not the Pincio.

Like Scheherazade spinning a nightly tale, Tomas depended upon his anecdotal powers to postpone what he dreaded. As long as he misled Anna and didn't delude himself in the bargain, he thought they could limp along like this indefinitely, delaying the moment when they either landed on their feet or somersaulted into quicksand.

*T*hat's nice and smooth now." Anna rinsed his face, stepped out of the tub and dried off with a towel that had the word *Spartak* woven into its nap.

Tomas waited in ankle-deep water. She hung the towel over his standing cock and headed into the bedroom.

Stretched out on the sheet, her legs apart, her arms pressed to her sides, she resembled a piece of Egyptian mortuary art. Wet black hair helmeted her head, and her eyes were rimmed in antimony. Reaching for him, she whispered, "Love."

Tomas skated a hand up the inside of her brown thigh. She was moist everyplace except where he put his finger.

"I'm so clean I squeak," she said.

He moved his mouth down her belly. It smelled of starch from the towel. Lower, he licked away layers of perfumed soap so that he could taste her. When Tomas loved a woman he liked to touch her with his tongue, sink it deep inside her as if whispering secrets. This was as close as he could come to confiding in her. If he told the truth, he knew he'd lose her again.

Sooner or later he was bound to lose her anyway. He had resigned himself to that and set about committing her body to memory so that something of her would remain after she was gone. Years from now, he would call her to mind just as he did Prague and he'd picture her inch by inch—the hard buds of her breasts, the tight slit of her navel, the soft slippery bud buried in a purse of flesh between her legs, the beaded membrane so seamless under his lips that he couldn't tell where he ended and she started. His lone defense against the sadness that would otherwise have haunted him was a conviction that he was preserving her, embalming her, in language.

Her pelvis lifted, her spine arched. Tension rippled up one leg and down the other. Tomas thought she was about to come, but she was reaching toward the night table.

"Not that," he said.

"Yes, that," she sang in the same cajoling voice she had used when shaving him.

"I don't want anything between us."

"And I don't want to argue."

"You act like I have a disease."

"For all you know I have one. Isn't that what you said?"

When she came back after Fletcher was kidnapped, Tomas had insisted on protected sex. She might have caught something from the American, he taunted her. Although he didn't believe this, it pleased him to insult her. It was such a small price for her to pay. But once he had made his point and was ready to do without condoms, it was Anna who insisted on using them to remind him that things still weren't the way they had been between them.

Ripping open the foil packet with her teeth, she fitted the sheath over him.

"Now I feel nothing," he said.

"Let's see if we can't change that." She urged him onto his back and lowered herself over him. "Feel anything yet?"

He shook his head that he didn't.

"Tell me if this helps." She rocked back and forth, hugging him in the cradle of her thighs. "Shut your eyes," she reminded him.

They were, she always told him, his worst feature, never deader than when filmed over with desire. He closed them and saw red, as though he had eyes like a crow's, which according to legend bled during sex. As Anna kept up her stage directions, asking him to do this and now that, he barely listened. Her instructions seldom changed. But then spontaneity wasn't what he expected from her. Where whirl was king, Tomas wanted stillness and release from any thought of Fletcher and from what he feared would happen to McClintock.

6

Zack's room was furnished with a telephone, but no outlet to connect it; a rabbit ear TV antenna, but no television; a console of dials for temperature control, but no air conditioner. Although clean and polished to a waxy gloss, it contained a couple of creepily intimate items that left him feeling like an interloper trespassing on the preserve of a registered guest who might return at any moment. A pair of support hose hung in the closet and a carton of panty liners lay in the bureau's bottom drawer. The bed—a foam mattress slapped down on a wooden frame—bore the imprint of a body that appeared to have slept in the same spot for years.

Beneath the wallpaper's *fleur-de-lis*, a capillary pattern of wires spread toward the ceiling. In the old days, Zack guessed, the room must have been bugged and monitored by cameras. Maybe it still was. Maybe Big Brother wasn't dead, just dozing at the controls until someone switched on the juice and got the poison pumping again. It was one thing to change political systems. It was a different matter to dismantle all remnants of a national intelligence network. They'd have to raze every building and reassemble it brick by brick.

On the off chance he was being watched, Zack concealed his money belt as he undressed. But he didn't bother to hide the .38. After the run-in with Misha, he'd rather it be known that he was armed.

After showering and shampooing the glass from his hair, he debated what to do next. Though anxious to get started, he was in no frame of mind to ask questions or answer them. It seemed best to avoid people until he regained his bearings. Above all, he didn't care to go downstairs for dinner and drink too much.

He stepped over to the window and gazed out at the city. A defect in the glass distorted the view, compressing street lights and lanterns into pinpoints that shone from the chrome of cars and the gun barrels and brass of soldiers. The immense dome of the Grand Mosque, robin's egg–blue during daylight, dark as India ink at night, simulated the curve of the earth and the course of the stars in their constellations.

There were lightning flashes at the horizon. Or were they artillery bursts, miles and miles away, so far they might have been across the border in some breakaway battle zone that had declared its independence?

He wondered what the hell had brought Paul Fletcher to this benighted burg. It had to have been more than money. What was he trying to prove? Zack couldn't imagine and thought that he might well ask himself the same question. Was he only trying to help Adrienne, showing her how much he loved her? Or did he want to show himself, after that setback in Switzerland, that he could still cut it in this line of work?

Fetching Eddie's memo from his suitcase, he stretched out naked atop the bed, sinking into the trough some stranger had hollowed in the mattress. A letter fell out of the folder. Addressed in Adrienne's familiar handwriting, it had reached him the day before he departed for Central Asia. He had read it and didn't need to again. Several lines would never leave him; they were stenciled verbatim on his brain.

"Ever since I was a little girl," she had written, "I have craved your love and approval. What I usually received instead . . . well, it wasn't without its

own value. I learned early that what happens to us as children is very important, but what doesn't happen, what we don't get or feel, has consequences
too. Please don't take this wrong. I know you were busy and it wasn't easy
raising me alone and dealing with your grief about Mom."

Zack put the letter back into the folder, and the folder on the floor next to
the bed. Outside, there was what sounded like gunfire. It carried him along
like a lullaby, taking him back to 'Nam and memories of the Corps, then to a
scalding stew of sadness and the desire to discover what part he played in all
that had gone wrong. How to unbraid the long skein of his failures from the
short rope that remained?

He couldn't evade the conclusion that if he had been a more attentive father, Adrienne wouldn't have fallen for Paul Fletcher. Much as it pained him,
his mind made the next, the inevitable, leap, and he decided that if he had been
a better husband, Stefanie would still be alive. She had died in an automobile
accident, south of Quantico, on a road slick with ice. The fact that, instead of
being with her, he was half a world away in Saigon and she was worried about
him, and that she had had a premonition something dreadful would happen—
logically none of this added up to his guilt. But as he reckoned the calculus of
responsibility, he had nobody to blame except himself.

*A* thunderous rumble rocked the bed beneath him. To Zack it felt like a
bomb. Sand sizzled against the windowpane, driven by the horror movie har-
monics of gusting wind. He stood up and the floor heaved under his feet. The
whole hotel was swaying. Plaster sleeted down from the ceiling. The rabbit
ears hopped off an end table and jumped around the room, chased by the giant
black beetle of the telephone.

Earthquake! As the word composed itself in his mind, Zack was already
running toward the bathroom. During seismic tremors, he knew the drill—
take shelter in a doorjamb. He braced himself in the metal frame and was confronted by a mirror that was fast losing its silver backing. Parts of him

disappeared—a hand, an arm, an ear dropped off. Just enough remained of his face to show how baffled and frightened he looked and how foolish—a naked middle-aged man, loose flesh jiggling at his midsection. He didn't want to die, not like this, at the ass-end of the universe, in the ridiculous predicament of watching himself go to pieces, convinced that when they dug him out of the rubble there would be nothing to identify his body.

He scrambled back and grabbed his billfold from the pocket of his pants. He didn't bother about the money belt. Let some rescue worker get lucky and rich. Stuffing the wallet into his mouth, Zack felt better knowing that he wouldn't die nameless.

*T*hen just as suddenly as it had started, the shaking stopped. The hotel was still standing and so was he. Once the dust died down and the window cleared, he noticed that a white dove, peaceful as a Paraclete, had lighted on the window ledge. Darting its beak back and forth, it plucked from under its wings white feathers that appeared to be snowflakes. Magically they floated up on warm air currents.

Zack dressed and went downstairs. The timed light in the hall clicked like a canary's heart. His own ticker beat a notch or two faster.

In the dining room, Tomas, Anna, Misha and a man in a Roman collar sat at a circular table, serenely eating and drinking, perhaps too numb from alcohol to have fled the quake. Bottles of vodka, bubbly domestic wine and imported scotch stood at each place setting. A fine talc had fallen elsewhere in the sepulchral room, but not a speck of it marred their platters of salami, pickles, cucumbers and tomatoes.

Now in a white Reebok tracksuit, Misha leaned far back in his chair, like a smug customer awaiting a shave and manicure. Beside him, the priest looked sickly and consumptive. Cigarette smoke and the overhead fluorescent light conspired to give him the green-gilled complexion of a fish about to be filleted.

Dapper in a counterfeit Lacoste shirt with an alligator on the chest that would swim away in the first wash, Tomas introduced Zack to Anna and Father Josef. "Misha, of course, you know."

Zack nodded. Misha blew a smoke ring in his direction.

"What the hell hit us?" Zack asked.

A smile hovered on Tomas's lips like a climber stranded on a cliff. "We have these little tremors from time to time."

"If that was a tremor, I'd hate to feel a full-blown quake."

"You would, my friend. Trust me, you would." He motioned Zack to a chair between the baboon and the emaciated priest. "Something to eat and drink?"

"Is there tea and that flat bread?"

"Of course." Tomas spoke Russian to Anna, who was running a pendant back and forth on a gold chain around her neck. Her Byzantine eyes skewered Zack. She crossed to the kitchen, glancing back at him. Under her skin-tight white slacks, black panties were visible as a negative triangle from the cleft of her buttocks to the V of her crotch.

"Ziggurat?" Misha shook a pack of Papirosis at Zack.

"I don't smoke."

"Americans! So stupid, so scared. How does one ziggurat kill you?"

"Father Josef comes here twice a week," Tomas said, "and we make a meal and he teaches us Italian. Anna's father was from Rome and she hopes to emigrate."

"I am Polish." Father Josef scrupulously downplayed his ability as an Italian instructor. "But I did my studies in Rome and I know Latin and there is a similarity in the languages."

"He's the only Pole arriving here not in a cattle car," Misha said.

"Many Poles were deported," Father Josef said, "by Stalin. But I come from Krakow two years ago."

"Very few travelers visit us by choice," Tomas said. "Which makes it a great honor to have you, Mr. McClintock."

"Did you come after the revolution?" Zack asked the priest.

"This revolution," Misha snorted, "is one big joke."

"When the people have their church back," Father Josef said, "they need a priest. They didn't have one since the war."

Zack asked, "Which war?"

Father Josef held up his thumb and first finger, his canonicals, the consecrated fingers that touched the Holy Eucharist. "The Second World War."

"Nothing is different," Misha said. "Communist becomes capitalist, dictator is democrat. All the same."

"Not for you," Tomas broke in. "Your life gets better and better."

Misha grinned and poured himself a shot of Johnny Walker Black.

Zack hoped that if he ignored him, Misha might shut up. Better yet, go away. "It must be a big change from Poland," he said to the priest.

"So and so. Some things good, some things not. People here don't so much believe in God and my parish is small. Mostly old women."

"His church is gymnasium for Russian army," Misha said. "It stinks of socks. I play there many times the game with a stick."

"He means hockey," Tomas volunteered.

"At least you have always the sun here," the priest said. "And in winter, there's fruit and vegetables."

"Before there were never any vegetables," Tomas said.

"Not for the *vory v zakone*," Misha said.

"True, the drones had no fresh food. Party officials hogged it all," Tomas explained. "When I was a boy, it was like sex. I spent so many hours dreaming about fruit and vegetables. I never believed they really existed. Now, in the bazaar, it's pornography." He caged his face behind the bars of his fingers. "There's so much everywhere, I hide my eyes and hurry away."

"This I do not believe one word," Misha said.

Anna undulated over to the table and placed a teapot and a *lepeshka* in front of Zack. Slipping an arm around her waist, Tomas lifted her onto his lap. She snapped at him in Russian. With a hula of her hips, she realigned her panties and sat in her own chair.

Misha laughed, and Tomas laughed with him. "She tells me not to touch her in front of a priest, but I believe she says this because of you," he told Zack. "She likes Americans."

"That's nice. Not everybody does."

"She figures they have two big advantages—lots of money and most of their teeth."

The hotel manager's talkativeness puzzled Zack. Everything he said seemed to imply its opposite; he might as well have been speaking in italics. Anna, too, had a hard time understanding him. Pawing through thorny brambles of English, she tried to pluck out a few intelligible phrases. But it was Tomas's smoothness, the honeyed language he slathered over the grit of his meaning that left Zack confused about his point. "You mention things changing. What about the wires in the walls of my room? Is the hotel bugged?"

"No, it's not like the old days. Someone was always listening and there was no privacy even for a man in his own bed. Whenever married couples had something to say, they went to the kitchen and banged pots and pans. That deafened the NKVD."

"I know women in Poland who still announce they are pregnant," the priest said, "by pounding the stove and screaming."

"I had some sympathy for the secret police," Tomas went on. "Imagine their poor eardrums. Their empty minds." He tapped a finger to his temple.

"*Otmorozheni,*" Misha said.

"Right," Tomas agreed, "they suffered from frostbitten brains. Imagine listening to married couples complain all day about the price of cabbage and all night about their sad sex lives. It's no wonder Communism collapsed—it was emotionally and mentally exhausted."

*H*e poured himself a glass of water as if to punctuate the end of the subject, but ran on with more anecdotes about the ironies of the Soviet system. "People accused the Party of being liars. They acted like they preferred the truth.

But no matter what they claim now, everybody was happy to live a lie back then."

"Not everybody," the priest protested.

"Those who didn't are dead."

"No, there were dissidents. There was Solidarity in Poland and Charter 77 in Czechoslovakia."

"A few thousand *refuseniks* in a population of how many hundreds of millions? It stands to reason that Communism couldn't have survived so long if the majority didn't cooperate."

"Not me," Misha belligerently proclaimed and pulled the cuffs of his sweat pants up his legs. There were blue stars tattooed on both kneecaps. "You know what means this?" he demanded.

Zack shook his head that he didn't.

"I kneel to no person, no power." He flicked the tassel of hair that grew at the nape of his neck. "You know what means this?"

Zack had had enough of this meathead. "I know what a rattail covers," he said.

Bewildered, Misha turned to Tomas who, despite his best effort to suppress it, burst into laughter. Neither Father Josef nor Anna understood, but Anna sensed trouble. She left the table for the lobby. A minute later Misha followed her.

"There goes a guy," Zack said, "who could start a fight in an empty room."

"Yes." Tomas was still chuckling. "In the old days, he would have been arrested for exhibiting symptoms of fascist delinquency and anarchistic nihilism."

"Not to mention dialectical errors and parasitic behavior," Father Josef joined in.

Zack broke the flat loaf of bread in half and fixed a salami sandwich as the priest and the hotel manager continued to joke about Misha. Clearly relieved that he was gone, Tomas said, "It's a mistake to make fun of him. Misha's nobody to laugh about. He's not stupid. He understands more than you think."

Father Josef salted a sliced cucumber, dipped it into a glass of vodka and took it like a host on his tongue. Chastened by what Tomas said, he drained the glass and busied himself stamping circles with it on the tablecloth.

"Do you come to us on business?" Tomas asked.

Zack washed down a bite of the sandwich with tea. "I suppose you could say it's personal business."

"You're not with the government?"

"I'm on my own."

"We're in a period," Tomas said, "when people aren't always sure themselves who they're working for. Or against. Some claim to be agents of a state when they're really in private enterprise."

"Must be hard to tell the players without a scorecard," Zack agreed. "But trust me, I know who I'm working for. I'm Paul Fletcher's father-in-law."

Tomas couldn't hide his surprise. "I didn't realize Fletcher was married."

"You knew him?"

"Of course. There aren't many Americans around. He visited the hotel sometimes to eat and have a drink. Do you hope to ransom him?"

"I don't have a million bucks, if that's what you mean. But his kidnappers aren't demanding money anymore. They want some kid flown to the States for treatment."

Tomas munched at a pickle. Judging by his expression, it was sour. "Nobody knows where that second message originated."

"Do they know where the first one came from?"

"Nobody's sure about anything."

Father Josef pushed to his feet. He didn't care to be part of this conversation. "Arrivederci to Anna. Tell her to attend Mass one Sunday," he said to Tomas. "Tell her to bring you." He shook hands with Zack and added that he too was welcome in church.

After the priest left, Tomas said, "You Americans go to church all the time, don't you?"

"Some do."

"My mother baptized me a Catholic. I went to Mass for my marriage. I haven't been since then. At school they taught us that religion is a knife severing the vein of progressive socialism." He made a cutting motion over the salami platter. "I fear it's too late for me to be redeemed."

He found it difficult to believe that Tomas cared to discuss religion. More likely, he wanted an excuse to quit talking about Fletcher. Normally in his work, Zack proceeded on the assumption that the best approach to any topic was oblique. But with this guy he suspected he could waste weeks circling a subject. He decided to force the issue. "You figure there's any chance Fletcher's still alive?"

"I'm sorry, but no. It's been too long. If the kidnappers didn't kill him, conditions have."

"Conditions?"

"There are too many competing interests in this town. They couldn't hide him here all these months. The desert's out of the question. That leaves the mountains, and he wouldn't last a winter."

"Doesn't anybody live up there?"

"Some do. But not Fletcher—soft from university teaching and years in a lab. You need to be hard and to have very little in your head to survive in the mountains."

"If he's dead, why the new ransom note? Why offer to release him?"

"Who's offering? Ask yourself that. Then ask about this boy. Who cares about him? Such children are like roaches—everywhere in the streets getting stepped on. Only the woman he lives with believes he's worth saving."

"You know her? You've seen the kid?"

"Yes."

"What do you make of him?"

"I'm not a scientist, but the boy doesn't seem to me so special." He fidgeted with the pickles, tomatoes and cucumbers, rearranging them on a platter as if to illustrate his ideas. "Dr. Medvedev thinks he's retarded and belongs in an asylum. The Mullah thinks he's Satan in human form. I have my opinions."

"They're good enough for me. I'd appreciate hearing them." Zack splashed vodka into a glass. The first sip felt like dry ice sliding down his throat and melting in his gullet.

"This boy of Kathryn's," Tomas said, "he's like the rest of us, only a little unluckier. We're leftovers from an experiment that failed. It blew up in our faces. Now we have to go on living in the bombed-out laboratory."

"Fletcher's lab?"

"You're being too literal. It's simple, really, if you remember what's been going on . . ." He gave a languid backward wave, signaling a long, long time. "This is the toilet for all the shit Moscow decided to flush away—a dump for political enemies, criminals, the population of dissident republics. Anything that was dangerous or had to be kept secret, they did it here. Atomic testing, biological research, new weapons—we were the guinea pigs. Fletcher was just another chapter in that tradition."

"Was it widely known what he was doing?" Zack asked.

"Not widely. But he was a talkative man when he drank, and rumors spread. Nobody was surprised. They had been through it before—chemicals in the food, rivers too polluted to freeze in winter, snow falling in black flakes, kids born with tumors. How can we believe this boy of Kathryn's was raised by animals when so many here have been reduced to beasts?"

Tomas had started to sound less like someone in love with the sound of his own voice than like a man attempting to hide how deeply he cared. But sincerity could be another disguise, Zack knew, and he probed for what lay beneath it. When he asked about Islamic fundamentalists, Tomas skittered off on a tangent, fuming about a former hotel employee, a bellboy called Bakshilla. "He swears the Koran has the answer. But he's replacing one form of propaganda with another. Instead of comrades meeting for self-criticism sessions, he has them in the mosque praising Allah and Mohammed and handing him their money. Hamas, the Hezbellah, holy wars in Baghdad and Algeria, he pretends he's in touch with all of that. You'd think he was bankrolled by Osama bin Laden. But he's full of hot air."

"So's a balloon. But once it's airborne it can cover a lot of ground. It can cross mountains."

"If Bakshilla crossed the mountains, he wouldn't carry bombs. His ambition is to be a moral policeman, the Minister for the Promotion of Virtue and the Prevention of Vice."

"To be a policeman, you need a gun."

"That's not Bakshilla. He'd rather frighten old women and young girls. He believes bananas are an aphrodisiac and told me to take them off the hotel menu."

Zack gave Tomas the laugh he was looking for, then said, "Haven't a lot of these Moslem sects made a regular industry out of holding hostages for ransom?"

"Believe me, Bakshilla had nothing to do with the kidnapping."

Zack knocked back the rest of the vodka and poured more. Wrung out after the long day—the ride up-country, the rock through the car window, the wrangling with Misha, topped off by a seismic tremor—he thought he should cut this talk short and get to sleep. But he found himself saying, "I understand Paul may be dead, but I have to know for sure. My daughter's young. I don't want her wasting her life, waiting around for a man who's never coming back."

"So you're searching for proof."

"Yes. If not his remains, then a witness, somebody who has even second-hand knowledge of what happened."

"Without a body, how could you ever believe?" Tomas studied him with dead eyes. "And please remember what's written: 'Who gathers knowledge gathers pain.'"

"The Koran?"

"No. The Bible. Father Josef could quote the chapter and verse. In your country, Mr. McClintock, it may be natural to ask questions. Here only powerful people have that right. For an outsider such as yourself, it's dangerous."

"I thought things had changed."

"They have. Now it's not the KGB or the state that asks questions. That privilege, like a lot of others, has been privatized."

"Are you suggesting there's someone in the private sector who could tell me about Paul?"

"I'm suggesting the opposite. I'm suggesting don't ask. And please don't repeat anything I've told you. If I could get out, I'd go. You should never have come in the first place."

7

*M*ost days, despite the heat and the threat of civil unrest, Kathryn Matthews crossed the city on foot to shop in the bazaar and sample the mood of the streets. The morning light was meridional, the air aromatic of fresh baked *lepeshka*. Round loaves of it lay stacked like paving stones outside communal ovens. School-age kids chewing long greasy corn sticks called out smart-aleck remarks about her height, her lanky arms and legs, and strawberry-blond hair. Soldiers and armed civilians shouted too. But the only ones she feared were the truculent, bearded men in front of the Grand Mosque. They shouted that she should cover her arms and lower her eyes.

Kathryn hurried on, her shadow spilling ahead of her as attenuated as a candle, her wind-tossed hair a guttering flame. Had she been merely pretty, she might have become accustomed to people staring at her, but her face, though difficult to forget, was not conventionally beautiful. It had a fixity of attention that suggested the long exposure of an antique camera. There was a strong set to her jaw which her mouth, no matter how it was made up, re-emphasized. The upper lip was thin, the lower one full, and when they opened there was an instant of adhesive tension before the defining qualities of her character—voluptuousness and stringency—parted company.

Kicking up fallen fluff from poplar trees, she circled a ceremonial arch. Heavy traffic ground around it like a great millstone. In the Russian quarter each shop sold a single product, and the word for it was scrawled in soap on the front window—*malako, syr, khleb, kalbasa*, milk, cheese, bread, sausage. But as she entered the old town, the simple coherence of the scene dissolved into arabesques, and the broad, bombastic boulevards dwindled to crooked alleys. At a fountain she watched a woman sink her arms elbow-deep in water, apparently rinsing a skein of wool. She was washing a lamb. A man lugging two gutted goat carcasses bustled along beside a teenage girl with a live chicken clutched to her chest. Local lore had it that carrying a live fowl heightened a woman's fertility. Then again, the girl might have been bringing the bird home for that night's dinner.

Men in quilted *chapans* lounged at the lip of a murky reservoir. A tree had taken root in a crack in the stone basin, and a stork had built its nest in the top branches. But there was no stork there now, no storks left anywhere in the country. Moslems complained that Jews had killed them off. Christians blamed the Moslems. But everybody knew it was the Russians and their pollution that had forced the storks to migrate by eliminating the frogs they fed on. Still, each time she passed it, Kathryn glanced at the nest hoping to spot a hatchling.

It came to her, as it did more and more these days, that she would miss these walks once she and the boy were gone. So while she had the chance, she felt she had better feed the appetite that gnawed her—a yearning to break through to this place and to deeper parts of herself. Among the other things she allowed herself to wish for—love, meaningful work, a sense of where her life was leading—she wanted to go home knowing that she hadn't let this experience slip through her fingers. To Kathryn the city was a book written in stone. She intended to take it with her to the United States and continue reading it at leisure.

With no pretext except pleasurably wandering, she strolled past mosques, a synagogue, several Christian churches—Catholic, Russian Orthodox, Armenian—each in a different state of dilapidation or desultory renovation. Tubes of bottomless plastic barrels sloped down from roofs, shunting debris to the ground. She saw doors painted blue to ward off the evil eye, and scorched alcoves where Zoroastrians secretly worshipped fire and celebrated the feast of Noruz. She passed into a burial ground strewn with wreaths, votive candles, jars of flowers and scraps of prayer scribbled on papers fluttering beneath pebbles. On the tombs, every inflection of color and fletched tile, each feathery application of gold leaf was meticulously precise, yet the overall design struck Kathryn as an explosion of fractals that only an expert in Chaos Theory could decipher.

Entering a precinct that appeared to have been constructed by giants for giants, she advanced like an inchling among monuments commissioned centuries ago by despotic megalomaniacs with no end of money and no shortage of slave labor. Pilgrims processed counterclockwise around mausoleums, kissing cold cenotaphs, conking their foreheads against marble. In a courtyard as big as a football field, women crawled under the *mihrab*, praying for children, begging for sons. Shards of glazed tile showered down in tessellated patterns that passersby reshuffled with their feet. Domes had split open exposing vaulted interiors, as ornately decorated as Fabergé eggs, and expanses of bare masonry, which resembled lost continents on maps sketched by cartographers under the sway of fantasy rather than geography.

*I*n the past, she had spent hours roaming around these ruined tombs, but now that the boy was waiting for her, she allowed herself only a brief visit. Eager to rush back to him, she felt that she, too, was on a leash. It yanked her from cubicle to cubicle in the marketplace. A shopkeeper who reckoned the bill on an abacus sold her eyedrops and refills of the antibiotic Dr. Medvedev prescribed. Farther on, she bargained for cheese and a honeycomb while shoals of small children swam around her. She gave them candy, chewing gum and spare change that weighed no more than balsa wood. The coins had holes at the center and might have blown away in a stiff breeze. But the kids were glad to get them and Kathryn was happy to give them.

Returning through the Russian quarter, she passed the post office, site of her most searing frustrations, the place where she collected infrequent letters and attempted to put through international phone calls. It was run by petty tyrants and sticklers for rules who were never offended by any bribe—unless it was too small. Now these same sadists, like many *budgetniki* on the public payroll, hadn't been paid in six months. So on the off-chance of finding cash, they had taken to ripping open envelopes from hard currency countries.

In the crowd outside the PO, an old man hawked hand-carved puppets that danced at the end of strings like dwarfs dangling from nooses. A blue-faced matron, who may have been drunk or choked by the cleaning solvent she was selling, unfurled a moth-eaten rug, flung dirt over it, then scrubbed it up. On-lookers couldn't have been more mesmerized had she climbed aboard the carpet and cruised around Pushkin Square.

When a man fell into step beside her, Kathryn kept her eyes down and continued walking. He wore a turban and around his waist, a silk scarf, the mark of the Naqshbandi sect. Moslem mystics, they were reputed to have preserved their beliefs in secret all during the Soviet era. A wild curly beard hid half his face, but she recognized him as a former bellboy from the Intourist Hotel. Now that he had become a Mullah, she didn't know whether to address him as Bakshilla or by some honorific title.

"Your arms will burn," he said. It was impossible to judge whether he was warning her about the sun or the fires of hell that awaited women in sleeveless blouses.

"It's hot." Kathryn said.

"In The Book it is written that women should stay in their place." He spoke English. From tourists at the hotel he had learned a little of a lot of languages, but all his sentences had a Koranic ring, as if casual conversation would be a moral offense.

"What's a woman's place?"

"Separate from men, as in the mosque."

"I'm going to my house. That's my place."

"I hear you have a child there. The Koran tells us that children are the ornament of this life."

She was relieved to learn that they agreed on one thing.

"I want to see him," the Mullah said. "I want to help."

"Thanks, but Dr. Medvedev's helping him."

"He is a doctor for animals. I heal men and their souls. This child suffers from a sickness I can cure."

"It's kind of you to offer—"

"I do not offer kindness. I insist on examining him."

"Doctor Medvedev's done that, and the boy's much better."

"Is he?" the Mullah asked, lifting his nose as if he sniffed a lie. "Does he eat and drink as humans do? Does he speak a language? Does he pray to Allah? If not, why do you say he is healed?"

"I didn't say healed." She quickened her pace until she realized this would only bring him to her house sooner. "I said he's getting better. But it takes time, and he needs special tests and treatment."

"I will treat him."

"What I'm talking about has to be done by experts with machines."

"Machines?"

Kathryn despaired of explaining the purpose of a CAT scan, an MRI and an EEG. "Look, you just can't see him. Strangers make him nervous and upset."

"But how is that?" The Mullah gloated at catching her in a contradiction. "You said he is better."

They had reached her house. Every winter grey mold furred its outer walls. Then during warm weather the mold turned brown and flaked off. While she and the Mullah argued, a mist that felt like caterpillar fuzz floated around them. She couldn't afford to underestimate the damage this man might do. As he harangued her for not letting him bring Allah's word to the child, Kathryn's neighbors leaned out their doors, listening. Some had already complained that the boy howled when the *muezzin* summoned the faithful to prayer. She didn't dare provoke them by disputing the Mullah's authority in public.

"All right," she said. "You can come in for a minute."

"Unlock the door. I go in alone."

"No. I have to be there."

"It is a scandal for a Mullah to be in a house with a Christian woman."

"You'll scare him. I'm the only person he trusts."

"Leave the door open and stand outside so he sees you."

"He might break free. He's fast. We wouldn't be able to catch him."

"Is he your prisoner? Is he so miserable he must escape?"

"Look," she said flatly, "either I come along or you don't go in."

Tugging fingers through his tangled beard, the Mullah capitulated and nodded for her to untumble the lock. From the living room, she heard the boy in the kitchen, his nails clicking against the floor as he scratched. She heard him and she smelled him—the wild, wet leaf odor that wouldn't wash off no matter how hard she scrubbed. The Mullah came in behind Kathryn, palpably relieved now not to be alone and grateful for the harness that hooked the kid by a leash to the wall.

Catching sight of the Mullah, the boy lifted his elongated jaw, reared up and growled. Kathryn whispered a steady stream of sibilants, soothing him with nonsense phrases and baby talk. As she stepped closer, he lowered his head and licked her hands. Like a cat caressing itself, he nuzzled her knees and surged in and out of her legs in a supple figure eight.

"You speak of him as a child," the Mullah said, "but he's a man. Why is he naked? You should cover him and cover your eyes."

"He tears off everything I put on him."

She fetched a plate from the cupboard, crumbled the honeycomb and set it in front of the kid. Crouching on elbows and knees, he gobbled the wax along with the sweetness inside it.

"You raise him like an animal." The Mullah gathered his robes in one hand and extended his other as if to show that he meant no harm or to make the boy believe he had more honey. "And he behaves like one. Let an animal doctor look after him and there's no hope he becomes human."

"Stand back. Don't scare him."

"What's his name?"

"I don't know."

"Even dogs have names."

"I was waiting to find out whether his family would come for him. I didn't want to give him a name if his mother and father call him something else."

"What mother? What father? This creature has no parents."

"Of course he does. They got separated from him. Or maybe they're dead. He's like any other little boy."

The Mullah shook his head, moving nearer. The kid craned his neck, glaring. Then he flattened himself to the floor. It might have been a submissive gesture. Or a warning. The Mullah came closer, chanting, "In all that Allah has created in the heavens and on earth, there are signs for righteous men."

"I agree," Kathryn said. "Allah created him and sent him to me as a sign, because I'm a teacher and I can help him."

"By letting him live naked in your kitchen? By tying him to a wall?"

"He was sick and I cleaned him. He was hungry and I fed him. He was frightened and I comforted him." It struck Kathryn that she sounded as oracular as the Mullah. "I'm teaching him to talk."

"Talk? This one will never talk. Not in a tongue we understand. Look at his eyes."

Instead, she looked at the Mullah's. They were black at the center and burned at the fringes. It was hard to say what they projected apart from their own piercing fervor. To Kathryn he looked like a shaman, some nickel-and-dime necromancer about to attempt an exorcism. Non sequiturs and formulaic phrases poured out of him. "Forbidden are carrion and blood and the flesh of swine," he declared as if diet were the issue.

"He doesn't eat meat," she objected. "He won't touch it. There's no truth to any of those stories. His eyes don't glow in the dark and he doesn't go out and hunt at night."

"You have no idea what he does while you sleep. You do not understand what you have brought into your house, into our town. Evil has many forms. But Allah knows them all and punishes devils in this world and the next."

Swirling the folds of his robe, he might have been a matador making passes at a bull, distracting him. Then he lunged, seized the boy's harness and hauled him upright. The kid slashed at him and swiveled around to sink his teeth into his wrist. But the Mullah gave him a savage shake and held him at arm's length. "Look at him and tell me he's human. Tell me he's not a beast or worse."

"You're hurting him. Put him down."

"They say the dog of a sheik is a sheik itself. Just so, the dog of the devil is Satan himself."

"He's a child," Kathryn cried. "Just a little boy who was abandoned and brought up alone."

"Brought up how? By who?" The boy leaned back his head and howled. "Only a wolf makes such a sound."

"Even if he was raised by wolves, he's still a human."

"Wolves don't raise human babies. They eat them. Then maybe—Allah alone knows—they become them. Don't you understand what he might do to you and the people of this town? Don't you know what could follow him here?"

Hanging from the harness and the Mullah's outstretched arm, the boy scrabbled his toes at the floor and gasped for breath. His howling stopped and in panic he started peeing. The pure force of the yellow jet jerked his penis erect. The spray went everywhere. The Mullah dropped him and jumped back, slapping at his robe as if it were on fire. In his frenzy, the boy broke the leash and clattered out of the kitchen. He and the Mullah raced through the living room, overturning furniture. The Mullah reached the front door first. The boy would have chased him into the street had Kathryn not caught his leash and pulled him up short.

Once the boy realized who had a hold of him, he stopped struggling and let her take him in her arms. He trembled and pressed his face to her shirtfront. Outside, the Mullah was trembling too, and his voice shook as he reeled from language to language—English to Russian to dialect. He was condemning Kathryn to a congregation of her curious and confounded neighbors who peered in at her and the naked boy she hugged to her chest. With words of execration echoing in her ears, she slammed the door and led him back to his corner of the kitchen.

8

*I*t was with relief that Tomas Vacek set out on foot across the city to deliver his report to Misha. In his Toyota Land Cruiser the trip would have taken no more than ten minutes. But he wanted to prolong his absence from the hotel and savor a rare sense of well-being. That others weren't as lucky heightened his appreciation of this moment when he felt safe and believed McClintock was too.

The modern section of town, constructed on a massive scale to impress the populace with Soviet might, had shed more masonry in the recent tremor. Unlike the ground-hugging mud hovels of the Moslem quarter, Russian highrises tended to crumble from the top down. The upper stories of a number of apartment towers were reduced to bare frames and rusty girders, reaching like broken ladders toward heaven. Between buildings, scavengers picked through the bricks, pipe and wire for anything they could use or sell.

Some of the destruction had been caused not by earthquakes, but by mafia turf wars, torchings by protection racketeers—all the vicious smash and grab tactics that passed for privatization in the aftermath of independence. Like prisoners on parole after half a century in solitary confinement, pedestrians skulked along the sidewalks with a strange gait, as if still in leg irons, alert to main chance and any opportunity for revenge.

Yet amid the squalor, there were stunning displays of privilege. In former government office buildings, pricey nightclubs and restaurants had opened, and smuggled luxuries could be bought from the backs of trucks that trafficked in commodities, ranging from caviar to kitchen appliances. The ravaged town was thick with dollar millionaires—a fact that would on any other day have rankled Tomas. Now he accepted it with equanimity.

At the gated entrance to a Christian cemetery, an aged babushka sat slumped on a bench selling flowers. A dog was draped over her legs like a lap rug. It raised its snout and growled at Tomas, and the babushka growled for it to shut up. Behind her, a vast tent of vines sagged over the tombs. In spots the tent had torn, and wingless angels, headless saints and shattered crucifixes poked through the net of frayed strings.

Crossing a bridge, he saw gypsies crouched on the river bank, washing clothes in the tea-colored water, pounding them against rocks. Behind them a colorful collage of socks, undershorts, skirts and head wraps was spread out to dry on the grass. Naked kids swam in the river, their gleaming black hair and brown bodies reminding him of Anna. The sight of human beings living like this sent a corkscrew through Tomas's heart. He would have saved them if he could.

But he couldn't be responsible for everybody. Last year, after an incursion from across the border by a band of guerillas whose identity was as mysterious as their motives, he had seen worse. Bodies and body parts had rafted down this river. Swollen purple, they floated by with birds perched on their heads, taking dainty pecks at the ripe meat.

Tomas trailed in the wake of a decrepit old couple. The stoop-shouldered man carried posters; the woman lugged a bucket of glue and a dripping brush. They used to distribute placards emblazoned with the hammer and sickle, the dates of glorious victories, Party congresses, performances by traveling orchestras and ballets. Now they stopped at a kiosk and pasted up a page of Koranic verses.

> Well have you deserved this doom:
> Too well have you deserved it!

He passed by them and into a park. Under a canopy of poplar and chenar trees, a delicately detailed mosque—the country's oldest and most venerated—was in a perfect state of preservation. To maintain its pristine condition, the townspeople concealed it under tons of earth whenever invaders approached the town gates. Centuries ago, after a murderous Mongol siege, nobody had survived to remember what lay beneath the mounded tumulus, and the mosque was lost for ages. Once it was rediscovered, pilgrims journeyed from all over the Islamic world to marvel at its façade of interwoven bricks, as intricate as a basket made of reeds gathered from the river that morning.

These days, so few believers visited the shrine that there was talk it would have been better to bury it again before the latest barbarian invasion. Thugs had taken over the park. Opium growers down from the mountains, gun runners, all manner of *shabashnuki*—the "self-employed," as Russians ironically put it—met here to buy weapons, change money and market information. Commandeering a cottage previously occupied by the mosque's caretaker, they had set up a combination clubhouse/clearinghouse. Twenty-four hours a day, it was hedged in by Mercedes and BMWs, sport utility vans and four-wheel drive vehicles, and above the cacophony of car radios and CDs, there was the nonstop babble of hard bargaining.

In Tomas's hand, the doorknob to the house throbbed like a live thing. But as soon as he stepped inside, the noise was muted by the cotton wool of cigarette smoke and dozens of close-packed bodies. The air had a meaty density to it and smelled of socks, marijuana and uric acid from lambskins that had been salted and cured, not tanned.

Misha summoned Tomas over to a pool table. Three men in identical porkpie hats and leather coats were with him. They had the braised faces and pale, shaved necks of country boys in town on business. Their ancestors might have arrived in cattle cars from Mongolia, courtesy of Stalin, fifty years ago. Or they might have ridden in on horseback eight centuries ago. No matter when they got here, it was always remarked of Mongols that they hailed from a land where even the butterflies sting.

Misha and the porkpie hats were munching cherries, spitting the pits into the pockets of the pool table. Two of the men brandished cues, but nobody seemed to know where the balls had gone.

Dismissing Tomas's suggestion that they move over to a corner to talk, Misha said, "Tell me about the American."

"He's not what you thought. I spoke to him last night. He didn't come to reopen the lab or replace the other guy." He felt squeamish about mentioning Fletcher by name. "He's here because of the second ransom letter."

Socketed deep in his skull, Misha's eyes registered doubt. "How can you be sure?"

"His daughter's married to the missing man. He's doing this to help her."

"Then he must have a lot of money on him."

"No, don't you remember? The last letter didn't ask for a million dollars. It offered a trade for the boy."

Misha was calculating, not recollecting. "It costs plenty to travel all that distance from America. And he paid me three hundred dollars with no complaint."

"I suppose he has something."

"He has to have thousands to fly the kid to the States." He glanced at the porkpie hats. Their lips were dark red from the cherries. "They'll snatch him and find out exactly how much he's carrying. Then we'll see how much more somebody will pay for him."

"They won't pay a penny for McClintock. Not after refusing to ransom the first one. He isn't working for the U.S. government. I told you, he's doing this for his family."

"You don't know who he's working for. And why do you care anyway?"

"I don't want trouble," Tomas said. "If you leave him alone, he won't learn anything and he'll go away."

"He's not leaving with his pockets full of *kapusta*," Misha said.

"You think he'll just hand it over to you?"

"If he doesn't, we'll send him where the stink comes from," one of the porkpie hats piped up.

This tickled Misha. He burst into laughter, but then began to choke. A cherry pit had stuck in his throat. He hacked and coughed it up.

"McClintock isn't worth worrying about." Tomas was aware of the wheedling tone of his voice and couldn't suppress it. "He's an old man. No threat."

"You're wrong," Misha said. "On the drive, he and I had an argument. He jumped on my back. He doesn't scare. He knows what he's doing."

"All the more reason not to bother with him. Why make him suspicious?"

"Maybe he's already suspicious. Maybe he's after you."

"No, he's only interested in Fletcher." In frustration, Tomas finally let the name slip. "Before he flies the kid to the States, before his daughter can do anything else in her life, he needs to know about his son-in-law."

"And when he finds out he's dead," Misha jabbed Tomas's chest, aiming at the tiny alligator on his knit shirt, "what then?"

"He gives up and goes home."

"Maybe not. Maybe he goes after us. You want that?"

"Of course not. But . . . ." As he reasoned with Misha, he moved his hands, polishing the air, painting a mural, anxious to smooth over every potential disagreement. ". . . the lab's closed. Fletcher's dead. The Americans won't come back unless you give them an excuse."

"I'd like them to come back and bring money."

"That's not what they'll bring. Look at Iraq, look at the Sudan."

"You afraid they'll hit us with rockets all the way from the Indian Ocean?"

"They'll hit somebody."

"So much the worse for somebody," Misha said. "Let them look after themselves. I want you watching McClintock."

*O*nce outside Tomas fell motionless in the undertow of music that swirled around the house. A tumult of buried feeling rose, as if from an ocean trench, and paralyzed him. As heavy metal competed with Armenian *patarks* sung in haunting strophelike psalms, he couldn't distinguish separate sounds or individual words. Instead he remembered what he had read on the wall: TOO WELL HAVE YOU DESERVED THIS DOOM.

Poised between parked cars, he gazed at the ground beneath his feet. Birds had marked the dust with the hieroglyphics of their claws. Tomas studied them for answers. But there were none there. Suddenly his brain was flooded with pious bursts of prayer that he had picked up from his mother. "Sweet Jesus have mercy on my soul. Blessed Mary intercede for me in my hour of need. Infant of Prague protect me."

Then a phrase from one of Father Josef's Italian lessons came to mind. *L'ultimo canto di gallo*, the last cry of the rooster. Shorn of all pride, Tomas was reduced to a final groan. He might have pleaded for forgiveness. But after what he had done, what hope could he have in God or anyone else? Examining his conscience was like lowering himself down a mineshaft with a lantern. He knew there was bound to be an explosion. Having accepted a bloody contract with Misha, there was no backing out now.

He gripped a chrome car door handle on either side of him. The day's scalding heat was stored up in the metal. He held tight and absorbed the pain. The most catastrophic choices in his life, Tomas was convinced, came as a consequence of previous bad choices. One flawed decision led inexorably to the next. Was this just another mistake? Or the final, fatal error?

Forcing himself to walk around the mosque, he circled it in a clockwise fashion to prove his indifference to religious protocol. He wasn't praying, wasn't performing some superstitious ritual. He was admiring the view, the exquisite latticework of brick turning crimson in afternoon light. One point in favor of pollution, it made for remarkable sunsets. The western sky was ribbed pink and purple. Wind flailed a rope against a flagpole. There was no flag. After the U.S.S.R. struck its colors, nobody had known what to run up in their place.

He retraced his steps across the bridge to the cemetery. Given the heaviness of his steps, he looked like he was carrying a graveyard inside him. Every man his age, Tomas thought, carried around the weight of his dead family, former lovers, lost friends and children. But he wondered how much room remained in his internal burial ground. And when would it break him?

A horse-drawn wagon, whispering on bald truck tires, rolled along beside him, the horse half-asleep in its traces, the driver barely awake with the reins wrapped around his wrist. After a day of begging, the city's cripples were being collected and delivered to wherever they spent the night. A boy helped those who couldn't climb aboard the wagon on their own. The flower seller and her lapdog both needed a boost.

Then Tomas noticed a man, or half a man, who hobbled along with rubber sandals strapped to his hands. He had to be hoisted up and wedged into place. Sight of him called to mind the old Party axiom: "Those who block the rails of history must expect to have their legs chopped off."

As the wagon wheeled onward, he was conscious of the adage swinging like a bell clapper in his brain. Dispassionate in its power, oblivious to his existence, the locomotive of history had plowed into Tomas. But he was still walking, and now somebody else was about to get splattered on the tracks.

9

*W*hen Anna grew bored behind the reception desk, she locked the cash register and told one of the chambermaids to stand in for her. This would infuriate Tomas, but she was confident that she could handle him. Blessed with the same faith in her sexual allure as a saint has in the existence of her soul, she found it exciting what she could accomplish with next to no effort. Deft as a magician plucking a rabbit from a hat, she had the power to change men's minds, change their shapes. With the lightest touch, just a look or a smile, she could coax Tomas into a column of coiled heat.

Upstairs, she put on her leotard and did dance aerobics to one of the cassettes she had stolen from Fletcher's apartment after he disappeared. It was music they had listened to as they made love. The music reminded her of what she had lost—a ticket out—as well as the way he used to treat her. Sweet, gentle and generous as Tomas was, she got tired of his melancholy garrulousness and missed Fletcher's boisterousness in bed.

Although she pretended to be aroused by Tomas's tales about Rome, they, too, had begun to bore her. Each evening as he reopened the plush casement of his memory, it was an effort for her to act fascinated by the jeweled images he dangled in front of her as though they were diamonds. For an hour or two, they distracted her from the dreary reality of her life, but later, when she came back to herself, she questioned what was true and what false.

Fluent in five languages, Tomas was, she realized, a gifted liar in every one of them. Even when he spoke Russian, she had difficulty following the convolutions of his sentences and felt like a prisoner of the present tense, while he was free to express himself in the subjunctive and conditional. Seductively textured as his descriptions of Rome were, she never trusted that he'd actually take her there. At times, she doubted that he had been there.

Last night, for instance, he mentioned that they would travel to Italy by train in a private, wood-paneled wagon-lit. The trip would last long lovely days, he said. But Anna had studied the map and she remembered Fletcher talking about flying to Frankfurt in five hours. Did the railroad even run as far as Rome?

When the music ended, she went into the bathroom, washed out her leotard and climbed into the warm tub. As she soaped herself, she reconsidered her arrival in Italy. Maybe a train wouldn't be such a bad idea after all. Tomas had made their compartment sound so snug and romantic, with the two of them at a window watching a landscape covered by snow. Hill towns and tiny farm villages would flash past in a shower of sparks fizzing up from the tracks. Aroused by the rocking motion of the locomotive, they would make love, then sleep until morning when the train crashed through forests of ice-encrusted trees, making a racket, he said, like a raucous tavern where revelers danced on broken plates. They would reach Rome as the city shrugged off the last tatters of night, and the street lamps along the Tiber winked out one by one. Flocks of seagulls would skim the water, trailing the confetti of their reflections over the river.

As he set the scene, Tomas passed his slippery hands between her thighs. Anna did the same now. Deep in thought, deep as a seed in its fruit, she touched herself as he had, tenderly at first, then faster, moving a single finger in a circle. She lifted the detachable showerhead and pressed the pulsing nozzle to her pelvis. She held it there until she thought she couldn't stand it. Then she held it there longer, until her knees shuddered and fell apart.

The trouble with Tomas, Anna decided, was that despite the severity of his face, he had a softness at his center—something like the fontanel on an infant's head before the skull hardens and closes. This might waken maternal instincts in some women, but it troubled Anna and made her wish Tomas brought the same passion to sex as he did to talking. Once, when she complained that he was dreamy and detached in bed, he replied with a Persian proverb: "I am there from where no news even of myself reaches me."

That was exactly Anna's point. A flesh and blood man shouldn't depend on proverbs nor fabricate a life from words. Raised on a collective farm where her parents tilled the chemically polluted cotton fields, she preferred harsh reality. Her earliest memory had been a desire to get away, to escape the fate that she feared was written for her. Moving to town had not been easy, and sometimes she felt her soul would shrivel to the degree where her one companion was the little girl she used to be. But she never mentioned this to Tomas or anyone else. Weakness frightened her, and she would only show hers when she saw some advantage. If she believed in any proverb, it was: "Kiss the hand you can't cut off." But she didn't confide this to Tomas either.

Anna stepped out of the tub and placed the immersion coil back in the water. She didn't want to waste it. Tomas might like a bath later. In the other room, with the cassette recorder off, the silence reminded her of Fletcher as much as the music had. He had never had much to say. It was enough that he promised to take her to the States; she didn't need him to describe the country.

He seldom talked about sex, never shared his fantasies or asked about hers. In bed, he pivoted her like a jeweler examining an uncut diamond, debating which facet to grind next. He manhandled her around the mattress, seized her by the ankles and scissored her legs wide. He folded her knees to her chest, split her open and plunged in. He lapped between her thighs as avidly as a lamb at a salt lick, flicking his tongue from the cleft in front to the crease in back. The first time he did this she shouted for him to stop, and he rolled away, daring her to get up and go if she didn't like it. When she stayed, he buried his face where it had been and, yes, though he never asked, she did like it. She liked the way he carved new channels of sensation, pushing her from pain to pleasure and back again, convincing Anna that her body consisted of nothing except nerve ends and every part of it was capable of a climax.

It was uncanny how much the new American reminded her of Fletcher. True, this man McClintock was bigger, older, more haggard. But about them both she noticed a quality that seemed to combine sympathy with the potential for cruelty. Far from repelling her, this intrigued Anna. She tried to guess his age. He must be over fifty. Still, she liked his hair, lightly salted with gray, and his eyes. Green as dollar bills, they glittered as if threaded with the kind of metallic strip she had seen in certain hard currencies.

As she dressed, she gave herself up to the grasp of an idea that only gradually developed. She put on a bra and a sequined blue khalat. She never wore panties except under slacks. They were just something else to clean and keep track of. She liked how it felt to go without them, to be conscious of her cunt, the faint smell of it when she crossed her legs. It was nothing to be ashamed of, that barely perceptible odor. She had never met a man who apologized for his prick.

After doing her lips and eyes, she added the final touch, fastening around her neck what she referred to as her "sexy necklace." A present from Tomas, it was a tear-shaped lozenge of amber with a fly trapped inside—a Spanish fly, an insect whose attributes Tomas had explained at needless length. Even on an isolated collective farm, she had learned such things.

*A*nna knocked at Zack's room. A ladder of quizzical furrows climbed his forehead when he opened the door and discovered her at the door instead of a chambermaid.

"Do I disturb?" she asked.

"No."

"Permit, please."

She walked in as far as the window, couldn't feign interest in the view and swung around to him.

"Your time here, it goes well?"

"Good enough."

"You like the city?"

"Haven't had a chance to see much of it."

"You stay long?"

Her questions had the mechanical lilt of a language lesson, a carryover from the Italian classes with Father Josef.

"I'll be around a while," he said.

Executing a slow three-hundred-and-sixty-degree sweep, she inventoried his belongings. There was nothing much except dirty clothes draped over a chair. "Sometimes Tomas makes a not such good impression," she said.

"Tomas is all right by me."

"Yes, but sometimes too much talk. Permit, please." She sat against the headboard of the bed and patted the sheet beside her. Zack stayed on his feet.

"We have a saying," she told him. "A man creeps down on the floor to feed the dog while the woman in his bed goes hungry."

He appeared to be parsing this for an American equivalent.

"Your house in the States," Anna said, "it's nice?"

"I like it."

Giggling, she clapped a hand to her mouth. "My English is little and it goes away. Tell me of your home."

"There's not much to say. It's a Cape Cod."

He perched at the edge of the bed so she could see his eyes, but not the .38 at the back of his belt. His complexion, she thought, was like water-worked rock, smooth in open stretches, craggy in the corners. As she formulated a sentence in her mind, a subterranean grumble broke the silence.

"The generator," Anna said, "it makes small music when it marches."

He smiled. She smiled, too. Raising the folds of the *khalat*, she let the material fall to her lap. "Hot," she said.

"Hot," he agreed.

She fiddled with the chunk of amber on the chain around her neck and whispered what sounded like "tsetse"—as in the fly that causes sleeping sickness. Lowering her hooded eyelids to half-mast, she looked at him drowsily and muttered "tsetse" again, meaning "sexy." When Zack didn't react, she reached over and touched him. For a moment, he didn't move. Then he set her hand aside.

"You don't like?"

"I'm flattered," he said. "It's the best offer I've had in years. But there's my war injury."

Lacquered with cosmetics, she looked like an icon doing a double take. "Excuse?"

"No excuses. That's just the way it is." He started to stand up.

She caught him by his belt and the money belt beneath it. "I do wrong?"

"You do great." He pried her fingers loose. "It's me that doesn't do so great these days."

"I fuck good. No one finds out."

Zack's shoulders sagged and shook. Anna thought he was crying. But as she leaned closer to him, she realized he was laughing.

"Happy now?" She stroked his hair. "A man your age looks good with hair."

"A man my age is lucky to have hair or anything else." He took her hands off him. "Look, honey, I'm fifty-five. I've been taking these pills. Some parts of me work perfect. Some parts not so hot."

As he hauled her off the bed, her *khalat* shimmered like the scales of an exotic fish. Her face, too, had the baffled look of a fish that can't figure out how the bait has become a hook.

"But how do I get to America?" Anna wailed as he walked her out of the room.

"I've been asking myself the same question all day," Zack said, and shut the door behind her.

10

*A*s amused as he was by the encounter with Anna, Zack was more amazed by his reaction. He had damn near let that little sweetie in her sparkling party dress catch him in a classic honey trap. No sooner would he have unzipped his fly, he assumed, than Misha and Tomas and probably the priest would have been pounding on the door, demanding bribes. Or demanding that he leave town. Yet the truly astonishing thing was that while he guessed from the start what Anna was up to, he had been tempted. Zack couldn't recall the last time he had felt the urge.

Now an opposing urge, almost as strong, welled up in him—the instinct to get out of here. Hire a driver, race to the capital and catch the next flight to Frankfurt. Once he was home he would explain to Adrienne . . . what? That he wasn't equal to the job, wasn't the man he used to be? He couldn't cope because some clown at the airport confiscated his pills?

No, he had come this far. He needed to carry through until he found Paul Fletcher or, at least, learned what had happened to him.

Going downstairs to the lobby, he crossed paths with Tomas who looked preoccupied, lost in non-thought. Zack had to call his name twice to get his attention.

"Could you give me directions to that woman's house?" Zack asked. "The one that's taking care of the kid."

"After our talk, I was hoping you'd decided not to bother."

"I want to meet her. Do you know where she lives?"

"It's not safe to walk there now. It'll be dark before you get back."

"I'll take a taxi."

"Not at night. The streets are too dangerous. Let me drive you."

"I'd be grateful."

Tomas led the way down to the hotel's underground garage where he kept a Toyota Land Cruiser.

"Where do all these new cars come from?" Zack asked.

"A lot of them are hijacked in Europe. It's best not to know the details." With a remote control, he raised a sheet-metal door, and they rolled out onto a side street.

"Sorry. There I go again with my questions. Just one more. You say it's dangerous. How does this woman survive?"

"She doesn't have any money. She doesn't get involved in religion. Nobody has a reason to bother her as long as she minds her own business."

Despite his matter-of-fact voice and the volume of cold air jetting out from the AC vent, Tomas was perspiring. The flinty surface of his forehead glistened. Zack couldn't believe the man was sweating over the subject of someone else's safety. But he wasn't about to ask and get another lecture about nosiness.

The Land Cruiser eased its shiny bulk through a street market where vendors hawked cigarettes smuggled in from American military bases in Turkey, clothing from China, caviar from the Caspian Sea, vodka from Russia and from basement stills. Men knelt next to squares of cardboard strewn with bent nails and rusty hinges, garlic bulbs and hardboiled eggs, melons and wormy cabbages. Dealers in amulets and philtres sold rabbits' feet, flattened lizards, snake skins, crab claws and live scorpions in jars. Then there were desperate women who milled through the crowd trying to find customers for corroded batteries, broken tools and dog-eared, out-of-date magazines.

"Trash from all over the world winds up here," Tomas said. "And these people live by selling it."

A fire hydrant had been uncapped, and passels of kids frisked under the spray, reminding Zack of summer days in Virginia when he had doused Adrienne and her friends with a garden hose. A portly babushka, half-mad or completely drunk, pushed in among the children and performed ponderous glissades on the wet asphalt. Dirt streamed off her skin in black braids, revealing vaccination marks, like rivets, indented in both her shoulders. She struck a pose, head pitched back, bosom heaving, arms outspread, a ballerina courting applause. The kids clapped, and she clapped back at them.

"This is it." Tomas pulled to the curb in front of a cottage and cut the engine. "I'll come in and introduce you."

"No thanks. I'd rather do this on my own."

"Okay," he agreed with visible reluctance. "I'll wait for you."

"I appreciate your concern. But I'll be fine. This could take some time. You'd better get back to the hotel."

Zack didn't give him a chance to argue. He climbed out of the Land Cruiser, and as Tomas drove off, he turned to Kathryn Matthews' house.

She answered the third knock, but didn't open the door until Zack identified himself and explained that he needed to discuss Paul Fletcher and the ransom letter.

Framed in the doorway, she was tall and slender, with high coloring and russet hair. Her expression seemed tentative, as if she had been expecting someone else, not a middle-aged man in blue jeans and a work shirt. If she was surprised, so was Zack—by how pretty she was and young. From the way Ms. Pearson spoke, he had imagined the boy lived with some whiskery, wild-eyed spinster.

"If I'm interrupting," he said, "I can come back later."

"You caught me ironing," she said. "I'm always ready to be interrupted when I'm doing housework."

Dressed in loose painter's pants, a sleeveless denim blouse and flip-flops, she showed him into the living room. There were two burgundy velour sofas that might have done duty in the first-class compartment of a train. An ironing board stood between them. Nervously Kathryn skinned the hair out of her face, tied it back with a rubber band and regarded Zack in three-quarter pro-file. "Are you from Paul's university or some other institution?"

"I'm his father-in-law. My daughter had almost given up hope until the second letter. We decided I'd better fly over."

Color flooded Kathryn's face. "I'm so sorry. This must be terrible for you and her. I thought the U.S. Consulate, or if not them, some quasi-governmental agency would handle things."

"No, there's no deep pocket." Zack felt awkward standing there, but since she didn't sit down or invite him to, he stayed on his feet. "Adrienne and I are going it alone and need to know a lot more. I'd like to meet the boy."

"Are you in this field, Mr. McClintock?"

"Call me Zack. What field are we talking about?"

"Behavioral sciences, neurological studies, linguistics."

"No, no, I'm in the opposite field." He laughed. "So far from those fields, I'm off the wall."

As the crimson faded from her cheeks and she watched him from the far side of the ironing board, he began to get the impression that she was a judge gazing down from the bench, readying herself to conduct an interrogation. Though he intended to ask questions, she had some of her own. "So what is it you do?"

"I run a business outside of Washington. Corporate security, risk analysis, that sort of thing. We've worked on a few hostage situations. So this isn't en-tirely out of my league."

"I don't know what you've heard," Kathryn said. "There've been such ridiculous rumors."

"I've got an open mind," he assured her. "That's why I'm here—to see for myself."

She nodded and motioned for him to follow her into the kitchen. It was a cheerful, yellow space with a sink, a stove and an icebox at one end. At the other end there was a dining table, four rush-bottom chairs and the kid leashed in the corner.

Zack couldn't recall what he had heard. It, along with everything else, suddenly flew out of his head. Nothing anybody had said could have prepared him for what he saw—a bony, underfed boy in a leather harness, crouched on knees and elbows, his chin resting on his crossed wrists. When he scrambled to a four-point stance and growled deep in his throat, the hair on Zack's arms stiffened.

Kathryn said, "Shhh," and the boy rubbed his face against her knees. "Don't come closer," she told Zack. "Give him a chance to get used to you. He had a traumatic run-in this week with the Mullah."

Lean and sinewy, with a fused steel tension to his limbs, the kid resembled a sprinter down in the blocks, listening for the starter's pistol, primed to spring upright and pounce. As Kathryn fussed over him, he remained preternaturally alert, twitchy, reactive to noise and motion. Head to heels, he was a brocade of nicks and scratches, bite marks, stings and scars in different stages of scabbing and mending. Though his hands and feet had calluses thick enough for him to walk on coals, he was agile and looked to have toes as prehensile as his fingers. His hair, where Kathryn had clipped it, was whorled and tufted as an animal pelt.

Zack remembered the boy on the road, the one Misha blamed for breaking his window. This kid had the same chipped teeth, the same crudely protuberant navel and drum-tight skin that revealed every rib, every notch of his spine. His eyes contained depths that you could tumble into and never touch bottom. It occurred to Zack that after he started taking the pills, he felt like he was trapped in a corner of his old self, just as this kid was trussed up in the corner of what might have been a suburban American kitchen.

"Can I get you something?" Kathryn asked. "Tea?"

He didn't answer. He sagged down on a chair, and she went ahead and began to brew a pot. He glanced around everywhere, anywhere, except at the boy. Thumbtacked to a corkboard were photos of Kathryn's friends and family. A birdcage of bamboo hung from the ceiling. It contained a light bulb, not a bird. He noticed the typewriter and file cards neatly stacked on a shelf, next to some spiral notebooks. He examined each banal object as if it might inoculate him against the naked creature on the floor.

Normally Zack had no problem with silence; he could hold his counsel for hours. He didn't regard this as the opposite of gregariousness, but rather as its complement. Either one could camouflage the core of a person, and he had been trained to glean facts from the most closemouthed sources. But he was grateful that Kathryn, after a little prompting, started volunteering information and seemed determined to convince him of something she suspected he would dispute.

"I look on it as a luxury," she said, explaining what had brought her here. "I like living in a country that most people wouldn't visit without a bullet-proof vest and a full body condom. It keeps me so busy coping day to day, I've quit obsessing about petty stuff. I read somewhere that an expatriate is a person who cures one form of alienation with another. But to take a positive view, I wanted a change and I wanted to be changed." She poured the tea. "If nothing else, it's so unstable here I have a ready-made excuse for my mood swings."

At the mention of mood swings, he took a closer look. She didn't seem the type. But since he suffered from them, too, maybe he wasn't the best judge.

She undid her hair, shook it out and fidgeted with the rubber band, stretching it over her spread fingers. "Whenever I feel lousy, I blame it on conditions, the late mail, the lack of news."

"I guess you'll be glad to get back to the States."

"That depends. I'm not leaving without the boy. If I have to, I'll work with him here."

"Work with him?"

"We're both learning as we go along." She wrapped the rubber band around her thumb. She wrapped it so tight the tip of her thumb turned blue. "Because of limited resources, I've had to study him at the same time as I'm teaching him."

As they settled into the conversation, the kid became less edgy. After circling several times, he stretched out at their feet.

"Teach him what? Study him how?" Zack asked.

Kathryn unwrapped the rubber band. Her thumb was white. "Have you heard of the wild child of Aveyron?"

He shook his head no.

"You must have seen the Truffaut film. They show it all the time on TV."

"Not where I live."

She gave him a sidelong glance, uncertain whether he was joking. Again in three-quarter profile, one eye appeared to wander slightly in what was either evasiveness or, Zack thought, a sleepy vagueness, a sly sexiness. She sugared her tea and squeezed in a little lemon. Her hands were freckled by the sun, just as his were by age.

"The wild boy of Aveyron," she said, "is the best documented account of what may have been an authentic feral child. This was two hundred years ago, in a remote region of France. They found a boy roaming in the forest. He was afraid of humans. Word spread that he'd been raised by wolves. He was captured and kept under observation. Priests, doctors, scientists, government officials, philosophers, they all examined him and wrote up reports. I've been trying to follow their example—at least what I remember about it."

Her mention of "capture" and "constant observation" set off painful reverberations in Zack. He managed not to show it, but was conscious of exaggerating his drawl as if he found this story and everything she said enormously droll. "What did they learn, those Frenchmen?"

"An amazing amount. Their data eventually became the basis for teaching the blind to read and the deaf to speak. It was instrumental in refining theories of language acquisition and educating mentally handicapped and autistic children."

"But what about the kid? They ever find his family? They ever find out how he wound up in the woods? And was he really raised by wolves?"

"Those aspects of the study were inconclusive."

"Doesn't sound like he got a whole lot out of the deal."

Kathryn refused to take him up on his wry tone. "Well, he did learn how to say a few words and to respond to sign language. In the end he was capable of performing repetitive tasks. When you remember the state of science and the primitive equipment available at that time, it's remarkable what they accomplished. And it's just as remarkable that they didn't do what they might have done."

"What's that?"

"There were doctors in the eighteenth century who believed human beings and animals were physiologically compatible. They thought they could change a patient's mentality by changing his blood. They experimented with transfusions of calf's blood to cure insanity and lamb's blood to calm hyperkinetic children."

"Do I want to hear the results?"

"Not unless you have a strong stomach."

"Try me."

"Animal blood clogs the circulation and lowers blood pressure in humans. Most of the time it causes shock and death."

"I bet that put an end to the experiments."

"No. They were slow learners." At last Kathryn answered Zack's wisecracks with her own. "Some doctors kept at it until early this century."

"Makes you wonder about doctors and scientists. Aren't you afraid some quack'll send this little guy through the same sort of wringer."

"That won't happen. The technology and therapies are much more sophisticated today. The best researchers in the country will jump at a chance to treat him."

"When you say treat him, do you mean cure him?"

She cocked her head, puzzled or perturbed. "Of course, he'll get health care. As for a cure, that depends what you mean. They'll certainly study and analyze him."

"Study and analyze him." He poured downhome treacle over the emotions churned up in him by the boy and the unexpected drift of events. "Please explain why they'd do that."

"It's obvious, isn't it?"

"Not to me."

"You can't conduct a controlled experiment that creates a feral child. Ethically, it's unthinkable. But if you discovered an otherwise healthy boy who grew up in isolation, in severely deprived circumstances that more or less replicate the Wild Boy of Aveyron's case . . . well, think of all the valuable research that would generate."

"About what it's like growing up in woods with animals for parents?"

"Are you doing this for a purpose?" she asked. "Just to provoke me? Or is it part of a test? No matter how you dumb down, you sound like you're from a think tank and you're here to put me through the third degree about my grant proposal."

"Hey, you got me all wrong. I'm just curious about the kid. I see why you want to go back to the States. But what's in it for him?"

"Fine! Since you asked on the best available evidence, he'll probably never learn to talk well enough to describe his experiences or deal with abstractions. The circuitry between the right and left lobes of the brain is hard-wired or lateralized at an early age. After that, it's too late for a child to access the hemisphere that controls language. But he'll get good medical care, a place to live and enough to eat. Now is that what you want to hear?"

"It helps." Zack took a chance, reached down and rubbed the boy's head. His hair felt like the bristles on a wild boar. "Now that I know what's in store for him, there's one other thing I need to get straight. How did Paul's kidnappers come to be so interested in the boy?"

"For months—long before he lived with me—everybody was talking about him. They'd seen him or knew someone who had. Everybody told a second- or third-hand version, and inevitably—"

"No, I'm not asking how the kidnappers heard about the boy. What I wonder is why they went from demanding a million bucks to trying to score a plane ticket for the kid."

"It stands to reason"—Kathryn spoke slowly, as if English were Zack's second or third language—"that when their original ransom demands were rejected, they moved to plan B. Or else the group that first grabbed him sold him along to another group. That's how it works sometimes—a hostage gets passed around until somebody agrees to negotiate."

"So what do you figure, Kathryn?" As he continued stroking the boy's hair, he sounded avuncular, easy-going, but was seething inside. Almost as much as the wasted effort, the pointless trip up-country and raising Adrienne's false hopes, it was the kid's being penned up in a room and run through a maze that infuriated him. "You figure Paul fell into the hands of a terrorist band that was too stupid to beat Uncle Sam out of a million bucks, but smart enough to understand the value of a feral child?"

"That's not a question," Kathryn said heatedly. "It's an accusation. You make it sound like I should know their motives. I just know that unless we act soon, it'll be too late."

"Too late for what?"

"There'll be another coup or a change in government policy and we'll never get him out."

"Paul or the kid?"

"Either one."

"I hear what you're saying and I have to tell you—maybe you already guessed—I'll need some proof that Paul's still alive before I get involved."

"Is it the money?" she asked. "Because if it's that—"

"The money's the easy part. I'm concerned about my daughter. I want to do what's best for her. She doesn't deserve more disappointment."

"I have no way of guaranteeing that Paul's alive. I'm not in touch with the people who kidnapped him."

"Maybe you know somebody I can talk to. It's a long shot, but someone must be in contact with the kidnappers. I'm willing to work through a go-between."

"That might take weeks. Months! Meanwhile, what about him?" The boy ducked from under Zack's hand and glanced at her. "It's cruel to hold him like this. I don't have the facilities to care for him. I'm just warehousing him."

"I agree. My advice, turn him loose."

"You don't understand. Without the harness and leash I can't control him. Once he got out to the courtyard, he'd go right over the wall."

"So let him go."

"He wouldn't last a week on his own."

"He lasted before you came along."

"He was dying when I found him. He'll die if I set him free."

"He'll die one way, one place or another."

"Thank you, Dr. Sartre, for your insight into man's existential dilemma." Her voice blistered with sarcasm. "But if you don't mind, I don't want him starving to death or getting gunned down by some moron with an AK-47."

"Would you rather he die in the States, in an institution where they'll stash him after he's worn out his welcome as a lab rat?"

"You have no right to say that." Kathryn pitched out of her chair. The boy scrambled off the floor in a clatter of nails. Straining at the leash, swinging his head from side to side, he was a parody of a child caught between bickering parents.

"Look, Kathryn, I'm not your enemy. But put yourself in my place. Everybody tells me Paul Fletcher's dead. The other thing they suggest is that you wrote the second ransom letter."

Her reaction seemed to him a strenuous failure to react. "If you believe that, there's no point in talking."

She stalked out of the kitchen, through the living room, past the ironing board. Zack trailed after her, but at the front door he wouldn't be rushed into the thrumming night. "What became of that kid in France?"

"He died in 1828," she said tersely.

"How old was he?"

"Who knows? He wasn't carrying a birth certificate when they caught him naked in the woods."

"How long was he in captivity?"

Kathryn gazed at the ceiling. She might have been calculating the years or the direction of his questions. "About twenty-five years," she said.

Zack whistled. "A long time. Still he must have been a young guy, only in his 30s, when he died. Where were all those doctors that treated him—all those scientists and philosophers that were supposed to be studying him?"

Kathryn appeared to hesitate between pushing him out of the house and providing an honest answer. Finally she said, "It's not clear how he died. A doctor named Itard supervised him for the first five years. You have to keep in mind, Itard was exploring unknown territory, improvising. Under the circumstances, his report was a miracle of deductive reasoning. Later he published a groundbreaking treatise about ear ailments and hearing impairments."

"I take it he wasn't there when the boy died."

"No. An old woman in Paris was paid by the state to look after him. She loved him and took good care of him. But she was illiterate. There's nothing much in the way of written material about the last twenty years of his life."

"A shame," Zack said, laying it on thick. "But I believe I've seen that bottom line before. It used to be on bumper stickers. 'MIAs never have a nice day.' "

Then he let himself out the door.

*B*y this hour every sign of blight had been softened by darkness. The ugly web of overhead wires and pipes, the smokestacks at the edge of town, were lost amid a pandemonium of stars spilling from a horned moon. They looked close enough for Zack to blink them away like eye floaters. It was almost possible to imagine the place without blast shields and sand bags, back when its beauty inspired lyric poetry.

But he was beyond caring about any of that. Start to finish, he regretted everything he'd done and failed to do today. He wished he had given Anna a swift kick in her sweet ass. He wished he had caught a ride to the capital. He wished he hadn't met Kathryn and asked questions that put her back up. Above all, he wished he had never seen that kid rise like a zombie from the deepest sump of his subconscious.

At the hotel he made straight for the bar. Finding it closed, he crossed the lobby to the restaurant where footsore women in slippers and bellboys in wrinkled tunics and tarbooshes were laying out dishes of cucumbers and radishes for dinner. Zack beckoned to one of the bellboys, tipped him five bucks and told him to bring a bottle of wine to his room. Not vodka, not bubbly domestic champagne or any of the rot gut the Russians had discarded as undrinkable. He wanted a European label.

Pleased to be of service, the boy fetched a quart of Chivas Regal, which, he announced, cost $75. In pidgin English and fractured Russian, Zack explained that this was Scotch whiskey, not wine. The fellow raced off for twenty minutes and came back with a bottle of Bordeaux. It, too, cost $75. The price was right, Zack said, as long as it included the courtesy of opening it. After a long and finally successful search for a corkscrew, he paid the boy and slumped into bed with the wine. His plan was to get drunk quick and sleep without dreams. He managed on one score—he got drunk—but he remained awake, tumbling downstream, through deadfalls and over steepled rocks, into nightmarish memories.

He had gone to Geneva at the behest of several gentlemen who identified themselves as high officials of the Haitian government. Determined to trace the illegal assets of Baby Doc Duvalier and repatriate the fortune to its rightful owners, they hired Zack for the express purpose of violating Swiss law. To gain access to Baby Doc's secret numbered accounts, they needed somebody to bribe bank officials, and Zack knew the people to go to. He had been there before. Within a matter of days he was in a position to pass along the information to the grateful Haitian gentlemen.

On the way to the airport for his flight back to the States, however, a car with a blaring siren stopped his cab. Two men scrambled out of an unmarked Mercedes, spoke sharply to the taxi driver and dragged Zack out of the rear seat. When he demanded that they identify themselves, they showed him their shoulder holsters, not badges. Zack broke and ran to the other side of the murderously busy autoroute. But they caught him, handcuffed him and frogmarched him over to the Mercedes. There was a third man who held a handkerchief to Zack's face as if to mop off the sweat. The cloth must have been chloroformed.

He woke in a windowless, brightly lit room. It took him an instant to understand that he was naked, handcuffed to a wall and lying on a bare mattress. They let him have some time—Hours? Perhaps a whole night?—to mull things over in a prone position, staring straight up at an incandescent light bulb.

Then the men came at him with questions. At first it was the three who captured him. But they were followed by relay teams of fresh cross-examiners. They weren't especially rough. They were simply relentless. They all asked the same thing: Who did he work for? Who hired him? Who had he bribed? What were the account numbers?

Zack insisted on calling the American Embassy. He demanded that they let him speak to an attorney. He swore he would say nothing until they told him who they were. Swiss police? Fiscal agents? Employees of another Haitian faction? But they didn't deign to answer. They just kept hammering away at him. They were in no hurry. He was here and he would stay, they promised, until he cooperated.

Zack vowed he wouldn't crack. He wouldn't give them the satisfaction. He also figured that anything he said might endanger the Haitian gentlemen and expose himself to legal jeopardy. Though it was bound to be clean and bright, he didn't care to spend time in a Swiss jail. So as they barraged him with questions, he sang to himself. He hummed. He thought about Adrienne and what they would do when he got home. He believed that the men would lose patience before he did.

As the intervals between interrogations stretched out longer, he thought it was working. They were growing weary and would get nothing out of him. But then they switched off the light, left him alone in the dark and sent an indescribable sound rushing into the room. It dinned at his brain like a dentist's drill. It entered his body, took possession of his bones, occupied him cell by cell, crowding out every other sensation. He soiled himself and couldn't smell it. He lost track of whether he was asleep or awake. Seized by an intuition that they were watching him around the clock, he tried to lie still, tried not to babble back at the noise. He didn't want to let them see him as weak and foolish, a pathetic specimen to be examined under a microscope.

When the sound died, he guessed he was dead. Then the light snapped on again, and he thought he was blind. The men reappeared, asking the same questions. He cursed and kicked at them, and to his humiliation, he started sobbing. Still, he refused to talk, and so the light blinked out and the noise boomed back on.

How long it lasted, how many days elapsed before he broke, Zack couldn't estimate. He only remembered crying, and finally the men cleaning and consoling him, and he to his shame letting them lead him around like an animal. He told them everything they wanted to know and kept on talking even after the questions stopped.

In the end, two men escorted him out of the room and shoved him into an elevator alone. A lab rat conditioned by repeated experiments, he feared that this was the next stage, a trick, another torture. For a full minute he didn't move. Then he pressed the button and felt the floor drop out from under his feet. In a shriek of stripped gears, the elevator plunged down the shaft in free fall. Before it hit bottom, he was already unconscious.

His first thought when he woke was that he was back in the windowless room for another bout of interrogation. But he came to in a sub-basement surrounded by men carrying picks and shovels. They might have been miners trapped by a cave-in. As astonished to see Zack as he was them, they hauled him to his feet and patted him down for broken bones. Groggily, he asked who they were, why they were here. Judging by their expressions, they were asking him the same thing. But they couldn't find a common language. They were Turks, laboring literally in the underground economy. Once this fact registered, he realized the wild elevator ride had been a mechanical malfunction, not an effort to rub him out.

The Turks ushered Zack onto a downtown street in Geneva. Dizzy, disoriented, he staggered through falling snow, wearing the wrong clothes, wandering the wrong way, wondering where the right path lay. He felt the same deep disorientation as he finished the bottle of wine and thought about Kathryn and the kid. He was in free fall, and there was no fixed point for him to grab hold of.

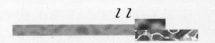

*A*s he drove back to the hotel after dropping Zack at Kathryn's, Tomas couldn't breathe. He felt his lungs go liquid, just as they had at soccer games when he was a kid and it fell to him to take a free kick. His own teammates used to mock him, he was such a choker.

He parked in the underground garage and knew he should return to the reception desk. He didn't trust anybody else to do the job right. But his one thought was to flee. It didn't matter where, just away from here.

Setting out on foot with no destination, he left the garage by the side entrance and let a route choose him. In the wayward course of his life Tomas had fled plenty of people and places—his wife, Prague, a passel of women. It sometimes seemed that the act of departure defined him and that whatever he didn't discard was finally who and what he was. But now the prospect of doing it again filled him with the woeful sense that he was the one being abandoned.

He wound up meandering through the bazaar. Camel heads hung from hooks, their long-lashed eyes serenely shut, sprigs of parsley stuffed up their nostrils. Below them on the cobblestones, lined up like shoes outside a mosque, severed hooves were footed to their reflections in shiny rounds of blood.

If McClintock was lucky, Tomas thought, that's what Misha would do to him—break his legs and send him limping back to the States minus his money. If he was less lucky, he'd end up like Fletcher, wrapped in chains and rolled into a mountain lake.

Beyond the meat market lay a maze of ruins. Shattered masonry crunched under his shoes. The few domes still standing were fissured with cracks, and sunlight filtered through them, casting chandelier-shaped shadows. Constructed to last for eternity, these mosques and mausoleums had foundations a dozen feet deep. Yet even they had crumbled. So what hope had he of remaining upright?

Passing from the ancient city into the Russian quarter, he skirted a monumental façade of bas-relief sculptures. Tomas's hard-edged features might have served as the template for their stony vacant faces, but he knew he lacked the epic grandeur of these heroic workers and warriors. He was more like the rebus of a man stenciled to a fuse box on the same building. Electric shock waves burst from the stick figure like swords from the Sacred Heart.

The road eventually brought him to Father Josef's parish. Hard used for half a century, the church's scruffy, breeze-block exterior recalled the desecration that the Russians had visited upon it. Tomas stepped inside where the congregation had painstakingly renovated parts of the nave. It smelled of beeswax candles, incense and altar wine—scents that transported him back to boyhood. The ceiling was freshly painted, and an amateur artist with his heart in the right place but his perspective slightly askew had attempted a *trompe l'oeil* cupola. The chalky blue oval looked like it had been hollowed out with a pool cue.

Pale and sickly and lost in his cassock, Father Josef was slumped in the front pew reading his breviary. As Tomas advanced up the aisle, he emptied his head of thought as if jettisoning luggage from a crashing plane. He was on automatic pilot with no time to weigh the question of where exactly he would land. He just knew that his chances were better if he lightened his burden. Startling himself as much as the priest, he knelt and whispered, "Bless me, Father, for I have sinned."

Father Josef smiled, taking this for a joke. "How are you, Tomas?"

"Miserable. I have to talk to you."

"Talk to me as a friend or a priest?"

"I need to confess."

The priest shut his breviary and shifted around to face him. His black cassock was so old it was iridescent in spots. "We could move into a confessional, but since nobody's around, why bother hiding in a box? How long has it been since you last received the sacrament of Reconciliation?"

"Years and years ago. In Prague, before my wedding."

"Christ is always happy to welcome repentant sinners. Please remember, there's nothing He won't forgive and no sin is so serious that you can't confess it and find peace through His grace."

"I don't know where to start," Tomas said.

"For a man living alone, separated from his wife, I suppose there have been sins of impurity," Father Josef prompted him.

The concept of purity as a religious stricture struck Tomas as outdated. Politicians had adulterated the idea ages ago. The Soviets had always called for a purification of bourgeois elements. Former Communist Party officials flying under false colors in the current regime promised they were pure of past contamination. Environmentalists cried out for pure water and air, and Moslems insisted that Allah alone could purify the population.

"There's Anna," Tomas conceded.

"No names. That's not necessary."

"But she's part of the reason I'm here."

"Did she suggest that you speak to me?"

"I haven't talked about this to anyone."

"She discussed it with me."

"How can that be?"

"Don't get upset," the priest said. "It came out naturally in the course of her Italian lessons."

"What came out?"

Father Josef patted his arm. "That she's waiting for you to marry her and move to Rome."

"She knows I'm already married."

He gave Tomas another paternal pat. " 'Only for death is there no solution.' That's what they say in Italy. The church's position on divorce hasn't changed, but there's a new attitude toward annulment. You may have grounds."

"For what?"

"For annulling your first marriage. It's not quick and it's not inexpensive, but the Vatican has been sympathetic to appeals from the former Eastern Bloc."

"Look, you don't understand . . ."

"But I do. Your situation in the Czech Republic couldn't have been much different from what I saw in Krakow. Many Polish couples married without sufficient reflection because of political pressure or to avoid military service. This violates canon law. Without the informed consent of both parties, a wedding is invalid."

Pulling a plastic vial from the waistband of his soutane, Father Josef shook some tablets into his hand and palmed them into his mouth. Though they may have been medicine, they smelled like breath mints. "The important question is whether you love Anna and mean to make her your wife in the eyes of God."

"With respect, Father, the question is more complicated than that."

"Of course, of course. There are steps to climb before you reach the altar. Even after an annulment, you'll need a civil divorce. Then you and Anna must take instructions. I won't marry you—no priest will marry you—unless you're more committed to this marriage than you were to your first wife. And it's imperative to express a sincere spirit of contrition and a firm resolution to amend your life. Are you sorry for your sins, Tomas?"

"I'm sorry for everything."

"There's a difference between self-pity and true contrition."

"Believe me, I'm sorry, especially for my son."

The priest sighed. "How sad to have a child so far away in Prague."

"No, I had him by a woman here."

Sucking on the tablets, Father Josef absorbed the new information. "The mother of this child, do you see her?"

"Not since the last truce. She lives in a village near the border."

"Does she know you're married? Does she know about Anna?"

"She knows I'm married. Not about Anna."

"And Anna, what does she know?"

"About my wife, not about the boy's mother."

"And the child?"

"He's a baby. He doesn't even know me."

"What do you want from me, Tomas. Really, why are you telling me this?"

"To be forgiven."

"Forgiveness isn't automatic. It's not as easy as reciting the Act of Contrition. You have a moral obligation to your child and to these women. God gave you free will."

To Tomas, this sounded absurd. His life was immutable, his options non-existent, his room for maneuvering terrifyingly slight. Why pretend he was free? He had a hotel to manage. It was losing money. He feared he was losing Anna again. Misha intended to rob McClintock and probably murder him and maybe Tomas too.

"You've made mistakes," the priest prattled on, "but none that can't be remedied by prayer and penance. You mustn't lose hope. Despair is the greatest sin."

"Worse than murder?"

"Much worse." Summoning a spasm of energy from his wasted body, Father Josef said, "To kill a man deprives him of physical life. But to despair is to kill your own soul, to murder your hope for eternal life. Like suicide, it's an unforgivable sin."

Tomas longed to end this jesuitical hairsplitting and shock Father Josef into shutting up and listening. "Okay, I killed a man."

The sickly priest responded with surprising equanimity. "There's nothing you can confess that I haven't heard before. Who did you murder?"

"Fletcher."

"Why? How?"

"I had my reasons."

"You kidnapped him for money? The million-dollar ransom?"

"No, because of Anna. He stole her from me, and I was envious and angry. When I found out he was taking her to America I had to stop them."

Father Josef raised his eyes to the *trompe l'oeil* cupola. From this angle, the illusion didn't work at all. The ceiling looked as flat as the old gym floor. "You really believed they were leaving?"

"Did she tell you they weren't going?"

"We've never talked about anything more complicated than Italian grammar. But you're not a teenager. You should know better than to take anything a woman says as literal truth."

"The truth is she left me and lived with Fletcher. That was bad enough."

"Enough to make you hate him? To kill him?"

"I didn't hate him. He was a good customer. He came to the hotel a couple of nights a week to drink and meet women. But when Anna left, I felt betrayed. I didn't want him dead. I just wanted her back."

"If you didn't mean to kill him, it's not murder," Father Josef broke in. "To commit a mortal sin, there has to be full knowledge and intent. If you struck him in the heat of an argument—"

"I never touched him. I was nowhere near him when he died. But I'm to blame for his death."

"Did you pay somebody to do it for you?"

"Nothing like that. I knew some things about him. I knew if I told them to the wrong people, he'd be in trouble."

"You knew he'd be murdered?"

"No. I thought they'd scare him, rough him up, run him out of the country. Then Anna would move back in with me."

"Don't make me keep guessing, Tomas. Tell me how all this happened."

Suddenly he wished they were in a confession box, speaking through a screen. Now he had nowhere to hide except behind his blank eyes pounded like nails into his wooden face. "Fletcher told me what he was doing at his laboratory," Tomas said. "The U.S. government sent him here to manufacture a chemical to kill off poppies. It sounded like science fiction to me, but Fletcher swore it was true. You can imagine how anxious certain parties would be to learn this."

"Misha?"

"More the people who pay him. Misha's one of the *guvnyuki*—just another shithead. But the man behind him, the *pakhan*, wanted to bomb the lab and kill everybody in the bargain. I convinced them it made more sense to kidnap Fletcher."

"But they did blow up the laboratory."

"That was later, after no one paid the ransom and Fletcher was dead."

"Does Anna know this?"

"No. She wouldn't be with me if she did."

"Are you sure he's dead? Wasn't there another ransom letter?"

"It has to be a fake. Misha told me months ago that they got fed up and drowned Fletcher in the mountains."

Father Josef dredged in as much air as his damaged lungs could contain. "You must warn McClintock."

"Why? That won't bring Fletcher back."

"His daughter is suffering, not knowing whether her husband's dead or alive. And McClintock's in danger."

Tomas clutched the sleeve of the priest's cassock. "You tell him."

"I can't break the secrecy of the confessional."

"I give my permission. I release you from your vow."

"Nobody can release me. You have your cross, and I have mine."

"But you only have to say that Fletcher's dead and he'd be smart to clear out."

"He'll ask how I know. He'll suspect that I'm in contact with the killers and try to track them through me. No, Tomas, this is your responsibility, your penance."

"If I warn McClintock, Misha will kill me."

"He'll kill McClintock if you don't. Do you want another murder on your conscience? Warn him, then leave the country with McClintock."

"I don't have any money. And there's Anna and the hotel and my son. I'll lose everything."

The priest's reply was swift, as if he'd been waiting his whole life for an opportunity to say, "What does it profit a man if he gains the world, yet suffers the loss of his immortal soul? I won't absolve you unless you right the wrongs you've done."

As Tomas stood up, blood rushed to his head. He had the feeling he was incense floating toward the *trompe l'oeil*. "You said despair was worse than murder. You told me there was no sin God wouldn't forgive. But you're killing me."

"Where are you going?" he called as Tomas turned away.

"There's no place to go. I'm dead."

12

*I*n the kitchen, the boy stirred and grumbled in his sleep. Kathryn envisioned his dreams as plain images in primary colors, and hoped that they were more consoling than the kaleidoscope of her present thoughts. People made dumb and desperate mistakes in the name of love, she knew. They blinded themselves to reality, committed crimes, even killed. Yet when she had sent off the second ransom letter, she figured she was placing a rational bet. Since the plan didn't involve a direct payoff, only what might be construed as a humanitarian gesture, she assumed the state department—even if not officially approving—wouldn't object if some foundation financed the boy's travel and treatment. She hadn't counted on Fletcher's wife and father-in-law picking up the tab, and she hadn't counted on Zack McClintock confronting her.

He reminded her of the American oil roughies who roved through this region before most foreign companies pulled out. There was a stringy meanness to him, a redneck recklessness. His tone, no matter how he pitched it, seemed to drawl, "I don't give a damn." But then she had noticed his eyes and had had second thoughts. For all his show of toughness, he had responded to the boy. He responded to her too—with ill-concealed anger. Was it just because she kept the kid cooped up in a corner? Or because she had dragged him halfway around the world on a snipe hunt?

Hit by a choppy storm of tears, Kathryn held tight until her emotions diminished to smooth waves of confusion and weariness. Since her divorce, her plan had been to have no plan, her abiding principle of advancement to burn bridges behind her. Refusing to consider how much longer her money might last, how much elasticity her nerves had left, she had proceeded on the assumption that her problems would resolve themselves and she would eventually return to the States. But now it occurred to her that if she told McClintock the truth, she would have to stay here if she hoped to keep the boy.

She could survive the summer and the cool, apple-scented autumn. It was winter that she dreaded. The melancholy of the boy's sleepy breathing called to mind the wind out of the east, its lonely, fluting, atonal music. Bleak as a Brueghel landscape, the town would turn treacherous with ice, and for weeks she would be confined to the cottage. Rusty orange icicles would drool from the rain gutters while sleet pinged at the windowpanes and speckled the courtyard, like rice outside a wedding chapel. The snow would melt on the cobblestones, but not in the seams between them, and the streets would become a symmetrical blanket of black patches stitched together by white thread. As the freeze deepened, the season would send a shaft of sadness through Kathryn, as awful as an arrow through the heart.

She started crying again and thought of the boy, her plans for him, none of them possible here. This led to thoughts of Dr. Itard and the wild child of Aveyron, and then to the old woman who had been left holding the leash that the brainy doctors and scientists had let drop. A step or two removed from a scullery maid, the woman, Kathryn had read, used to walk the wild child through Paris at hours when pedestrians wouldn't gawk and he couldn't dash out in front of a carriage and throw himself, excited, upon the horses. Kathryn pictured them in the Luxembourg Gardens under a pearl grey sky, hand in hand beside the pond, a shriveled old lady in a shawl, a young man as motionless as the park's statues, only his eyes following the flight of pigeons, the flash of fat carp in the fountain. Two people as wistful as the dead looking back at the living through the long warped lens of eternity, neither of them capable of saying a word that would make the other less lonely.

It hit Kathryn that in twenty years she would be close to sixty. Was it conceivable she would still be here with the boy? The idea overwhelmed her. Yet she could imagine worse things happening if she didn't warn McClintock.

*T*he next morning she hurried to the hotel, rehearsing what she intended to say. She would propose a different trade and save McClintock time, guaranteed trouble and money in exchange for a single promise; her confession to him had to remain confidential. If it got around that she had forged the ransom letter, she feared expulsion from the country and prosecution in the States. She wanted to leave herself some chance for a future, no matter how slight.

The hotel lobby smelled of floor polish and sour milk. The usual contingent of toughs in track suits sat on hassocks smoking cigarettes and chewing sunflower seeds. Behind the reception desk, Tomas wore a suit in a smooth synthetic fabric that clashed with the coarse planes of his face. When Kathryn asked for McClintock, he answered with an insinuating half-smile and a room number. "There's no phone," he added. "But you can go on up."

The elevator worked today and so did the Muzak. Serenaded about some guy flying high in the sky, his idea of nothing much to do, she studied her reflection in the polished silver panel of buttons. For the first time in weeks, she had changed out of slacks into a blue shirtwaist dress with a hemline six inches below her knees. Despite the heat, she had draped a white sweater around her shoulders to prevent fundamentalists from hissing disapproval at her bare arms. She had also applied makeup, not just sun block, and thought she resembled a Kelly Girl arriving to take dictation from a traveling salesman.

Kathryn knocked at his door, paused and knocked louder. Zack warbled incomprehensible words as if under water. When she knocked a third time, he moaned, "Later!"

She didn't trust herself to postpone this. "It's Kathryn," she said. "From last night."

Something—a belt buckle?—clanked against porcelain. Zack coughed or choked, and a toilet flushed. Then he crossed the room barefoot to open the door. He was in blue jeans, nothing else, and cradled his sunburned arms across a powerful chest tufted with white hair. He appeared to be balancing a jar that he was afraid might break at any instant. " 'Scuse me. I can't seem to find my shirt and shoes."

Kathryn spotted them beside an empty wine bottle that had rolled and unraveled a red stain across the parquet. The sheets were on the floor, too, twisted like a rope ladder or a noose. One way or another, he appeared to have been plotting an exit.

"I meant to stop by your place first thing this morning," he said as he shot back the drapes. Blinding light splashed through the room. "The rate I was going, I guess I'd have been lucky to get there by afternoon."

"What have you been celebrating?"

"Just drinking up a little Dutch courage and composing an apology." His jeans rode low on his hips, the money belt cinched the flesh around his waist. "I had no business talking to you like that. It's not my place to say what you ought to do with the boy."

Kathryn stepped between him and the window, shading him from the sun's glare. "I wanted to apologize too. I wasn't completely candid when—"

"No, no." He waved that she shouldn't bother. "I was way out of line."

He fetched his shirt, then fumbled with his socks and shoes. His fingers trembled as he tied the laces. Kathryn resisted the urge to help him, dismissing this as an overstimulated maternal instinct that the boy had stirred up.

"You're the expert," he said. "You know the kid's requirements. I don't know my ass from my elbow. But I'll do what I can to help you get him to the States."

"But your daughter——"

"My daughter, I have a hunch, if I know her half as well as I think, she'll be happy that I'm helping you."

"Even if Paul's dead?"

"We always knew that was a possibility. As long as I do everything I can to find out what happened, she'll want to see something good come out of this."

McClintock's abrupt change of heart, and especially the undertone of contrition, gave Kathryn pause. It was difficult to fathom so much remorse. She needed a few minutes to make up her mind. "Why don't we go downstairs," she said, "and get something to eat?"

He grimaced. "I'd a hell of a lot rather not have anything on my belly just yet. But I could do with some fresh air."

*O*utside, it was hot, but not as bad as it would be in a few hours. Contrary to her habit, she chose a route that avoided the bazaar and its ant-army of shoppers. The gingerbread geometry, the warren of streets there, would distract her when she needed to concentrate. Wondering whether she could justify reverting to the original scheme, she led Zack to the river.

Along the road, laborers were excavating what smelled like a sewer. A sign swore it was an architectural site. But who could say? The city was forever tossing up its past, and as Kathryn had learned, it was sometimes as hard to distinguish treasure from trash as it was truth from . . . from varieties of truth.

Next to the river the damp ground bore strange tire tracks. They started and stopped at regular intervals, and sometimes ran six abreast. She recognized them as the prints of rubber-soled sandals fashioned out of discarded tires. In the shade of a stand of birch trees, a woman in chartreuse leggings decorated with royal blue chevrons hunkered behind an upturned crate, selling vodka and bottles of Thunderbird wine.

"It can't be the real stuff," Zack said.

"Who'd brew fake Thunderbird?"

"You got a point there."

"I like to imagine a con man cornering the market on Ripple and Thunderbird," Kathryn said, "and exporting it worldwide."

He chuckled, then clutched his aching head. "They say you can't con anybody who doesn't want to be conned."

She had the impression—no, she simply preferred to believe—that they were speaking in code, that maybe Zack knew what she was up to and had decided to accept the ruse. Where was the harm? Whatever it cost him to fly the boy and her to the States, she could always pay him back once she got settled. And if by some fluke Fletcher were still alive, she wasn't putting him at greater risk by not admitting the truth about the second ransom letter. The only trouble was finding a way to protect Zack.

Willows arched over the river, and mercurial light strobed from the silvery undersides of their leaves. Men were swimming in the scummy water; others sunbathed along the shore. They all had something hideously wrong with them—missing limbs, slick pink depressions where meat and muscle had been gouged out, grotesque skin grafts and crosshatched scars with stitch patterns like centipedes. A few of them were paralyzed, and their friends stood on the shore and dunked them into the cool stream. Their stringy arms and legs quivered like spaghetti in boiling water.

"Afghanistan?" Zack asked.

"Wrong generation, wrong war," she said. "This is from recent fighting. There used to be a rehab center around here."

"*Used* to be a rehab center?"

"These days there aren't any doctors and nothing much in the way of medicine. But the wounded gather there anyhow, hoping for the best."

As they pushed on, Zack said, "Ever think the kid maybe got caught in the crossfire, his folks were killed, and he came out of it . . . I don't know, shell-shocked, suffering from PTSD?"

"Were you in the army?" she asked, shrugging the sweater from her shoulders.

He nodded.

"Vietnam?"

He nodded again.

"Then you tell me—does he act like any post-traumatic stress case you've seen?"

He shook his head no.

"Don't get me wrong," Kathryn added. "Despite the impression I may have created last night, I'm not God. I'm not one hundred percent sure about his neurological symptoms. He needs to be examined by somebody who's trained and has the right equipment."

They had entered an orchard where little boys climbed the trees to steal fruit. Gobbling cherries by the fistful, they stuffed the excess into tin cans. Kathryn stopped where two of them in nothing but underpants clung to a branch, their cheeks striped red like savages in war paint.

"Aren't they terrific?" she said. "I love the kids in this country. There's a girl who sweeps the tea shop. I'd like to steal her and take her home."

"Why don't you have a few of your own?"

She couldn't tell by his tone, but judging by his expression, he seemed to expect an answer. "That's something I'm saving for when I'm in the States—motherhood, carpooling, soccer practice, retirement to Tampa and shuffle-board."

"Any room in your schedule for a husband?"

"Is this a proposal?"

"A survey."

He sounded as if he had fallen back into last night's conversational style, plaiting strands of wisecracks into every sentence. Blitzed as he looked, this had to have been an effort. "I was married once," she told him. "We didn't have kids. At the time, I thought I was lucky. What about you? Any kids apart from your daughter?"

"She's the only one. My wife died when she was little."

"You never remarried?"

"No. In the army I had to move around a lot. After the army I traveled even more." He handed each boy a dollar bill. With no better place to save it, they shoved the money down the front of their underpants.

"Peacock proud as Chippendales," Kathryn said.

"Hey, you're funny, you know that?"

"You are too. We're a couple of comedians. All that's missing is a straight man."

But she knew there was something else missing—from her reasoning or her ethical fabric. The more time she spent around McClintock, the worse she felt about not leveling with him. This duplicity wasn't like her—or what she wanted to believe about herself. Yet she couldn't imagine an alternative. When she got down to the irreducible facts, she just didn't think he'd help her—she feared he'd hurt her—if she told him the truth.

As they walked on through the orchard, she said, "You asked last night about people who've taken an interest in the boy and might know something about Fletcher."

She let the sentence hang there. Zack was squinting ahead at a row of electrical pylons that had collapsed into gleaming metal chrysanthemums. Next to one of the bombed pylons, two fellows in full fencing regalia practiced with epées. Their blades clattered like cutlery, their voices slurred through mesh masks.

"I see why you've stayed here," Zack said. "It's nonstop entertainment, isn't it?"

"Around the clock," she agreed. "Getting back to the boy, have you talked to Tomas?"

"Yeah. First night here. He advised me to leave."

"That's not bad advice," she felt obliged to concede. "You can ask only so many questions before people understand what you're up to, and you're in trouble. Or they totally misunderstand and you're in worse trouble."

"Who else should I speak to?"

"Dr. Medvedev. And there's the Mullah."

"Tomas says he's a phony."

"That's the standard line on Bakshilla. But he has his followers."

"Would he know who wrote the last ransom letter?"

Kathryn let herself swim in Zack's soft, sea-glass green eyes. There were lies, she knew, and there were damned lies. Then, as Disraeli had declared, there were statistics. So many ways for people to fuck each other over. But among the myriad deceptions, there were some that protected the person deceived. That's how she salved her conscience. By suggesting stone-cold leads, she thought she could keep McClintock from blundering in dangerous directions.

"Bakshilla might know something," she said. "Why don't we start back? I'll show you where he lives."

13

*I*n a residential district of slummy, slab-constructed buildings, Kathryn guided him to the entrance of an apartment tower that was surrounded by chicken pens, rabbit hutches and guard dogs staked to chains. Zack urged her to get back to the boy and went in alone, up a staircase where people, mostly women in bandages or on crutches, waited in line on the steps. He might have been in a housing project in Harlem or southside Chicago. Cryptic frescoes of graffiti covered the walls, handrails had been ripped loose and wires sprouted from busted light fixtures. Some pilgrims glared at Zack before giving ground, but most made way gracefully, kissing their fingers and touching their hearts as they moved aside. The sickest among them were laid out on litters. When he reached the top landing, a woman on a stretcher was being lowered to the ground floor via a contraption of ropes and pulleys.

Stern, bearded men guarding a door greeted Zack with gusts of questions in Russian and guttural dialect. He explained as best he could that he was an American here to pay his respects to the Mullah. A boy who spoke a bit of English said, "Yes, please." The kid wore a nylon windbreaker with a sheriff's badge on the breast pocket and a label that read "Texas Ranger Man, Made in

Italy." After listening to Zack, he disappeared into the apartment. Almost at once, he returned, murmured, "Yes, please" again and motioned for Zack to follow him.

Inside the door in a jumble of slippers and sandals, Zack stepped out of his shoes, as custom decreed. They passed a cubicle that contained a water tap and a Turkish toilet. Cartons of canned goods, soap and paper products lined the long hallway. A history of shortages had taught indelible lessons in the wisdom of stockpiling supplies.

The boy left him in a room light-years removed from the rest of the squalid tenement. Hand-loomed kilims cushioned the floor in overlapping layers to a depth of six inches. Tapestries were tented from the ceiling and swagged to the walls, concealing the windows and the whelming vastness outside. The plump Mullah sat cross-legged on a dais, like a potentate in a seraglio. Beaming at a crippled old crone who held out a handful of crumpled bills, he daintily plucked the dollars one by one from her arthritic fingers.

As she left, he beamed the same beneficent smile at Zack. "Welcome, please, and forgive the poor English I practice on you."

Zack sat on the carpet in front of the bearded cleric.

"What a weather we are having," the Mullah said. "Do you hate it, this heat?"

"It doesn't bother me."

"Good, good. Neither me." The baggy white garment he wore was grape-stained with sweat at the collar. "Allah is kind. He makes us a hot land of dry deserts. But he makes miracles, too. With water our fields become a paradise."

The Mullah clapped. An attendant peeked his solemn face around the door. Zack caught the word *chai* as the Mullah spoke. The attendant entered the room and busied himself at a samovar.

"You are American?" the Mullah asked.

"Yes."

"We have many believers there. Michael Tyson and Michael Jackson have converted to Islam."

"I read about Tyson."

"Yes. And Jackson too."

"Are you sure about that?"

The Mullah was more interested in the former heavyweight champ. "Tyson heard Allah's call in prison. Changes in a man's heart occur anywhere. Even on the moon. The astronauts, they say, have heard His voice in space."

"They're very religious, the astronauts."

"Yes, they pray for safe journeys. Allah always answers. But anyone who prays to animals or men or any god except Allah is punished. Not just in this life, but in the next."

The attendant served glasses of sweet tea on a brass platter. Holding his glass in two fingers, the Mullah toasted Zack. "Fraternal felicitations."

"Amity and concord." Zack raised his glass. The temperature of the tea shocked him. A tiny sip singed his tongue.

"I see you know the Russian sayings. Maybe you drink alcohol to them at the hotel. But the Book warns us, 'Satan seeks to stir up enmity and hatred by means of wine.' "

"I won't argue with that," Zack said. "Is it true you worked at the hotel?"

"Yes, I cannot lie, because if we lie, we will be punished. Before Allah called me, I was in the world. I was a sinner. Now I am a teacher and a healer. The sick flock to me and I touch them and by the mercy of God they are cured."

"When you worked at the hotel, did you meet an American by the name of Paul Fletcher?"

"Everyone knows of him. But I avoid politics. I am busy with books." Reaching up to a shelf, exposing a purple patch under his arm, he lifted down a leatherbound volume and passed it to Zack. "This is the labor of my life. I give it to you for looking, not keeping. You cannot read it, I think, but you can see my writing."

Riffling the pages, Zack murmured in admiration, then returned the book. "Very nice. The reason I mentioned Fletcher—"

"The Koran," he said. "I translate it into our language."

"The Koran into Russian—that's quite an accomplishment."

"I make a small correction. I tell you this in friendship. Russian is not our language."

"Sorry for my ignorance."

"We used to speak Russian. We used to obey the Russians. We had no choice." He shoved the book back onto the shelf. "Now we are free to speak our own language and pray in the mosque. Life is becoming beautiful. If we keep a pure heart and practice our faith, we are happy. But no politics." He wagged an admonitory finger. "Islam has nothing to do with politics or power on this earth."

"Glad to hear that. Seeing Iran and Iraq, a person might think otherwise."

"That is not a normal situation. Neither is Afghanistan and Tajikistan. There they have fighting and not even food to eat. They should read what is written: 'Did Allah not find you an orphan and give you shelter? Did He not find you in error and correct you? Did He not find you poor and enrich you?'"

Zack ran a finger around the rim of his glass, teasing a muted tune from it, and let the Mullah rattle on. He couldn't decide whether the man was crazy or cagily avoiding talk about Fletcher by tossing out quotes.

"In the time of the Russians, people think they know who they are." He rocked as he spoke. "They have papers that say Uzbek, Turk, Armenian. They think, I am that, I am this. But when the Russians go, people aren't sure any more. Catholics have to bring in priests to explain what is the church. Jews forget the Bible. They even forget the dyes for carpet colors. Always the Jews used to make carmine from crushed bugs they pick from mulberry trees. Now somebody must teach them. But with Islam, we remember who we are. You know why?"

Zack confessed that he didn't.

"Because the Koran is written. In the beginning it was written on palm leaves and flat stones and in the hearts of men." He thumped his chest. "And I translate it for everybody. This is hard."

"I'll bet it is."

"The hardest part is paper. You cannot write books without paper and we have very little. Also there are few pens and typewriters and not much money. This subject, you see, is complicated."

"I'd like to make a contribution to your cause." Zack took a ten dollar bill from his pocket.

The Mullah slipped the money into the recesses of his robe. "You understand well our problem."

"I do. And I respect your decision to stay out of politics. But when I ask about Fletcher, it's personal, not political. He's married to my daughter, and she wants me to bring him home if he's alive. Or bring back his body, if he's not. Can you help me?"

The Mullah turtled his head down on the pliable column of his neck and assumed a meditative pose. Zack settled in, too, rearranging his haunches. It was hard to find a comfortable position. The money belt cut into his belly, and his lower back ached where the pistol pressed against his spine.

"You live at the hotel?" the Mullah asked.

"That's right."

"So you know the place it is and the people there?"

"I wouldn't say I know them, but I've seen them."

"Look, please, after yourself so that no bad thing happens to you. It is evil, that hotel. It stinks in the nostrils of Allah—the music, the dancing, the drinking of whiskey and the singing of songs about money and love. It was bad to work there. I wanted to leave and worship Allah. But each day is no change and I start terribly to cry." He dragged his fingers through his beard, describing the tracks of his tears.

"Then I learn a big lesson. I learn the high bosses know nothing of the low laborer, but the laborer knows everything about the bosses. Their secrets are my strength. Little bit, little bit, I become powerful and understand that the world must be cleaned. The middle of Islam is beautiful, but all around it is dirt. Each one hundred years a man appears and his job is to save Islam."

"And you're that man?"

"Allah alone knows." Modestly he lowered his gaze. "There are 124,000 prophets. Jesus is one. Mohammed is the greatest. When the need comes, a new man comes."

Zack suppressed the urge to voice a fervent prayer that the new man not arrive before he was safely back in the States. He was starting to suspect that Tomas had been only half right about the Mullah. Although he might be a phony, he was a genuine phony, the real article, one who believed in his own cant and in the prison he was building brick by brick for himself and his followers.

"Do you think people at the hotel had something to do with Fletcher's kidnapping?" Zack asked in order to nudge him back onto the subject.

The Mullah pondered the question. "Possible. But to know . . . more swift is Allah's scheming. Our angels are recording their intrigues. And we will punish them."

"Who's we? Who's them?"

"*We!* Not just me, but those in this room we cannot see. Nobody escapes Allah's eyes. Fletcher did not escape. They will not escape."

"Fletcher didn't escape what?"

"His fate. In the hotel he drinks. I see this many times. I am sorry for your daughter. But it is true, and now he is punished."

"As I understand it, if Fletcher was punished for anything, it was for making a chemical to kill off the poppy crop."

The Mullah raised his tea, sipped it and said, "Of this I know nothing."

"In some countries," Zack went on, "Moslems control the opium production and trade it for weapons."

The Mullah's face—what little of it showed above his beard—darkened. He moved a hand toward his heart. Or was he reaching for a shoulder holster?

"The world is very large," he said, "and we live in a small crack of it. We know that good sometimes comes from bad. Allah created man out of clots of blood. So who is to say what He creates from poppies? There are medicines, are there not?"

"You're the expert on Allah. But you and I both know what men make out of poppies. And Fletcher was making something to stop it. Then he was kidnapped and the ransom note said Islamic fundamentalists were holding him."

The Mullah's hand was now inside his robe. Zack arched his spine and reached around as if to rub the small of his back. He didn't intend to let anybody lock him in a closet with the Koran. He gripped the gun butt.

"This is not true," the Mullah protested mildly and let his hand fall to his lap. "Here no Moslems are holding hostages. If somebody says other, he lies to hurt me."

"But different groups, maybe across the border, they might have kidnapped Fletcher. Are you in touch with them?"

"I do not judge men who fight a *jihad*. There are worse sins, I think, than shedding blood. As for selling drugs to our enemies, I don't do it, but I don't condemn it. It is no more than they deserve. Still, I am not with such people." Recrossing his legs, he added, "For you and his family, I hope Fletcher is alive. I hope it, but I do not believe it."

"Why not?"

"It has been too long."

Zack released his grip on the pistol. "There was a second letter. You have any idea who wrote it? Who'd offer to exchange Fletcher for the boy?"

"This is a big question." He clapped his hands and the lugubrious disciple brewed more tea. As the Mullah accepted a full steaming glass, he asked, "Do you know what is *djinn?*"

For a second, Zack thought he meant "gin." Indeed, he knew gin all too well. But it quickly became apparent that the Mullah was referring to a different spirit, a force more evil than alcohol. "Some believe that the boy belongs to the American woman, that she had him by a man in town. But you have only to look at him to know this is not true." He brought the glass to his lips, blew on it and drank.

"I agree. The boy isn't hers."

"No, she is *his*. He is not her pet. He is her master. He is a *djinn*."

"Do you think she wrote the ransom letter?"

He shook his head vigorously; whiskers rasped his collar. "She might have put them on paper, but the words are his."

The image of the kid dictating to Kathryn made Zack smile.

"You take this for a joke?" the Mullah demanded.

"I don't see the boy trying to trick somebody into buying him a plane ticket to the States."

"Why not?"

Why not, indeed? Everybody else in town seemed to be working a scam. Why not the kid? With disappointment, Zack realized he would learn nothing helpful from this loon. "Maybe you're right," he muttered.

"But he must not be allowed to leave." Hot tea slopped out of the Mullah's glass, over his hand. He shook his stinging fingers. "Allah's wish is for a man to stay in the place where he is born. Better your own weeds than somebody else's wheat, we say. For a man to leave the sky and land and weather of his home is like losing his heart through his throat."

"But you said he's not a man. He's a *djinn*. Why would you want him to stay here?"

"It's not what I want. It's what Allah wills. And, thanks be to Allah, I am not afraid to keep the boy where I can watch him. If he goes to America, he will devour the world."

There was so much he might have said to the Mullah, so much he was tempted to tell the folks on the staircase hoping to be made whole again. And as for the boy, no matter whether he remained here or moved to the States, Zack feared the world was far more likely to devour him. But he kept all this to himself, thanked the Mullah, shook his hand, and following his example, touched his fingertips to his heart.

14

*I*n the unvarying evening ritual, Tomas lounged in the bathtub with Anna, his soapy palms coasting over the glazed swells of her body. Sitting behind her, with his legs around her hips, he stared at her back. Broad in the shoulders, it tapered to the waist, an inverted triangle bisected by the groove of her spine, each notched vertebra as smooth and distinct as a bead on a rosary. Running his fingers up and down the linked cartilage, he resumed the well-rehearsed narrative that was required to keep her quiet while he entertained his own thoughts. Her needs were so simple he could satisfy them without being entirely here in the present or there where he promised to transport her in the future.

As usual, memories of one city served as a map for the other. Rummaging through his recollections of Prague, he described the life they would live in Rome. Yet even while he conjured up images, capturing them in the lovely off-light of an aspic, he mentally replayed Father Josef's words about despair, the worst sin. How could he hope to rekindle hope? Where would he find the courage to warn McClintock? He couldn't bear to admit that he had allowed

Fletcher to be gangstered into a watery grave only so he wouldn't be without Anna at this hour of evening.

"Rome wasn't made for the bourgeoisie," he said, soaping her breasts, basting them with what appeared to be meringue. "It was built for rulers and aristocrats and the poor who served them."

"Will we have servants?" Anna asked.

"Naturally."

"Will we live in a palace?"

"Let's not exaggerate. We'll live in an apartment on the *piano nobile* in a building overlooking a piazza."

Whole blocks of Rome were as cheerful as a citrus grove, he said, and on side streets the fruit juice and Neapolitan ice colors turned to burnished earth tones. They would take their early morning coffee and evening Campari at a café he knew where the waiters raised and lowered the umbrellas like crewmen reefing the sails on a luxury yacht. Flowers blown from window boxes would lie scattered as coins on the cobblestones.

"Don't stop," Anna said.

He plowed on, confident he could keep this up forever. It was like sex. No longer an adolescent half-complaining, half-congratulating himself that he was chained to a monster with a mind of its own, Tomas was a grown man in full command of his abilities. He recalled the Vltava, transformed it into the Tiber and pictured fishermen on bridges, tethered by string to their shadows in the river. Yet even as he spoke of the Eternal City, he feared that the only eternity he would ever know was his KGB file preserved in some dusty office, logged onto a computer leading to an information highway that double-helixed into infinity.

"Hey!" Anna bounced her rump in his lap. "Did you fall asleep? Why'd you stop?"

While the familiar brain tape reeled through his head, he wasn't aware that he had quit talking, transfixed by the water trickling down Anna's spine, threading one ivory bead to the next. She bounced again and swiveled around to face him. Moisture had crimped her hair into tighter curls.

"Where are you?" she asked, irritably. "You look a thousand miles away."

"I have a lot of things on my mind."

"So do I. But I don't act like you—mysterious as a spy."

"Don't say that. It's no joke, calling someone a spy."

"Fine. You tell me what you are."

"A man lost in love."

"Bullshit. In bed you're barely there these days. Then you disappear from the hotel and hide for hours. In an emergency, how could I reach you?"

"I'm not hiding. And don't worry. In an emergency, I'd be there."

He hefted her breasts in both his palms. She batted his hands aside. "How would you know I needed help? People ask where you are and I have to lie to them. It's humiliating."

"Who asked?"

"Nobody. I meant *if* they asked."

"Let me know whenever anybody asks about me."

"You're doing it again," she pouted. "You're so suspicious, it's like you've gone underground."

"I haven't gone anywhere. I just feel—"

"Feel what? From what I can see—" she glanced down—"you don't feel a thing."

"I feel like a spare part for a machine that's obsolete."

"You don't make sense."

"I miss the way things used to be."

"Between us?"

"No, in the life here."

"I don't! I miss Italy. I miss what we're going to have there. *La dolce vita.* That's what Father Josef says he lived in Rome."

"The sweet life," Tomas sighed.

"If a sick old priest can enjoy himself, just think how much fun we'll have."

"I'm beginning to believe we already had *la dolce vita* and lost it when the Russians left."

"You talk like an idiot."

"No, listen. Don't you remember? There was no worry about jobs or money or a place to live."

"Right, just everybody in jail together eating slop."

"But once you accepted that reality, you could relax."

"Everybody in the same cell with guards and Party members and goons and secret police? I don't call that relaxing. Then if you tried to get out, if you so much as hinted you might be thinking about it, they sent you to the uranium mines."

"But within those limits there was a whole world." Tomas became almost as animated as when he showed Rome through the prism of Prague. "You could travel to Moscow or go skiing in the Tatra mountains. You could fly to the Black Sea and spend a week in the sun. Now nobody has the money to travel except the mafia. What's the point of being free?"

Anna scrambled out of the tub, shedding water like a spaniel. "Are you telling me we're not going to Rome?"

"No, we're going. But it'll take time. Business has been bad and everybody has his fingers in the till. I miss the days when people were too scared to steal. I'm tired of free enterprise."

She reached over to touch him, murmuring in a small voice, "Come to bed with me."

As he lay down beside her, he returned to the choreographed script and told her what he intended to do. Then he teased her, delaying, postponing, talking. But the predictability of his dialogue and Anna's stage directions deepened his depression and brought on a chilly detachment. While Anna moaned *Amore*, practicing her Italian, and Tomas whispered endearments and lewd diminutives, he stewed with regret at his life. He saw himself as a stooge for thugs, frightened into operating a mail-drop for black marketeers, drug dealers and killers. Every room in the hotel bore their marks—cigarette burns, bloodstains, bullet holes. As he catalogued the damage, Tomas shut his eyes so that Anna wouldn't say how ugly they were.

"Wait." She fumbled for a condom.

"No. Not that."

"Let's not argue."

Ignoring his protests, she fitted the sheath over him and was about to lie back when he grabbed her by the hair. He forced her head down to his lap. "You like rubbers so much, eat this one."

She flung her face to one side, screaming. He wrenched her around and rammed himself into her mouth. That shut her up. "Like it?" he asked. "Like how it tastes? You think I like wearing it?"

She bit him and tried to pull back. But he smacked her until she stopped struggling. As he pumped his hips up and down, he felt himself shrivel with every violent thrust until gradually he slipped out of the condom. Choking, she gagged up the latex, and they tumbled off the bed in opposite directions. Tomas held onto the headboard, afraid he would hit her if he had his hands free.

Sputtering to find something sufficiently wounding to say, Anna screamed, "I'm not going to Rome with you."

"We never were going any place."

"I believed you about Italy."

"You believed Fletcher about the United States. Where did that get you?"

"That's why you hate me. Because he loved me and was taking me to America while all you do is talk, talk, talk about Rome and fucking."

"You asked for it."

"I asked for more than words, but that's all I got from you."

She stepped into her slacks, fastened her bra, and thrust her arms into a blouse. She called Tomas a liar, a pig's bladder pumped full of hot air. Even as she berated him, he expected her to break down at any second, surge into his arms and beg for another chance. He knew she had no money, no place to live. But she tossed her meager belongings into a canvas bag. Then she stalked into the bathroom and swept her miniature cosmetics off the window ledge into a makeup kit. "What are you doing?" he asked.

"What's it look like I'm doing? I'm leaving."

"You don't want to do that."

"Why? You don't care about me."

"You're wrong."

"No, I'm right. You don't even care about yourself."

She pushed past him, out of the bathroom. When the door to the corridor didn't slam, he thought with some satisfaction that Anna had changed her mind. He was convinced he would find her in the other room. But it was empty and she was gone. He heard a noise like an engine cooling or a clock ticking. He didn't recognize the beat of his own heart.

*A*s Anna crossed the lobby carrying her belongings, she bumped into Misha. He made no move to give her a hand with her bag, but he did ask why she was crying.

"Tomas and I had a fight. I'm finished," she said. "I would never have gone back to him if Fletcher was still alive."

Misha seized her roughly by the elbow. "Who told you he's dead?"

"Nobody needed to say it. Let go of me."

"You sure Tomas didn't say something?"

"I don't have any interest in Tomas or the things he talks about."

She yanked free and stepped out of the hotel into the humming darkness. Insects sizzled against her face. Moths blundered about, beating powder from their chalky wings. Misha followed her through the blizzard of bugs, swatting his arms.

"Where're you going?" he asked.

"As far from here as possible."

"Ride with me. You don't want to be on the streets at this hour." He held her elbow gently this time and guided her toward his BMW. Misha was right, she knew. It was dangerous to wander around the city at night. Until she decided what to do, she was better off with him.

As they coasted down the driveway, he punched on the high beams, and light sluiced through the sand-scratched lenses like silver through a sieve. He offered her a cigarette, a Czech brand, Femina, that sounded to Anna like a personal hygiene product. She smoked one to steady her nerves. He offered a beer, too, from a case on the back seat. She said no thanks, but opened a can for Misha.

"It's Mexican beer," he said, drinking as he drove. "I bought a share in a truckload from Pakistan. Tastes like shit. A good beer should be like a good woman—full-bodied and not too bitter or long-lasting in the mouth. What about you?"

"I prefer champagne."

"You move out on Tomas, you won't be getting much of that."

"Then I'll do without."

He headed down near the river where whores huddled around twig fires, waiting for tricks. She didn't put it past Misha to choose this route to give her a graphic example of what became of women who lacked a man's protection. At the thought of ending up here, having sex back in a copse of poplar trees, she almost started crying again.

"Really, what did Tomas tell you about Fletcher?" Misha asked. "He must have said something."

"He was jealous of Paul. He never mentions his name to me."

"Did he say he knew what Fletcher was doing?"

She let this sink in. "Everyone knew that. It was no secret Paul loved me and we were planning to move to America."

"I mean what Fletcher was doing in his lab. That's why he got snatched— because of what he was making."

"And Tomas knew?" Instantly she wished she hadn't asked. If Misha and Tomas were mixed up in Fletcher's disappearance, that information was no good to her now. "Actually, I don't care about Tomas or Fletcher anymore."

"Soon the new American is going to disappear," Misha said.

Anna made as if to cover her ears. "Why are you telling me? I don't want to hear it."

"Why not? Are you hot for him? Does he promise to take you to the States?"

"I have no more interest in America or Americans."

"That's right. You're from Italy."

Anna didn't respond to his taunts. She was too busy guessing where he was taking her—in his car and in this conversation. She couldn't allow herself to feel much about what he and Tomas might have done to Fletcher.

"You ought to visit your family in Italy," Misha said. "But to do that, you need money. And you need to know the right people."

"I don't have any money. I don't know anybody." To her shame, this sounded like the bleating of a sheep—a pathetic admission that she was at the mercy of a man whom she knew to be merciless.

He drove to an apartment tower in the modern town and parked behind it. "I keep a place here. You're welcome to stay."

Anna considered refusing, running. But whatever he had in mind, Misha was no more reluctant to do in the open than indoors, and nobody would dare come to her rescue.

In the dark, with his hand on her arm, they descended a flight of stairs to a basement entrance. Untumbling locks in a sheet metal door studded with brads and bolts, Misha said, "Excellent security."

As they came into a cinderblock bunker not much bigger than a storage bin, Anna smelled disinfectant and moldy cardboard. Misha switched on a light. A single bulb in a wire basket swung at the end of a black cord. Moths had crawled into the basket and now beat themselves to death in a vain attempt to escape. The magnified shadows of their wings flickered across Misha's face like a mask that he repeatedly put on and took off. Apart from a cot, there was nothing in the room except boxes of black market cigarettes, whiskey and watches. This gave her some hope. She didn't believe he would kill her in a place packed with valuable goods that might get broken or blood-stained.

"It's not as nice as the hotel." Misha bolted the door. "But it'll do until you make up your mind."

About one thing she had already made up her mind. If he wanted sex, she wouldn't say no. She prayed that that was it—that secretly he had always desired her.

He sat close beside her on the creaking cot, but kept his paws to himself. "How would you like to make a lot of money? Enough to move to Italy?"

She suspected he meant to turn her out as a streetwalker. Or would he bring johns here? "It's good of you to let me spend the night. I'll have a friend pick me up in the morning."

Misha wasn't impressed by her fictional friend. "This new American, he's asking questions. He's also carrying a lot of cabbage. Those are two good reasons for him to disappear."

"What does that have to do with me?"

"Not much. You just have to deliver a message and lead him to me. Then you'll be a rich woman."

"What message?"

"Tell him you know where to find Fletcher."

"He won't believe that."

"It doesn't matter what he believes. He'll have to go with you to make sure. That's what he's here for."

"Go with me where? How?"

"You'll drive my car. I'll let you know where."

"Why not do it yourself?"

"I can't drive him and get things ready at the same time."

"Get what ready?"

"You don't need to worry about that. Just bring him where I say, collect your money and buy a ticket to Rome."

"How much are you paying?"

"Twenty thousand dollars."

The figure frightened her more than anything else Misha had said. The size of the payoff was proof that he planned to kill her too. No sensible person could expect to have so much money and go on living. She fought to stay calm and find a way out.

"When do I deliver the message?" she asked.

"When I say so."

"When do I get the money?"

"As soon as I take it from him."

"Why not tonight? He's at the hotel. I'll go to his room."

He patted her cheek. It wasn't a love tap. "I'll tell you when. Trust me."

After Misha locked the door from the outside, she killed the light so that she wouldn't have to watch the moths. Of all the words he might have chosen, his mention of "trust" had triggered in Anna a tumult of emotion. It was what Tomas told her and what Fletcher had always said. To her, "trust" now meant disappointment and death. She considered committing suicide to screw up Misha's scheme. She'd open a whiskey carton, break a bottle, and slit her wrists. No, better yet, break all the bottles, crush the boxes of watches and cigarettes, destroy his entire stash and leave him to scrape her decomposing corpse out of the bunker.

Then another idea dawned on Anna.

15

*M*ulticolored as coral, immense clouds reared in craggy reefs over the city as Kathryn waited for the evening's first flashes of heat lightning and the thud of artillery rounds behind the mountains. Or maybe the thudding would be thunder, and she could count the seconds as the sound traveled from the flash-point to her ears. Seated at the kitchen table, she was wool gathering and noodling at a blank page in a spiral tablet. The boy lay on the floor at her feet. Normally he slept on his side, arms and legs tucked to his chest. Now he rolled onto his back and let his limbs sprawl. As he sank into REM cycle and his eyes twitched behind their lids, he looked less like a self-protective animal, more like a sleeping man, immodest and sexual.

Kathryn watched him with a frank curiosity that she thought argued for her scientific objectivity. She speculated whether his new sleeping position reflected increasing confidence and adaptability. Then again, from her own restless nights, she knew that one way to counteract the heat was to open your body like a book and expose every inch of flesh to the dry air.

"Keep in mind the Heisenberg Uncertainty Principle," she jotted. Reducing the concept to its bare bones, she added, "The act of observing has an effect on the object observed."

Like a nurse with a thermometer, she shook the ballpoint pen, which had started to skip. The pause gave her a chance to consider to what degree the results of her observations had been influenced by a pattern that she imposed on events. As she grew close to the kid and drifted farther from herself, did her experiments appear to unfold in a particular way just because she willed them to?

She scribbled in the notebook, "To what extent does the Uncertainty Principle apply to both parties? Certainly there must have been times when he and I have reversed roles. I know I've changed since he showed up. I just can't judge how much. The effect I've had on him worries me far more. I hope our day-to-day proximity hasn't domesticated him to the point where he's of less interest to scholars and researchers."

*A*t sundown, as the *muezzin* summoned the faithful to prayer via an amplified recording, the needle got stuck in a dusty groove, and the nasal voice chanted the same *sura* until whoever had fallen asleep at the switch woke up and nudged the machine. Still, it was a lovely, mournful cry, and the minaret that Kathryn saw through her kitchen window was a lovely, mournful sight. Having taken a glancing hit from a Katyusha rocket, its rusty steel girders clung to scraps of pocked masonry and mosaic like a dowager clutching her last shreds of dignity.

As if in answer to the *muezzin*, the boy cut loose with a short, skirling howl, then flopped onto his side and subsided back into sleep. She resisted the urge to stroke his downy spine. For the moment, she wanted to restrict herself to the role of straightforward academic, not surrogate mother. Holding to the Greek adage that stories happen to those who can tell them, she longed to believe that she could produce a study of lasting importance. As she started to jot another note, loud knocking at the front door interrupted her.

She hurried to the living room and lit a lamp. The coiled filament barely brightened the bulb, giving off a faint glowworm of illumination. "Who is it?" she called.

"Zack."

When she opened up for him, he glanced toward the kitchen. "Did I wake the whole family?"

"Not me. I was thinking. Or thinking I was thinking." He had caught her in a tee shirt, cut-off jeans and bare feet. Her reddish hair hung unwashed to her shoulders. Kathryn was too annoyed at herself for slopping around like this to apologize for her appearance.

"Thought you'd like to hear what the Mullah said."

"Have a seat." She nodded to the identical velour sofas. "Something to drink?"

"What do you have?" He stayed on his feet, to all appearances as ill at ease as she felt, dubious about the wisdom of dropping in unannounced.

"Tea, apple juice, mineral water."

"How about a warm glass of milk and a fig newton? You sound like some-body's mother," he said. "No offense. I'm sure you'd make a great one."

"Wasn't that the wolf whistle of the nineties? I read it in the *New Yorker*. 'You'd make a terrific mother.' Let me see if I have something stronger."

He followed her into the kitchen. The boy scrambled up, straining at the harness, excited to see Zack. "Have you given him a name yet?" he asked.

"I'm holding off until I know him better."

"Come on, he's gotta have a name."

"Like a pet?"

"Like a person. Are you waiting to see which one he becomes . . . a pet or a person?"

"You sound pretty perky," she said. "Like you had a nip before you came." Under the harsh kitchen light, Kathryn knew how her face looked without makeup. She hated the bitchiness in her voice, but hated even more having Zack see her like this.

"I've had a little," he said. "Not enough to make me obnoxious. I was going to suggest we eat dinner at the hotel."

"No thanks. I don't care for the clientele."

"Hey, I think I'm the only guest."

"I'm talking about the palookas that loaf in the lobby. And that little slut-muffin who hangs around Tomas. I bet she has great talent as a tummy tosser."

"Haven't had a chance to catch her act."

"I'm sure she'd be glad to arrange a private performance."

"You and the Mullah sound like charter members of the same chapter of the Moral Majority. He treated me to quite a sermon about the sinfulness of the hotel."

Kathryn checked a cabinet over the sink. "I've got vodka. You can spike the apple juice."

"Hold the apple juice. I'll drink the vodka neat."

She poured him a generous shot in a coffee mug and herself a modest amount in a glass.

"If you don't mind," Zack said, "I'll just sip this a bit at a time—no clever toasts and down the hatch like the Russians."

He took the coffee mug to the table and sat near the boy. When he held out his hand, the kid sniffed it, then licked his fingers. "He likes me."

"Don't flatter yourself." She picked up her notebook and put it away, then sat opposite him.

Zack sampled the vodka. It had a lemony afterbite that puckered his lips. "Sure you won't let me buy you dinner?"

"*Buy* me dinner? You mean no dutch treat? A real old-fashioned date? How fifties of you."

"Are you mocking the decade or my age?"

"It's the New Millennium. Learn to live in it."

"I'm a man of the times. Perfectly housebroken and politically correct."

"Sounds boring."

"Well now—" he dragged out his down-home drawl, dripping with syrup and grits—"that depends on the company I keep."

Kathryn decided to quit needling him. "You mentioned talking to the Mullah."

"Yeah, in stutters and farts, we talked. I'm not sure how much he understood or how well I followed what he said."

"Whenever he's lost for words, he quotes the Koran." She noticed that Zack kept his eyes on the boy as they spoke. The boy's own eyes tracked back and forth between them, switching from speaker to listener a beat slow.

"He reminded me of a storefront preacher," Zack said. "I gave him ten bucks, but I never got the impression that he might cough up better info if I sweetened the pot. He flat-out denied knowing anything about Paul's kidnapping or his whereabouts. Should I believe him or go back and squeeze harder?"

"I'd let him be." She folded her knees up under her chin, bracing her bare heels on the chair's edge. "I mentioned him only because he has this fixation about the boy."

"Fixation doesn't half describe it. He's got a real mad-on against him. Claims he's the Devil's spawn."

"Sometimes the Mullah doesn't make sense. But I don't believe he's any threat."

"I'd feel more comfortable if I knew how close he was to the fundamentalists who wrote the first ransom letter."

At his mention of that letter, Kathryn feared he would leap to questions about the second one. She gazed out the window. A flash of lightning lit up the minaret like a neon bulb. Then it went dark, and she counted to twelve before she heard a rumble. Zack was peering in the same direction. "Why don't I freshen your drink and fix us something to eat?" she said.

"I didn't mean to barge in and bum a meal."

"It's no trouble. I'm hungry myself. I'll do something simple and quick."

"I'd like that," he said.

While she gathered cans and boxes from the food safe, Kathryn watched Zack watching the kid. The ruddy, weather-beaten man and the naked boy locked eyes, electrifying the space between them with the tensile strength of their absolute mutual absorption. They reminded her of herself counting off the seconds between a lightning flash and a thunderclap.

Despite his claim to the contrary, Zack looked no more housebroken than the boy did. A bridling, barely restrained wildness seemed to link them. But while the boy's essence could be distilled to a single impulse—the desire to be free—Zack, she supposed, had a well-practiced ability to conceal what he wanted. She bit her tongue to keep from wisecracking that he resembled a do-gooder plotting the liberation of a porpoise from a marina.

He touched the kid's head, testing his spiky hair, then came over to the sink where Kathryn was filling a saucepan with water.

"What do you do when you're not searching for missing persons?" she asked.

"Sometimes I search for missing paper. Corporate espionage is a boom area."

"You spy? You steal company secrets?"

"Just the opposite. Crooks walk off with in-house reports or patented material, and I run them down."

"Sounds exciting."

"Nah. Mostly I sit at a desk in front of a computer."

She punched the point of an old-fashioned can opener into the top of a tomato tin. Zack took it from her and prised up the lid. "Sending out stern letters threatening litigation is about as exciting as it gets," he said.

"I don't believe you." She set the pan of water on the stove to boil and emptied tomato sauce into a second pan. "Some of it must be fascinating."

"It's like being a dermatologist. You don't cure folks, but most of the time you don't kill them either."

"Are you implying there are times when you do kill them?"

"Never clients." He kept his pitch as light as hers. "Not unless they refuse to pay. That's another thing I do—I go after missing money." He splashed more vodka into his mug.

"Missing from where? Banks? Corporations?"

"All of the above, plus countries. After a coup, you've got dictators that'll hightail it to Switzerland with the national treasury. A new government takes over and they hire somebody to hunt down the missing assets. That's me."

"Now that *does* sound interesting. Tell me about it."

He paused. She could see that he didn't want to talk about this. Or else he wanted to so badly he didn't trust himself.

"A typical case was Haiti," he finally said. "After Baby Doc skipped off to the Riviera, the new regime was raring to crack into his numbered accounts."

"A noble enterprise." Kathryn snapped dry pasta in half and dropped it into the boiling water.

"At the start, that's what I thought. I didn't give a shit about breaking Swiss law or bribing bank employees. I figured that was fair. After all the Duvaliers did to Haiti, a family of fat cats starving their own people, I was ready to do whatever it took." His voice had grown barbed, and the drawl was gone. He topped up Kathryn's glass, then refilled his mug. "But whenever you ride out like a white knight, you're apt to limp home like a clown."

"Did something go wrong?"

"Only everything." He appeared to catch himself and change what he started to say. "I had a little dustup with the Swiss authorities. And after I handed over the secret account numbers, the new team in Port-au-Prince told me they would handle it from there."

"And keep the money for themselves?"

"Well, I never noticed any rebound in Haiti's GNP. From pictures in the papers, it doesn't look like people there have gained weight."

"What a rotten business."

"You asked."

"I don't mean your business. Just the way of the world. Pigs with their snouts in the trough." She forked up a strand of spaghetti and let it cool on the drainboard. Then she tested it by biting it between her front teeth.

"It needs a few more minutes."

"You're the boss."

"I like it al dente. What about you?"

"Sounds good."

When she drained the spaghetti into a colander, a cloud of steam wafted up, and the boy released a small cry of amazement. Craning his neck, he followed the condensation as it sailed off and evaporated against the ceiling. Kathryn mashed a handful of pasta, poured on tomato sauce and placed it on the floor for him. Then she served Zack and herself. He took a taste and pronounced it perfect.

"You're generous. My Italian ex-husband would turn up his nose because there's no parmigiana or wine."

"I could have brought a bottle from the hotel." He hoisted his coffee mug. "I know I said no toasts, but this dinner deserves one. What should we drink to?"

"Peace and freedom."

"You sound like a child of the sixties, a girl with flowers in her hair."

"At the moment mine's dirty enough to grow flowers."

"It looks fine. I like your hair."

It embarrassed her how susceptible she was to compliments, how deeply his praise moved her. "Eat your food before it heats up to room temperature."

"And you have a nice sense of humor."

"So you've said. Thank my mother. She stressed that a woman should be fun to be with."

"To your mother then." They drank, and Zack asked, "What else did your mother teach you?"

"Nothing practical. When I was a kid, she never told me to finish my milk or wear my boots when it rained or go to bed early. She's an interior decorator. Her idea of maternal advice was telling me that understatement is always in vogue and the three primary colors are beige, taupe and aubergine."

His eyes swept the room. "I see the understatement, but not the recommended color scheme."

"All right. Now you're embarrassing me. I keep planning to fix the place up. You know, buy carpets and handicrafts in the bazaar. But I never get around to it."

"You're rebelling against your upbringing," he razzed her and tipped more lemon vodka into her glass and his.

"That's my downfall," she said. "I'm a rebel. What's yours?"

"I got a long list. Number one, I have a lousy temper."

"Now there's a character flaw any *real man* will admit."

"That's what my daughter says. Men will always tell you what they're feeling as long as it's anger."

"That must be a drawback in your business."

"Downright tragic at times."

Kathryn laughed, and they continued trading quips in lieu of conversation. Aware of her own tendency to bare her soul in throwaway lines, she recognized a kindred spirit in Zack. Listening to him was a bit like watching a man open a vein and spill his heart's blood for a prank. With every self-deprecating sentence he seemed to proclaim, "Look at me. I don't feel a thing." But that wasn't the way he had spoken about Haiti.

As they finished the pasta and started in on a bowl of fresh fruit, Kathryn began to feel the vodka. The not unpleasant tipsiness reminded her of evenings in Ann Arbor when she invited her classes home for potluck dinners. As a graduate instructor, she hadn't been much older than her students, and there were usually a few fellows with crushes on Kathryn. At that age, it was so easy for them to imagine—if he was cute and smart, it was easy for *her* to imagine—that she had more than education to offer. In self-defense, she used to adopt a joshing, bantering style, not unlike the way she dealt with Zack now.

Still, she didn't forget that this was no lovesick sophomore she had in her kitchen. His profession was tracing people, catching suspects in inconsistencies. Though he sounded rueful and ironic, as if he didn't take himself seriously and didn't expect her to either, that might have been calculated to lower her defenses. He seemed like the last man on earth to throw his weight around, but she knew that the Haitians hadn't hired him for his nice green eyes.

Under the circumstances, it made no sense to drink more, yet Kathryn didn't stop him from refilling her glass. She decided to show him to the door right after dinner, but he insisted on helping her, and they wound up doing the dishes together. He washed, she dried, and the two of them sidled past one another in that cramped space with the boy's agate eyes following their every movement.

Something she said about the University of Michigan prompted Zack to talk about Annapolis and the year he fought in the Brigade Boxing Championships, coached by his best friend Eddie. "Neither of us had spent a day at sea, but Eddie was already talking like a tough old salt. He called a kitchen the galley, a bed a rack, the door a hatch and a toilet the can. Well, in the very first round I got smacked in the nose, and Eddie threw in the towel, screaming at the ref, 'Stop the fight. He's got a busted snot locker.' Nobody ever let me forget that."

Then as Zack laughed and the boy grumbled low in his throat, Kathryn recounted a comic version of her botched university career, the unfinished degree, the dull clunk of young minds closing in her classes. It all sounded so funny. "How could I encourage them to work harder when in my own courses I was just grinding away to get A's and stringing them like beads on a choker I stuck my neck into without knowing why?"

She filled him in on her failed marriage and flight from America, her arrival in Central Asia intoxicated by the idea of oceanic expanses that had vanished for centuries from the world map and were only now reemerging. She stayed on, she said, because the local black humor matched her frame of mind.

"I'll be sad to leave," she listened to herself say in a voice she scarcely recognized. "I'm not ready for the suburbs and the country club and dancing to 'Strangers in the Night' with a hubby in white shoes and a pink dinner jacket."

"Jesus, I'm glad you told me before I showed you my wardrobe and Sinatra albums."

She laughed too loud and tried to picture him twenty years from now. White-haired, heavier, she thought, but saved by good bones and great eyes.

A moment later she was letting him lead her into the living room and shut the kitchen door behind them. They sat on the same sofa. The velour prickled her bare thighs. The glowworm gleamed feebly in the light bulb, and she was conscious of a tsunami of sexual desire spreading through her. It was as if a storm had broken and she just happened to be out in the downpour and got soaking wet.

In the distorted distance at the end of the couch, she noticed that Zack had lifted her feet onto his lap and was kneading them, massaging her arch, knuckling the high scoop of her instep. In a craving that shocked her, she wished he would take her toes in his mouth and gently suck them. She had never before imagined feet as an erogenous zone.

"I can't believe you're doing this," she said. "I can't believe I'm letting you. They're filthy."

"They're fine."

"Are you a foot fetishist?"

"An apprentice masseur."

"You seem awfully experienced for an apprentice."

"I swear it's a first for me. If it's not for you, don't say it. I'd get jealous."

As he caressed her ankles, then her calves, she concentrated on his hands. They appeared to have a life, a personality, of their own. Tan and thickly veined, they were strong, competent, consoling, and she considered giving into them, literally putting herself in Zack's hands. But among the other things she felt, there was a lingering wariness, a sense that having gotten off on the wrong foot with him, she couldn't right herself. Still, she didn't say

"Stop," until he slid his fingers along her inner thigh to the frayed edge of her cut-offs. "I think we better——"

"Better what?" he asked.

"Better think about your getting back to the hotel."

He nuzzled her neck, nibbled at an earlobe, kissed her cheek, moved his mouth to her lips and lingered there. It was the longest kiss Kathryn could recall since college. But when she slipped a hand inside his shirt and eased it around to his lower back, he pulled away. It wasn't a graceless gesture, more, she assumed, a prelude to the suggestion that they move into the bedroom.

"This is when I usually say I have a war injury," he told her.

She prized a man with a sense of humor, but there were limits. "That's rotten luck," she deadpanned. "I bet you're hardboiled about it during the day, but at night it's another matter."

He was baffled.

"Don't try to stump me with Hemingway dialogue," she said. "I've read *The Sun Also Rises* sixteen times."

This—or was it something else?— deepened his bewilderment. After an instant, he stood up.

"Have I compromised your professional integrity?" she asked, prepared to be offended.

"I guess I got my signals crossed. I wasn't sure what you were reaching for." He pulled a pistol from the back of his belt.

With a heartclot of anxiety she thought he was about to shoot her. Instead he set the .38 on an end table, removed his money belt and switched off the lamp. He touched her face with his fingertips, tracing the curve of her lips like a blind man locating the precise spot he planned to kiss. When he took off her tee shirt and shorts, she pressed against him, as if stanching a wound. She lifted her legs and locked her ankles around his waist and dissolved into a quivering wishbone that convulsed and snapped at its center.

·  ·  ·

*A*fterward, she wanted him to spend the night, wanted to wake up with him in the morning and find out how he looked over breakfast. But the wish was so strong, she decided she'd better bury it. There was too much he didn't know about her, too much she didn't dare tell him. And all the questions either of them might have been tempted to ask presumed an intimacy that exceeded a single bout of sex. Besides, she preferred to have the pistol out of her house and the money belt back where it belonged.

Before he left, Zack paused at the door. "The Mullah told me some people figure the boy's yours by a guy in town."

"Do you believe him?"

"Of course not."

"What if it were true? Would that make you less willing to help?"

"It wouldn't matter."

Then he kissed her and stepped out into the moon-bright street.

*Book
Two*

*2*

*A*fter that first night, Zack McClintock had difficulty making sense of what he felt. It should have been a simple matter. What does anybody in solitary confinement, famished for sunlight, fresh air and human contact, feel when the cell door miraculously swings open? Grateful, of course.

But a strange disquiet underlay his gratitude. In part, he feared that the cell door might slam shut again. In part, he feared that it wouldn't. Over the years, scar tissue had hardened around him in an airtight shell. Now that the shell was cracking and the outside world entered him more deeply, he found himself in the rare position of yearning to talk.

Every day he returned to the cottage intending to tell Kathryn the truth about what had happened when the Haitian job went haywire. He wanted her to understand what it was like to be handcuffed to a wall, to have cherished notions about your strength, about yourself, systematically destroyed.

He thought he was skirting around the edges of the subject, coming at it from an angle, as he knelt down and roughhoused with the boy on the kitchen floor, much as he had with Adrienne when she was little and he tickled and teased her until she whooped with giggles. He told Kathryn that a boy this age needed to be outdoors, getting exercise. He led the kid into the courtyard and romped with him. He dropped the leash, raced him to the wall and playfully wrestled him down off it. Back inside, he pointed out to Kathryn that the boy was packing on weight and muscle. Another month or two and he would be manhandling them. But he never said a word about Geneva.

He also never asked her again about the second ransom letter. He assumed she had written it. Who else could have? But to confront her seemed cruel. Then, too, if he pressed the issue, that might end their time together, and he didn't want that.

He supposed she had her reasons for sleeping with him. Why coax her to spell them out? The crucial point was not to delude himself. He derived some satisfaction from viewing the situation with clarity—a man making love to a much younger woman, a stock comic character, middle-age crazy. When this ended—and how could it not?—he knew where he would land. Like somebody who had jumped off a forty-story building, he was doing fine so far, but rocky ground was rising fast.

To his surprise, Kathryn acted as though they had a future and indicated this by asking about his past. She invited him to talk about Vietnam, his friends, the places he had lived, his plans. When he mentioned his home in Virginia, she praised the Medical Center in Richmond and the excellence of the research facilities at the university in Charlottesville. Maybe she and the boy would wind up living near him.

Zack mulled over her words with the same slow deliberation as he drew her close in bed. Into the teeth of his tumbling silence, she dropped tantalizing scraps of conversation and never seemed upset that he didn't respond in kind. She gave him a key to the courtyard gate and asked him to use it when he came and went. She explained with a grin that she didn't care to scandalize the neighbors. The two of them were in this together, she implied, secretly plotting . . . what? a secret caper?

He was acutely conscious of the subjects they didn't discuss. The fault was his more than hers. He never mentioned the problem of arranging a passport and visa for the boy, or of transport to the capital and plane tickets to the States. Then there was Ms. Pearson at the U.S. consulate. He anticipated trouble from her, perhaps active interference. But he said nothing about this to Kathryn.

He did, however, insist on continuing the effort to find out about Paul Fletcher. He asked Kathryn to show him where his son-in-law had lived, and with her translating, he spoke to a few neighbors who professed to remember little about Paul or his disappearance. They visited the scorched heap of his bombed laboratory and learned nothing from it. They stopped by Dr. Medvedev's compound. The irascible old Russian struck Zack as having a grievance stuck like a bone in his throat. He gnawed it to the bitter marrow, but offered little of value about Fletcher.

In the evening, Zack watched Kathryn work with the boy. She spent hours speaking to him, repeating phrases and short sentences. Pressing his fingers to her throat, she encouraged him to imitate the sounds she made. The kid was mesmerized and floated in the acoustic cologne of her voice like a baby in amniotic fluid. At such moments the boy seemed content to remain in this room. But Zack knew, from pulling him down off the courtyard wall, where he would go if given the chance.

And Zack? Where would he go? When he first landed in Central Asia, he couldn't conceive of staying an hour longer than he had to. Now as the days passed, he wondered what, if anything, awaited him elsewhere.

After the lesson ended, Kathryn sat at the table jotting notes in her journal. "It's a record of my experiments," she explained.

"Am I one of them?" he asked.

"One of what?"

"Your experiments?"

She smiled. "I'd say you're a finished project, not a work in progress."

Though he smiled back at her, he said, "I'm not sure I like that—being finished."

"I meant fully formed, mature, in your prime."

"That sounds better."

"I'm going to wash my hair," she said. "You take over here."

Alone with the boy, he was tempted to do just that—resume where she had left off. If he weren't so self-conscious, he would have talked to him. Or maybe it was guilt, more than shyness, that dissuaded Zack from speaking. Since he was aware of what the kid wanted, he couldn't bring himself to natter nonsense phrases. And much as it was on his mind, he didn't consider recounting his own experience of being chained to a wall. That would only lead where his every line of thought converged—on the idea of letting the boy go.

Kathryn returned to the kitchen in a bathrobe and positioned herself in the window, backlit by the last rays of evening sun. Unwinding a turban-like towel, she released a cascade of wet hair and went about drying it by shaking her head from side to side. With her eyes shut, she swayed like a Sufi dancer, her lovely face that of a woman lost in a trance.

The spell extended to Zack. He was about to rise and wrap her in his arms. Overcome with tenderness, he longed to embrace and protect her, just as he had watched her do with the boy. But then she opened her eyes and said, "You know, I think I love you. So it's hard to admit that I haven't been leveling with you."

"If this is about the letter—"

"No, it's Anna. Tomas's girlfriend at the hotel."

"What about her?"

She moved next to him, as though she might sit on his lap. Instead, she stayed on her feet and placed a hand on his shoulder. "I didn't tell you because I thought it would hurt your daughter. But a couple of months before Paul was kidnapped, Anna left Tomas and started living with Paul."

"Jesus, I wish you had said something."

"I hope you understand why I didn't. If Paul's alive, I don't want to screw up his marriage. If he's dead, well, there's no point putting your daughter through more pain."

"Anna may know something about his disappearance."

"I doubt that."

"Still, I have to talk to her."

"Now?" She hadn't taken her hand off him.

He spent half an hour assuring Kathryn that he didn't blame her and wasn't angry. At least not at her. His fury was directed at Fletcher. And at himself as it dawned on him that when Anna came to his room that time, she might have been hustling him for something other than sex. Whether she had information to trade or something to hide, he had questions to ask her.

Zack left by the courtyard gate shortly after nightfall and walked along dim, deserted back streets until he was several blocks from the cottage. Then he cut over to a boulevard that felt safer than the dark tunnel of alleys. His footsteps echoed off the blast shields in front of office buildings. In places where sandbags plugged ground-floor windows, the noise of his heels was muffled and he heard the furious pulse of blood in his ears. The thought that he had flown here to save Fletcher after the son of a bitch had been cheating on Adrienne fed Zack's rage.

A soldier stepped out of a doorway straight into his path. Before it registered that he was about to be arrested or robbed or both, Zack had the barrel of an AK-47 in his ribs. The soldier motioned for him to empty his pockets. Zack brought out a wad of bills. The soldier wanted more and started to reach around toward his back pockets. Zack was afraid he would find the money belt and the .38.

He signaled that he had nothing else worth stealing. The soldier didn't buy it and crowded him toward the doorway. Zack wasn't about to let himself be pushed into the building. He pulled the pistol and banged it into the man's mouth. His front teeth broke off; the Kalashnikov clattered to the pavement. As the soldier clapped a hand to his bleeding lips, Zack kicked his feet out from under him and rolled him into the gutter. He grabbed the assault rifle and ran. Someone shouted. He didn't look back. He yanked the clip from the AK-47 and slung it across the street. Farther along, he heaved the rifle under a parked car. Though nobody was chasing him, he didn't slow down until he had jogged through the hotel gate and up the drive.

At the front entrance, he crouched and gulped for air. Only after his breathing subsided did his feelings—quite a few of them—catch up with him. Fear was down near the bottom of the list. Anger was right at the top. He couldn't believe how badly he had wanted to squeeze the trigger and blow the soldier away. That was what scared him most—how close he had come to killing the guy, how abruptly the familiar emotions had foamed up in him.

Inside, he spotted Tomas at a dining room table, drinking alone.

"Where's Anna?" Zack asked.

The smile that never quite touched his eyes had vanished from his lips as well. "She's gone."

"Where?"

Tomas shrugged. "Anna and I are taking a vacation from each other. She left a few nights ago and I haven't seen her since."

"Do you expect her back?"

"At my age—at your age—expectation is a waste of time. I accept what comes."

Zack was about to tell him exactly what would come next if Tomas didn't stop talking in riddles. He'd stick the .38 in his face. That would get his attention. But Zack had sufficient purchase on a cooler, more calculating corner of his brain to realize that he had better go up to his room and think.

What he thought was how long it had been since he had shot anybody. More than thirty years. Yet memories of Vietnam swarmed up as if they had happened yesterday. He could smell the mud and remember the earth opening its maw and him throwing fresh meat into it. Like so many men, he had gone there to do good and stayed on to cause catastrophe. It made him question in what measure his instinct to rescue was always just an excuse to wreak havoc. Much as he might argue that he was here only for Adrienne, he knew it was more than that. Now there was Kathryn and the kid. If he wasn't careful, he'd lose more than he had brought with him.

. . .

*T*he next day, a chambermaid slipped Zack a scrap of paper covered in barely legible, childlike block letters. "I no wear is Fletcher. Meat me outside, Anna."

The chambermaid couldn't or wouldn't tell him more.

This had a bad feel, a bad taste to it. Twelve hours earlier he had been searching for Anna. Now she sent a message. There was every reason to suspect that Tomas had orchestrated this. A blatant setup, a chance to shake him down for money. Or maybe much worse. Still, Zack felt obliged to follow through.

Fighting a nervous tic—the need to keep touching the pistol tucked in at the small of his spine—he crossed the lobby, and with a curt wave to Tomas at the reception desk, he advanced out into the heat which shimmered with intimations of relentless punishment later in the afternoon. Already the asphalt burned through the soles of his shoes.

A woman draped from head to ankles in a *burqa* lingered at the bottom of the driveway. Poised in front of a whitewashed gate pillar, she resembled a Rorschach of black ink. Zack would have sailed on by her if she hadn't spoken. The words filtered through the veil over her face as if from a faulty radio speaker. Mesh fabric masked her eyes so that he couldn't see in, but when she called his name, he recognized Anna's voice. "We go," she said.

"Where?"

"To Paul."

"Hold on. Where is he?"

"I take you."

"Is he alive?"

"Soon we are there." She walked him around the block, toward some lacy acacia trees.

"I'm not going anywhere until I know whether he's alive."

"A life," she said.

Misha's teal green BMW was parked in the shade of the trees. The uncial lettering on its license plate looked worm-like. "What's Misha got to do with this?" Zack asked.

"Nothing. He lets me drive his car. We do not walk. Too far."

After she unlocked the Beamer, she bent at the waist, gathered the hem of the *burqa* and shed it in one smooth motion. Balling up the baggy tent, she stuffed it into the back seat. Under it, she wore her white stirrup slacks and a fitted burgundy top.

Zack buckled himself into the passenger seat. Perspiration purled down his spine and printed the damp diagonal stripe of the seatbelt across his denim shirt. Avoiding his eyes as she drove, Anna focused on the chaos of traffic and pedestrians.

"Who put you up to this? Tomas?"

"No Tomas. I hear you look for Paul."

"Heard it where?"

Anna didn't answer. She stabbed at the control panel. "Cold you like?" She hit the AC button and jets of air feathered her curly hair. From the tape deck Barry White serenaded them in smarmy baritone. "I can't lose with what I use," he sang. "I'm qualified to satisfy."

Zack envied the man's confidence. At the moment he was hyper-alert to every prospect of loss. Anna, by contrast, appeared supremely at ease. Yawning, she didn't bother to cover her mouth. Her pink tongue curled like a lazy cat's.

"Does Paul know I'm in town? Does he know you're bringing me to him?"

"We never so much talk."

"Is he alone?"

"Always."

"Why are you doing this?"

"Money. Maybe you pay me." Her candid admission of greed was the first reassuring thing she had said.

For several minutes she rode the rear bumper of a tiny green vehicle manufactured to sweep streets. When she sped past it, Zack noticed a paraplegic beetling along at the wheel of the contraption. On the northern fringes of the city, between a few last derelict apartment towers, flocks of sheep and goats grazed on pebbles, munching at wiry plants and plastic bags. Coils of smoke, thick as cables, chained decrepit factories to the flawless majolica bowl of sky.

"How much farther?" Zack asked.

Anna flicked her fingers, suggesting they were so close it made no sense to waste time talking.

Arid and wind-scoured expanses of desert undulated ahead of them in heat mirages. Zack darted a glance over his shoulder. No one was trailing them. The asphalt in either direction appeared to drain into silvery lakes. Presently, the road was intersected by a gravel track where a UNESCO flag hung in tatters from a pole. Anna turned onto the track. Stones rattled against the fenders and clanged the undercarriage of Misha's car.

"Jesus, where are we going?" he asked.

Lifting a hand from the steering wheel, she waved vaguely, as if shooing away flies.

"This is bullshit," he muttered. But she drove on.

At regular intervals, steel rods had been hammered into the hard ground and linked by long strips of plastic tape—the kind that Zack associated with crime scenes. In spots, the tape had torn loose and had been whipped by wind around the rods in a barber pole pattern. Inside this staked-off area, an abandoned archeological dig was strewn with marble fragments, the pulverized remains of mismatched body parts almost indistinguishable from slag.

"When goes away the UN," Anna said, "people steal the good pieces."

They plowed on through sand ground as fine as pumice. The tires spewed khaki clouds in their wake. Ahead of them at the corrugated horizon, a series of domes looked, from a distance, to be the size of beehives or bread ovens. As they got closer, the domes loomed as large as church cupolas and acquired distinctive characteristics. In different styles and states of repair, they were ribbed, they were stepped, they were tiled, they were fringed with weeds like the down on a newborn baby's head. Two had fallen in and resembled fractured skulls.

"What the hell is this?" Zack said.

"Tombs."

"Is he dead? You told me he's alive."

"I show you."

She parked at one end of the desolate stretch of tombs. Zack could see that a narrow cobbled lane ran the length of the necropolis. Climbing out of the car's refrigerated air, he felt clammy sweat prickle his skin. Immediately, grit attached itself to the perspiration. As it dried, he seemed to be turning into a pillar of salt. He wished he were inanimate, inaudible—not crunching through stones with Anna twittering ahead of him, urging him on.

Sunlight glinted off the ceramic domes and soaked blood-red into those constructed of unglazed brick. He studied the empty street from end to end but refused to start down it, having no way of knowing who might be in the mausoleums. He grabbed Anna's arm. "Stay right beside me."

They detoured around in back of the tombs, on a path that paralleled the cobbled lane. He had clear sight lines between the domes, but nobody in the tombs could see him. He watched Anna. Her kohl-rimmed eyes and heavily made up face showed little emotion. Then a bearded goat clattered out of a crypt and startled them both.

"This is far enough," Zack said. "Where is he?"

Anna pointed nowhere in particular.

"Tell him to come out," he said.

"He's there." Now she pointed to the third dome on the right and pulled him toward it.

He held her arm tight. His free hand was easing around for the .38 when he heard something in the shale behind him. The goat, he thought, and turned to make sure. He flinched by pure reflex and never really saw the roundhouse right Misha swung from his heels. It caught him flush on the forehead. Zack fell as if he had been bludgeoned by a baseball bat. There was another punch, then a kick that toppled him into a tomb. In the instant it took Misha to catch up to him, Zack realized he was being beaten with brass knuckles. Rolling into a ball, he wrapped his arms around his head.

Rather than stomp or kick him again, Misha heaved him to his feet as effortlessly as he would pluck a handkerchief from his pocket. Then he tapped the brass knuckles against Zack's face like someone exploring a wall for a hollow panel.

"Mr. Question Man." Misha was laughing. "Ask this, ask that. Now I ask. Knock, knock! To know, where is Fletcher? In the place where you go!" With the precision of a carpenter wielding a ball peen hammer, he cracked Zack's cheekbones, his nose, his jaw, his teeth. "Now you tell me where is your money."

Through the deep inner flashing of his eyes, he saw the tomb dissolve around him. Hooks and blades of calligraphy seemed to scythe off the vault and tattoo the inside of his skull. He could smell Misha's foul cigarette breath but couldn't make out his mug. He tried to speak, but his mouth was full of blood. Close to unconscious, he pulled the .38 from his belt and squeezed the trigger, blowing a hole in the big Russian, front to back. The noise in that enclosed space was deafening; the concussion scaled a few tiles off the ceiling. He fired again, and bright fronds of blood fanned out on the faience behind Misha. Trailing a streamer of intestines, he slumped against the wall. While Misha didn't make a sound, somebody was screaming. Zack felt sonic waves shiver through the broken bones of his face. The noise died when Anna smashed the back of his head with a brick.

*F*or a time, there was nothing. Then prying apart the glued lids of one eye, he confronted absolute darkness and believed he was blind. Vision and sensation returned slowly. His brain was a roiling pond of eels and sting rays. Somebody scrubbed his face with a rough sponge. A medic, Zack thought. He was wounded, and a field doctor was cleaning a bullet hole. Ham-fisted, the medic buffed the sponge like an emery board against Zack's busted teeth.

He flailed a hand to get him to ease up. When the guy wouldn't quit, he grabbed his beard. He felt a tongue slobber between his fingers. The goat had clambered into the crypt and was licking Zack.

He sat up and was sorry that he had. His head lolled on the feeble stem of his neck. Gagging, he spat out bile and bits of tooth. Skittish at his vomiting, the goat retreated to the tomb entrance, silhouetted against stars. Zack couldn't guess how long he had been out, but day had become night.

Misha lay in a gold rectangle cast by the moon, a man in a gleaming casket. Stiff with rigor mortis, the fingers of his right hand clasped the brass knuckles. His Reebok jacket had bloated with blood; his pockets and wrist cuffs were full of it.

Zack patted his own pockets. Anna had tugged them inside out and stolen his money belt. Crawling around on his hands and knees, he found the .38 on the mausoleum floor and wedged it under the waistband of his jeans. When he went to stand up, the walls moved. He climbed out of the crypt with a blazing pinwheel in each eye and floundered along the cobbled lane, hauling himself hand over hand through the necropolis, reeling from one tomb to the next. But once he reached the stony, open plain, he had nothing to hang onto and fell. He righted himself, staggered a few steps and fell again. The goat was tailing him, butting his legs. Every time Zack collapsed, he felt the wet slithering tongue lick his face.

Amid the metal stakes and strips of plastic tape, he shuffled through shards of marble ears and hands and eyebrows. He slipped and lay stunned like a figure that had fallen intact from the frieze. In his fuddled state, he blamed the goat for tripping him and took a futile swipe at it with his fist. The next time the goat got near him, he fired a round from the .38 that left the animal without a head and Zack with another coating of gore.

Once at the paved road, he believed he had a chance. He could flag down a ride to town. When a car cruised into view, the drumming of tires on the asphalt jangled his bones, and he shouted and shook his arms. It felt like the jig-saw puzzle of his face was shattering. To the driver he must have looked de-mented, dangerous. The car rushed by, and so did the next one and the next. Squeezing his head between his hands, Zack screamed for somebody to stop. Then he screamed for the pain to stop. Crouched in a cyclone of sand, he con-sidered stepping into the high beams of a car and putting an end to this.

Instead, he walked and fainted and walked again. With no landmarks to gauge the distance, he counted steps, figuring sixteen hundred strides to a mile. Blood squelched in his shoes. He would have stayed down the next time and slept where he landed, but rage and revenge drove him on, dual engines that wouldn't let him rest. He wanted to get his hands on Anna and he wanted his money back.

He lost the capacity to count consecutively and started repeating numbers, singing cadence. When had he last done that? Parris Island? He remembered fifty-mile hikes with a fifty-pound pack on his back. Now the dead weight hung inside his head, quivering like a cut-glass chandelier.

As the moon rose, he made out the curved mass of the Grand Mosque and angled away from the road toward it. Indifferent to the ripe stench, he stum-bled through a garbage dump. Farther on, guard dogs protecting garden plots threw themselves into frenzied barking, but shied away from the scent of his blood and the goat's. Something popped under Zack's feet. It sounded like rotten plywood. His shoes plunged through, and he pitched forward, flinging out his hands. He might have landed on a xylophone upholstered in fur. It was a dead camel, its hide flattened to a frame of bones.

Entering the ancient city through the shuttered bazaar, he wandered in a warren of butcher shops and abattoirs. The few people on the street at this hour passed wraithlike in and out of obscurity. Any other night, they would have frightened him. Now they were the ones terrified by this specter that ap-peared to have sprung from the blood-slaked cobblestones, his face a ghastly smear.

He knew he would never make it to the hotel. He sensed it was a mistake to try. That was the first place they would search for him. Anna, the goons in the lobby, somebody was bound to take exception to what he had done to Misha and hunt him down. So he stopped at Kathryn's cottage but couldn't manage to fit the key into the courtyard gate with his numb fingers. He ended up smacking the front door with the flat of his palm. When she called, "Who is it?" he could barely murmur, "Me. Please."

Much as he wanted to warn her what he looked like, he couldn't bring himself to speak again and set off more turbulence in the free-floating slivers of his face. She opened the door, and Zack dropped through it like a hanged man through a scaffold.

*W*hen Anna failed to show up in the following week, Tomas welcomed the opportunity to be alone, lower his emotional temperature and indulge in a bout of melancholy. He convinced himself he had been more than generous to her—he had been profligate—and now had every right to derive petty satisfaction from not having paid her for the past month. He wagered she would be back for the money, if nothing else.

Meanwhile, he continued the evening bath ritual but no longer bothered to warm the tub with an immersion coil. He found the cold water bracing and it carried minor-chord memories of Prague winters. That was his favorite season, and since he no longer needed to reinvent the city for Anna in terms of Roman analogues, he was free to recall the gauntness of grey skies, the lonely street lamps haloed in drizzle, the castle a sugar-spun confection that freezing weather changed into a stone-hearted, steel-helmeted sentinel. On the icy Vltava, rowboats full of rotten leaves rocked against moss-covered wharves. As the river reached flood stage, tree branches sharked through the water and battered the pylons of the Charles Bridge so that pedestrians felt the impact in their feet.

Submerged in the tub, only his nose and eyes visible, Tomas intuited that there had always been something autoerotic about those sexually charged evenings when he invoked Prague, Anna fantasized about Rome and they both bathed in illusions. But what, after all, was autoeroticism except a form of nostalgia? In the past, he had boasted that his greatest weakness was women. Now he suspected that his sexual self-indulgence had hidden a deep sentimentality, a tendency toward pity that actually amounted to self-pity.

From here on he swore he would change and adopt the pragmatism of the Koran, which counseled that "women are your fields; go then, into your fields as you please." It wasn't too late for a dose of reality. And the reality was he could live without Anna.

Not that he didn't expect her to return, not that he had lost confidence that he could switch her on and off like a water tap. He shivered—a delightful sensation in Central Asia in midsummer—and decided that once Anna came back, he would be brutally honest and confess that he had never been to Rome. If she wanted to stay with him, she had to accept him as he was. And accept her own situation. No more daydreaming—

The bathroom door rocked back on its hinges, ruining his reverie. Tomas scrambled to his feet, then sagged into the soapy water and concealed his sex with a washcloth as four men crowded into the space between the tub and the toilet. Three of them had on leather coats and porkpie hats, like the men he had met through Misha. This might well have been the same trio, but nobody had exchanged names or pleasantries then and nobody did now. The fourth man was wispy and frail, much smaller than the others, and he wore an auburn toupee and photosensitive glasses. A leather purse the size of a camera case swung from his wrist.

"Where's the cunt?" he demanded.

To show them that he wasn't shaken, Tomas glanced under a corner of the washcloth and quipped, "There's no cunt here."

"Yes, there is," the little man said. "You're a cunt."

"Well, if I'm the one you're looking for, maybe you should tell me why."

"The Gypsy that lives with you, where is she?"

"I fired her. And she's not a Gypsy. She's Italian. Maybe she moved to Rome."

"No chance. She moved in with Misha."

"Then you're asking the wrong man. Ask Misha."

"I'm asking you." Though he spoke in a dialect devoid of hard consonants, there was nothing soft or sibilant about what he said.

Tomas stared up at the sun-braised faces staring down at him and lost his appetite for playing it cool. He had been questioned countless times by one brusque authority or another, and he knew the rules—never tell an obvious lie, never concede more than necessary. "I haven't seen Anna since she left the hotel. What does Misha say?"

"Misha's not talking much at the moment."

The man put his purse on the toilet lid, unzipped his trousers and flipped out his cock. The color of an eggplant, it seemed wildly out of proportion to his size. He shook it lazily in Tomas's direction, then started peeing into the bathtub. Tomas shrank back and started to stand up. The porkpie hats pushed him down into the water.

"Misha's dead," the little man said, pissing on him.

"I don't believe it."

"You better. It's true."

Urine scalded his chest and hissed in the soapsuds. The men wouldn't let Tomas turn away. He feared he was about to get a face full of it. But the spray stopped at his throat, pelting his Adam's apple. "Two gunshots in the belly," the little man said. "Blew his guts out."

"Where?"

"At the tombs. His body was there long enough for dogs and crows to chew him over. There isn't a lot left."

"Who did it?"

"That's what you're going to tell us."

"I don't know anything."

"You just need to know one thing—where's the cunt?"

"She didn't do it," Tomas said. "Anna doesn't own a gun."

"Maybe you gave her one."

"She left me. I wouldn't give her shit."

He flapped his dick, flicking off the last drops. "Maybe you shot Misha yourself because she was fucking him."

"I haven't been out of the hotel. Ask anyone. And I don't care who she fucks."

He zipped his fly and rinsed his fingers at the sink. "Maybe it was the money. You and the cunt decided to keep it for yourself."

"What money?"

"The American's."

"I don't know anything about him or any money."

"The cunt was supposed to drive him to the tombs so Misha could rob him. Instead, Misha's dead and she's gone."

"And McClintock?"

"He's gone too."

"Have you checked his room? He's still registered."

"He's not there." The man in the toupee retrieved his purse, unzipped it and pulled out a miniature pistol. Smaller than a cigarette pack, it might have been a toy, perhaps a lighter in the shape of a luger. But Tomas knew better. It was a PSM, an automatic pistol that the KGB had favored. It fired a tiny cartridge with a steel core that could penetrate a car door or an armored vest.

"I swear," Tomas said, "I don't know anything."

"Then you're really no good to us, are you?"

In an instant he digested this. "If there's any chance Anna was in on the killing with McClintock—"

"He's got a cock. I'd say there's a chance."

"I'll find her. There are places I can look for her."

"Better get busy."

"I'll need time."

"If I were you, I'd get dressed and get going right now. We'll be looking for her too and if we find her first . . . Like I said, what good are you?"

He aimed the PSM between Tomas's legs. When he squeezed the trigger, the gun jumped and gave a quiet hiccup. The slug drilled through the soap-suds and a centimeter of ceramic-covered, case-hardened steel. As dirty water drained out the bullet hole, Tomas cowered in the tub, petrified to move until the men left the bathroom.

3

*E*very word Kathryn whispered made Zack wince. And when he spoke, it was as if someone had shaken a hornet's nest inside his head. He clapped his face between his hands to stop the buzzing and stinging. His black eyes had closed to slits. His nose was broken and bent to the side, and his jaw looked broken too. Because of his raggedly split lips and shattered teeth, he had trouble talking, but wouldn't stay quiet until he had laid out a list of instructions. No matter who knocked at the door, he told her, she shouldn't answer it. In no case should she let anyone know he was here. He didn't need a doctor. He made her promise not to bring one in. If she'd help him into the bathroom and prop him up at the sink, he'd be fine once he washed off.

Fastening his hands to the faucet, he swayed like a drunk on a stormy deck and shut his eyes against the ghoulish misshapen mask that leered at him from the mirror. Then he bent toward the water, groaned and kept on going. His forehead hit the porcelain basin, and he slid to the floor unconscious.

Kathryn rushed to the kitchen for the first-aid kit and a sewing basket. The boy sensed something wrong, he smelled it—Zack's blood, Kathryn's fear, the acrid combustibility of the air. His shoulder muscles spasmed, and he leapt about, mewling like a scared pup. She murmured soothing sounds as she hurried from him to Zack and continued to croon a kind of baby talk to steady her hands and calm her quaking belly.

With a pair of pinking shears, she scissored at his shirt, slitting the seams and tearing off blood-drenched rags. To her surprise, there were no cuts on his arms and chest. All the damage appeared to be to his face. It looked as if he had smashed through a windshield. Then she saw the wound on the back of his head. Dabbing at it with a damp towel, she couldn't judge how deep it was. There was too much blood. Afraid that he had fractured his skull, she hesitated to apply pressure to stop the bleeding.

When she tried to move him from under the sink, he was far too heavy for her to lift, and so she dragged him. His head rolled gruesomely, painting a red brushstroke across the floor, and the pistol fell from his belt. Kathryn picked it up and hid it in a bureau drawer. She had to get help or she feared he would bleed to death. Despite her promise, she went for Dr. Medvedev.

At this hour few people were ever on the street except thieves and soldiers looking for bribes. But no one bothered Kathryn, who raced through the town like a woman who had already been beaten or robbed. When she reached the veterinarian's compound and banged at his door, the animals began barking and braying, and Dr. Medvedev complained that she had disrupted his first sound sleep in a decade. While he dressed, she waited in a hallway where two fifty-gallon oil drums exuded a sulfuric odor. He came back, crabbing that he wasn't the rescue squad, some special emergency service for Americans.

"I'll be damned if I'll drive my car and have it hijacked," he said.

"But there's no time to waste."

"Then find someone else. Does it no longer occur to people that there are certain professional courtesies?"

"I'm sorry. But I didn't have anybody else to turn to."

"That's my point. There used to be places to turn. Before, people bitched about the government. Now you depend on a veterinarian. Is this dialectical growth?"

"I'll pay you. I have some dollars."

"Don't insult me. I'm not one of these frostbitten brains with gold fever. One of these bandits ready to kill to get rich."

Lugging his leather bag, he hobbled on bunioned feet to her cottage and never quit grousing. Zack was still out cold on the bathroom floor. Kathryn suggested they carry him into the bedroom. The doctor preferred the kitchen, and together they hoisted Zack up onto the dinner table where he sprawled like a corpse on a morgue slab. "Now I don't have to break my back stooping," Dr. Medvedev said.

The boy reared upright, leaned into the leash and whimpered. Maybe he recognized the doctor by sight or scent. Maybe he associated this scene with his own treatment. Any other time Kathryn might have conjectured whether recall and empathy were uniquely human reactions, but at the moment she was preoccupied.

Interrupting his stream of invective about "hooligan anarchists," Dr. Medvedev instructed her to fetch a bowl of hot water and a bar of soap. After stropping a straight razor, he tested the blade on his thumb, then lathered Zack's scalp and shaved off a tonsured patch of hair. The gash had sliced loose a crescent-shaped hinge of flesh. He gently pressed it flat and applied an oval bandage like a skullcap worn by a Moslem.

"Shouldn't you stitch it?" Kathryn asked.

"And stick a needle into his brain?"

"Is his skull fractured?"

"Do I have X-ray vision? How should I know?" He turned his attention to Zack's face, suturing cuts.

"Please, don't shout. You're scaring the boy."

"The boy?" He scowled at the kid who strained to watch him. "It doesn't bother me to have him hop around. I am surrounded all day by animals making a racket. What bothers me—" setting aside the needle and thread, he tested Zack's pulse, then his blood pressure "— is the destruction of our city. It used to be a wonder of the world. Read Marco Polo. Read Ibn Battuta.

Genghis Khan couldn't destroy it. Tamerlane didn't. But after a couple of years of capitalism, it's falling apart, and social parasites prey on the population. Who is this man anyway?"

"You met him. He visited you to ask about Fletcher."

His bristling eyebrows arched in shock. "Ah, yes, Fletcher's father-in-law. I never would have recognized him." He pumped an ampoule of painkiller into Zack's arm.

"Will he live?" Kathryn asked.

"To the degree that life is possible under the present system, I suppose he'll survive." He shoved his yellow-white hair back from his forehead. "Do you have vodka?"

She presumed he meant to substitute it for a disinfectant, but he simply wanted a drink. She poured him a glass and prayed that it would put an end to his ranting. Although he went on talking, the vodka diverted him from politics, and he verged as close to personal conversation as he ever had with Kathryn. Munching a cucumber that she set out with salt, he sighed. " 'Against troubles, vodka inside and outside.' That was our slogan in the camps. Prisoners were convinced that it was healthier than *koumiss*."

"What's *koumiss*?" She served herself a thimble of vodka. The boy had stopped fidgeting and rubbed himself against her legs. She stroked his hair.

"Fermented mare's milk. Peasants claim it cures everything, even tuberculosis. But where I did my time, it couldn't cure the weather. In November, not even winter yet, the guards estimated how many of us would croak during the cold months, and they ordered us to dig that number of graves. Once it got to be December, it was too late. The ground froze and it took dynamite to dig a hole."

Dr. Medvedev slumped into one of the kitchen chairs and lit a foul-smelling Prima cigarette. Kathryn didn't object. Smoke curling toward the ceiling, the tired lilt of his voice recounting events faraway and fifty years ago, offered some relief from what lay on the table in front of them.

"We wore clothes around the clock." He tapped cigarette ashes into the cuff of his trousers. "We didn't even undress to sleep. If we took off our boots, they turned to ice under our beds and stuck to the floor. In the mines, it was so cold I'd shut one eye to keep it warm. Then I'd open it and shut the other before it froze. At night we built big fires and sat closer and closer around them as it got colder. Finally, we were sitting almost in the flames, our faces burning, our backsides shivering. You understand? We were cooking and freezing at the same time, and all the while drinking buckets of bad vodka. I had finished my medical studies, so I should have known what to expect."

"People got drunk and fell into the fire," Kathryn guessed.

"Some did, but the bigger problem was that alcohol lowers the body temperature and thickens the blood. Men's hearts burst. Just exploded, boom! in their chests, and they keeled over dead. '*Zgorel to vodki*,' we said. He burned himself to death with vodka."

"Why were you there?"

"Deviationist ideas."

"I don't understand."

"I planted a bomb to destroy a Trotskyite cell."

"You killed them?"

"No, the bomb didn't detonate. I bungled the triggering device. Still, they caught me and sentenced me to six years to redeem my guilt with hard labor."

"After they did that to you, why are you still a Communist?"

"Because I believe," he declared with the kind of frantic orthodoxy she hadn't heard since the last time she talked to the Mullah. "I believe in the idea, the ideal, not the idiots in charge."

"You believe they were right to throw you in prison?"

"It's not a question of right or wrong." Pinching out the cigarette, he saved the butt in his pocket. "Sending me to the mines was a subjective error that had nothing to do with the scientific validity of the concepts I believe in."

Kathryn stretched out her long legs as if this would smooth the curlicues from the conversation. "I don't understand how you can ignore what you lived through and believe what you haven't seen."

"But I have seen it. Up here." He touched his temple. "Isn't that how we all survive?"

"Through hope?"

"No, hope is pie-in-the-sky heaven. I'm referring to down-to-earth rationality. Men can formulate pictures of reality in their minds, can they not?"

"Don't you ever miss Russia?" she changed the subject. "Wouldn't you rather live there?"

His dirty disheveled coat exaggerated the slope of his shoulders, the weariness of his shrug. "I'm too old to go back. And there are things for me to do here." He plunked his empty glass on the drainboard. "Now I must sleep. If you don't object, I'll wait until daybreak before I go home."

"Use my bed. I'll stay with him."

"There's nothing more you can do."

"Still, I'd rather stay."

"As you please. But I'll make do with the sofa. Haven't you read Russian novels? It's our favorite place to sleep and very often to die. On couches. Afterward the corpse is laid out on a table."

Seeing the anguish this remark caused on Kathryn's face, Dr. Medvedev extended a hand as if to touch her hair. He stopped short. "He's going to be all right."

"Wouldn't he be better off in my bed?"

"He's as comfortable one place as the other. And honestly, I don't have the energy to move him."

He tottered into the living room and sank down on the sofa. The cushions groaned. Or maybe it was Dr. Medvedev who groaned after a day of dealing with yapping animals and humans.

Kathryn edged her chair closer to the table. As long as she didn't look at Zack's ruined face, she could imagine he was sleeping, not numbed by medicine and pain. Reminded of the time when she first found the boy, she wanted to touch him, somehow signal that she was there. She yearned to lie down beside him, curl up in the crook of his arm and offer consolation in the course of receiving it. Although nothing compared to his, her misery deepened by the minute. In a process as painful as the reknitting of bones, she puzzled over her options. She couldn't unwrite the ransom letter. She couldn't hope for him to forgive her. What should she do?

Frightening as it was, she finally forced herself to look at his face—battered, lopsided, livid. This was what she had sought from her years in Central Asia—a scar or a beauty mark. She didn't care which. She just wanted to be transformed. But it was Zack who had been changed forever, and Kathryn knew that it was her fault and it wasn't over yet. The blows might keep coming until everything she loved had been beaten beyond recognition.

*4*

*I*n the Beamer, on the way back to town, Anna had difficulty driving and thinking at the same time. She paused on the roadside buffeted by sand whipped up by outbound traffic, throttled the volume of Barry White and dithered over what she had done and what she should do now. She delivered McClintock to the tombs expecting Misha to murder him. For fear that Misha would kill her next or at least cheat her out of the money, she intended to hit him with the brick. But when McClintock shot him, she didn't wait to find out what the American would do to her. As she saw it, bashing in his head was self-defense—after which it made no sense not to strip him of his money belt.

Now she needed a plan. No, two plans—one to get to the capital, a second to get out of the country. Without a title to the BMW, she didn't dare attempt to cross the border. If nobody carjacked it along the way, customs guards were sure to confiscate it at the frontier. She could drive to the capital, but the road was full of bandits and it would be easy for Misha's friends to track her in the Beamer. Even hiring a chauffeured car struck her as too risky. Once it became known that she had dollars, she was afraid she would be robbed.

The safest way to travel, she decided, was the bus that ran on an erratic schedule based on reports about the level of violence along the road. Until the next one left, she had to find a place to hide.

Returning to town to a busy street in front of the Palace of the People's Revolution, Anna parked the BMW and strolled off in her white stirrup slacks, with the *burqa* over her arm. Once she entered the anonymous congestion of the bazaar, she draped herself in the yards of cloth and effectively vanished. But she still had nowhere to go. Tomas and the hotel were out of the question. She didn't put it past him to hand her over to Misha's friends. Only as the Catholic church came into view did it occur to Anna that she might convince Father Josef to shelter a repentant sinner.

*I*nside the drab cinderblock building, she was surprised how clean and quiet and beautiful it was. She regretted that she hadn't accepted Father Josef's earlier invitations to visit. Admiring the polished wooden pews, the gleaming gold tabernacle and sky blue ceiling, Anna believed that she could live here happily for a long time.

Dressed in civilian clothes, Father Josef was sweeping the sanctuary and looked more like a janitor than a priest. When he saw a woman in *purdah* swan down the center aisle, he dropped the broom. Then there was the added shock of Anna's voice behind the mesh veil.

Normally he would have insisted that they remain in the church where the sight of a woman with a clergyman wouldn't cause scandal. But when Anna began crying, he showed her into the rectory and gave her a glass of mineral water.

Removing the *burqa*, she drew a deep quavery breath and unburdened herself of a sad tale. She had moved into the hotel with Tomas, she said, because she loved him and believed he intended to marry her. But he not only didn't love her anymore—he meant to corrupt and exploit her. Tired of sleeping with her himself, he wanted her to have sex with other men and share the money with him. When she refused, he threatened to have Misha and his mafia friends turn her out as a street prostitute.

"Tomas wouldn't do that," Father Josef protested.

"Do you think I'm lying?"

"No. But there must be a mistake. I'll talk to him."

"No, don't! He's after me. That's why I wore the *burqa*—to hide from him. If he finds out I talked to you, I'll wind up with the women next to the river. I'd rather die. Please let me stay."

"The rectory's barely big enough for me, Anna. And I can't live with a woman. You know that."

"Just for a few days," she begged. "Just until the bus leaves. I don't have much money, but I can cook for you and clean or anything you ask."

"I have to consider my parishioners. They're mostly old women and—"

"They won't know. During the day I'll keep out of sight. At night I'll sleep anyplace—in a closet, on a chair, behind the altar. Don't send me back to Tomas. I'll lose my mind. I'll lose my soul."

She abjectly lowered her eyes and noticed that his scuffed brown shoes were military issue, probably the discards of some dead soldier. Her mother had always maintained that you could learn a lot about a woman by her shoes: quality footwear couldn't be counterfeited. She had never received guidance about men's shoes. Momentarily, Anna debated bribing Father Josef with the promise of a new pair. Instead she said, "While I'm with you, I'd like to become a Catholic. I want to learn the prayers and be baptized. Will you teach me, Father?"

Finally he relented, but stressed that in his precarious position, ministering to an atoll of Catholics in an ocean of nonbelievers, he had to remain beyond reproach and avoid the slightest appearance of evil. He asked her to wear the *burqa* and sleep out in the courtyard, in a lean-to previously occupied by the custodian of the gymnasium.

The lean-to's slanted wall was green, like the flap of a tent. In place of a screen, the lone window was covered by a *pandjara*, a decorative wooden lattice that let in air and light. The sun streamed through it, casting a filigree shadow on the cement floor like the ornate design on a carpet. Anna sat at the center of this arabesque, unbuckled the money belt from around her waist and unzipped it.

At the sight of so many dollars, she uttered a small cry that mixed amazement with avarice. She had never conceived of such a great sum of new bills, all crisp and flawless, in denominations of tens, twenties and hundreds. It took her a long time to count out the twenty thousand she had been promised. Then she counted twenty-eight thousand more. As she struggled to translate the total into a value system that she could comprehend, the sheer monumentality of the task stumped Anna. Yet while she had never heard the Marxist tenet about quantity changing quality, she immediately knew that this much money made her not just rich, but an altogether different person.

With trembling hands she tucked the bills back into the canvas belt and strapped it around her under the *burqa*. From the day she departed her village for the city, she had viewed her body as her only asset, and with cold clarity she had learned its secrets and mastered its intimate vocabulary. Unlike those girls who profess to be embarrassed by a blunt naming of the parts—what men call this, how they ask for that—she had never been prissy. Now she wanted to be every bit as matter-of-fact about money as she was about sex. But she felt squeamish and started to rationalize her sudden wealth like some silly farm girl justifying the loss of her virginity.

There was so much good she could do. Father Josef, for instance, she could help him. She vowed to make a donation to his church, but not such a large one that he would wonder where she got the dollars. She'd buy him a new pair of shoes and some furniture to replace the flimsy folding chairs and tables in the rectory. He had a sweet tooth for chocolate, and she'd supply him with giant bars of Toblerone. She'd fix bowls of *plov* and skewers of mutton, fatten him up and put some color in his pasty cheeks. Then when the time was right, she'd catch the bus to the capital and fly to Italy with a clear conscience.

. . .

*T*he next day, in her *burqa*, Anna went to the bazaar to shop. But not for Father Josef. She bought a box of tampons. Back in the lean-to, she emptied the box and pulled each cotton plug out of its cardboard tube. Then she spent hours rolling the bills, all $48,000 of them, into cigar-shaped cylinders and inserted them into the tubes. After she repacked the tubes into the box, she was confident she could leave it in plain sight. In her experience no man ever rooted around in tampons.

Despite some delight at her cleverness, a dull anger welled up as she thought about men and their superior attitude. What mattered to them was what they stuck in you, never what you might like. To be in bed with Tomas, to have him inside her, knowing that he didn't intend to take her to Italy, was humiliating. How could anybody blame her for what she had done?

*I*n the succeeding days, she came to prefer the lean-to to her life at the hotel. Every morning she lay awake, gazing at the complexity of the *pandjara* and listening to Father Josef say Mass. His prayers flowed across the courtyard as murmurous as a river and instilled in her a sense of well-being that rivaled the security of the womb. Although she hadn't the remotest conception of the meaning of his words, the ribbons of pure sound provided a brief stay against the menace of the world.

After Father Josef's few daily communicants dispersed, Anna cooked him breakfast at an outdoor grill, then joined him in the rectory for catechism lessons. In addition to Catholic doctrine, he continued to instruct her in Italian, and resuming where Tomas left off, he taught her about Rome. But he might as well have been speaking in parables about an altogether different place. Emphasizing the sanctity of every square inch of the city, he described streets named after popes and apostles and a financial institution called the Bank of the Holy Spirit.

Even the jail in Rome, Regina Coeli, meant Queen of the Heavens, and Father Josef claimed that when inmates exercised in the yard, women congregated on the Gianicolo Hill, behind the prison, and shouted the names of their men. Giovanni, Pietro, Paolo, Lorenzo—they chanted as though singing the litany of the saints. Many of these women, Father Josef said, were prostitutes yelling messages to their pimps. Yet no choir of angels sounded more beautiful.

Was the anecdote part of her religious education, Anna wondered? Or was he warning her about the pitfalls of Rome? Did he fear she would join that chorus of tarnished women? She could have set his mind at ease. She had no intention of getting involved with men ever again. Not that she thought it was such a serious matter—what Father Josef called sins of the flesh. Having a man's cock inside you was nothing compared to blowing a hole in his belly or busting his head with a brick. What forgiveness could she expect for that?

Almost as confusing to her as Father Josef's remarks about Rome were the paintings on the rectory wall. In one a naked, wistful man had been tied to a tree and shot full of arrows. That was St. Sebastian, the patron saint of archers, Father Josef explained.

In another, a woman with blood spilling down her bare chest lifted a silver platter on which her severed breasts rested in pools of gore. An angel hovered nearby, poised to whisk the platter away. Where? Why? Like Anna, was the woman embarrassed by her tits, their saggy shape and sad downward tilt? Or was this a mystery she couldn't understand until she converted to Catholicism?

Father Josef told her it was a portrait of St. Agatha. "She's the patron saint of female problems. You should pray to her."

"Pray to her for what?"

"Strength. Peace."

She did as he urged, but strength and peace, particularly peace of mind, eluded her. Every time she checked at the bus station, all departures had been cancelled. There were rumored to be rebel incursions on the road and uprisings in formerly safe areas. No one claimed that barbarians were coming. The barbarians had already arrived, and everybody dreaded something worse was on the way.

Anna believed that only the *burqa* protected her from oblivion. Each trip to the market became a test of her courage and the flimsy camouflage. It seemed to her that she survived with no more than a child's faith in magic, the dream that she was invisible if she shut her eyes. She passed people she recognized and wondered whether she had fooled them or they were tricking her. The curtain of flowing cloth, the woven face veil that transformed her field of vision into the cross-hatchings of a graph—this wasn't a disguise she could count on forever. Sooner or later somebody was bound to unmask her.

She started to spend longer stretches of the day in the lean-to. Sometimes she recounted the money. Sometimes she practiced the prayers that Father Josef taught her. When she asked him about paradise, he explained that it was a word of Persian origin that referred to a walled garden. "You're halfway there," he said. "After all, you live in a courtyard. That's a kind of walled garden."

"But I have to leave soon."

The priest didn't disagree. "You knew it wasn't forever."

That night, as moonbeams slanted into the lean-to through the *pandjara*, spreading an antimacassar of light, Anna knelt and pictured herself as St. Agatha, seized by rapturous faith and yearning, her face etched with orgasmic glory, her soul swooning. She pleaded that this wouldn't be all she would ever know of paradise.


*O*ne day she grilled *shashlik* for their lunch, sizzling the skewers of meat and fat over a charcoal fire. If Father Josef was correct, condemned souls burned like this for all eternity. Anna had seen farmers scalded by chemical fertilizer. She knew the smell of napalm and the incinerated stench of soldiers torched in their tanks by Molotov cocktails. On firsthand terms with fiery hell and saturated with memories of suffering, she swore she would do anything to be saved.

Deafened by the snap and hiss of the meat, she didn't hear the men cross the courtyard, didn't see them until they were on top of her—three Mongols in leather jackets and porkpie hats, and a little fellow with a henna-dyed toupee and photosensitive glasses. They tore off Anna's *burqa*, wrestled her into the rectory, and tied her to a chair. She screamed, got slapped and sat there dumbfounded in the white slacks and fitted burgundy body suit she had worn for a week.

Opposite her, Father Josef was lashed to his own chair with sashes and cinctures stolen from the sacristy.

"We don't have any money," the priest said.

"Shut up." The man in the toupee cracked him with a purse that swung from his wrist. He told the three porkpie hats to search the rectory and the church. They pried open the tabernacle, tipping over ciboria and chalices. Communion wafers scattered on the floor with the sound of a bad hand of cards flung on a table. They smashed wine cruets and ripped vestments at the seams and peeled them apart.

"For the love of God, stop them," Father Josef begged. "This is a sacrilege."

The man in the toupee bent over Anna. "Where's the American?"

"I don't know."

He hit her with the purse. It had something heavy inside it. Her head resounded like a thumped melon.

"Don't lie to me. You drove him to Misha."

"Misha told me to," she gasped. "He asked me to bring the American to the tombs, and that's what I did."

She darted her eyes at one of the porkpies who ambled in from the church empty-handed. The little man ordered him outside to the charcoal grill. Seconds later, he carried back the skewers, brandishing them like bandoliers. The gobs of mutton and fat still hissed.

The man in the toupee set down his purse and grabbed one of the skewers. After blowing on it, he ate the fat, but spat out the gristly meat. A mouthful plopped onto Anna's shoe. "Tell me what happened to Misha."

"My job was to bring the American there. That's all."

He slapped the skewer across her thigh. She yelped. It hadn't hurt much, but she hated getting a grease stain on her stirrup slacks. She planned to wear them when she flew to Italy.

"When I drove the American to the tombs," she started over, "Misha started punching him and asking questions. But the American had a gun and shot Misha. He shot him twice. So I hit the American over the head with a rock and ran away."

"You didn't run. You stole Misha's car."

"How else was I supposed to get to town? I was afraid."

"Afraid of what?"

"That the American might catch me and shoot me, too."

"How could he do that after you bashed him with a brick?"

"I didn't wait to find out how bad he was hurt. I don't even know whether he's alive."

"Unless you buried him someplace, he's alive."

"I didn't do anything like that. I hid with the priest and told him I wanted to convert. He knows nothing about this. Don't hurt him."

In prompt reply to her wish, he whipped the skewer across Father Josef's cheek, raising a red welt. "If you didn't do anything wrong, why ditch Misha's car? Why hide?"

When she was slow in answering, he slashed the priest again. This time he drew blood. Anna moaned as if it were she who had been hit. Father Josef said nothing, simply slumped lower. His concave chest curled over the cincture that bound him to the chair.

"Why didn't you tell anybody Misha was dead?"

She wanted to save Father Josef. She wanted to save herself. "I panicked. I was scared of being mixed up in a murder."

The two men had finished in the church and found nothing. The toupee sent them to search the courtyard. Anna forced herself not to watch them approach the lean-to. She faced the peculiar little man. As his photosensitive glasses cleared in the indoor light, his eyes took shape behind the lenses as if on a sheet of developing film. "Why didn't you warn Misha the American had a gun?"

"I didn't know."

"You're talking shit."

"Why would I hurt Misha? He promised me money."

"Because the American promised you more."

"No, I—"

Her voice faltered. The little man had raised the skewer over his head. "I'm getting tired of you," he said. "No more lies."

"I'm telling the truth."

He drove the sharp end of the skewer down into Anna's meaty thigh. Metal struck bone; the skewer bent. When he let go, it quivered like an arrow in her throbbing muscle. Blood blossomed on the white slacks, and she bellowed like a woman in childbirth. No space was sufficient to contain so much agony. It filled the rectory from its foundations to its rafters and echoed out into the courtyard.

The man grabbed another of the skewers that the porkpie had eaten clean. "This is nothing," he said. "This is the start." He flexed the skewer, then waved it in her eyes like a magician flashing a wand. "Where's the American?"

"For Christ's sake," Father Josef implored her, "tell him what he wants."

"I've told everything." She shook her head from side to side. "The last time I saw him, the American was in the tomb, covered with blood."

"He's not there now, you lying cunt."

"I don't think she knows anything," the priest said.

He flailed at Father Josef. "No wonder Tomas got sick of you. You're a dumb bitch—so dumb you think you're smart."

"Did Tomas send you after me?" she sobbed. "He's out to punish me because I left him."

She couldn't find a safe place to fix her eyes. Avoiding the skewer that vibrated in her thigh, she focused on the one he waved in her face and tried not to flinch, not to betray the terror that shut down every corner of her brain except the small sliver that believed she had a chance. She blanked out everything but the money. As long as she kept that, she could endure anything.

The two porkpies recrossed the courtyard carrying the empty money belt. Anna was relieved that they hadn't bothered with the box of tampons. Even as the little man twisted the belt around her neck, she didn't think he would choke her to death, not as long as he didn't know where the money was.

On the toupee's orders, they ripped off her bodysuit and bra. Her breasts drooped, the long nipples aimed down at the dreadful thing quivering in her leg.

"Please," the priest begged them. "Please, don't."

The little man gripped her plump arm almost tenderly. The next time she refused to tell him where Zack and the money were, he jabbed the skewer into her bicep in slow increments, like a doctor sinking a hypodermic into an hysterical patient. The point passed through the muscle, pinning her arm to her rib cage.

She screamed, "No, no."

But Father Josef shouted louder, "For the love of God, have mercy."

The toupee took a third skewer and scanned the remaining surfaces available to him, the curves and declivities of brown flesh. Nudging Anna's right breast, he exposed a half-moon of pale skin under it.

"Save yourself a lot of trouble and tell me where you hid the money."

She gazed at the painting of St. Agatha on the wall behind him and prayed for strength. "The American's pockets and his belt were empty."

"But you kept the belt for a souvenir?" He pricked her nipple. Blood beaded it.

"I kept it because . . . because . . ." Her kohl-rimmed eyes skittered left, right, up, down, anywhere to escape his pitiless gaze. "I just kept it."

He shoved the metal shaft up into the soft, pale half-moon. Its tip reappeared out the top of her breast and stopped just beneath her chin. Though

Father Josef bleated and moaned, Anna didn't make a sound. Her screaming was all in her eyes, in her sinews and the twitching tendons of her neck. As she shook, sweat sprayed from her kinked hair, and two men had to steady the chair to prevent it from tumbling over.

"What a stupid whore! Don't you care about the priest? You say he knows nothing. Are you so selfish you'd let him die?"

He snapped his fingers, and one of the porkpies slapped a skewer into his palm. He pressed the end of it to the priest's right ear. Father Josef's face went ash grey. His trembling lips made it appear that he was counting to himself. But Anna realized that he was praying. Transfixed by her bare bleeding torso pierced in three places, maybe he viewed her as a martyr like St. Sebastian who understood suffering, yet was powerless to end it.

The little man pushed the skewer into Father Josef's right ear until its tip jutted out of his left ear. All sound in the rectory ceased.

He concentrated his goggle-eyed gaze on Anna. He leaned close to her, so close she could see the intricate netting of his toupee and smell on his breath the cumin that she had seasoned the *shashlik* with. "Last chance," he said. "Tell me where the money is. Simple as that. The money or your life. You choose."

She looked down at her body. The priest had convinced her that it was the temple of the Holy Ghost. It didn't belong to her. It belonged to God. As for the money, she wouldn't give it up even though it didn't belong to her, either. She knew now that the little man had never intended to let her live no matter what she did. Anna glanced at the painting of St. Agatha presenting her amputated breasts to the angel and imagined herself about to fly away.

He laid the skewer against her left eyelid, repeating, "The money or your life." Then he inclined an ear as if to listen to her confession.

When he heard her whisper the Ave Maria, he accepted that as an answer, and her life ended in an instant of piercing light.

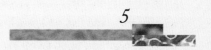

5

*Z*ack dreamed he was dead, then woke up disappointed that he wasn't. Befuddled by pain and pain killers, he feared he was back in Vietnam, dying in a field hospital from a shot that tunneled into his head and out his mouth. It felt like he had no face, just a suppurating sore where it should have been. He had seen soldiers like that, infantrymen with every last human feature erased. Now he believed he was one of them.

Fragments of awareness fell on him with the mercilessness of blows. He remembered Misha banging him with brass knuckles and screaming questions. Now in his head-spinning nausea Zack submitted himself to a similar inquisition. Had things happened to him because of who he was? Or was he who he was because of all that had happened?

As if in answer, a chimera reared up in front of his unreliable eyes. Zack had the sense that he was seeing himself from a double perspective—simultaneously at an enormous distance and very near.

Then the chimera changed shapes and became part of Zack. As he recognized the kid leaning into his harness, sustained at a precarious angle by the leash, he knew his own kind. They both did. He spoke to the boy. Or believed he had. He listened to him and thought he understood. He slipped under the buzzing surface of the here and now into a silent no-world, then revived again to find the kid still watching him. Convinced that he wasn't so much convalescing as coalescing, Zack felt that he had plunged from a great height and gone to pieces. Now he was being fitted back together in the boy's almond-shaped eyes.

As the circumference of his consciousness expanded, he followed Kathryn's movements around the kitchen. She wore a baggy XL tee shirt—her notion of a nightgown—and had on lipstick as red as paprika. It stung his eyes, the lipstick, yet he couldn't stop staring at her mouth, searching for the tiny indentation on her upper lip that let him know when she was close enough to kiss.

She hovered over the table and regarded him as if she had something troubling to confide. She asked how he felt and was satisfied by the few words he said. That he was capable of speech at all appeared to delight her, and she spoke to him as she did to the boy, with precise inflections, as though teaching Zack to talk.

She tilted a cup to his cracked lips and coaxed him to swallow some pills. The water was like fire on his chipped teeth, the pills like chunks of coal in his throat. She fixed soup and urged him to suck it through a straw. Then she mashed meat and vegetables into gruel and spoon-fed him. When she asked what he remembered, he considered claiming that he suffered from amnesia. But that was no way to protect her or the kid. Somebody might be after him. Misha wasn't smart enough to operate alone. Once his friends discovered that he was dead, they'd search for his killer.

He recounted events in a sequence dictated less by chronology than a determination to tell Kathryn the truth without scaring her too much. But with each installment of the story, narrated during scattered periods of lucidity, he noticed the whirlpool of panic in her eyes. What frightened her most, it seemed, wasn't that somebody might barge into the house gunning for him. It was what he had done to Misha and was ready to do again if he had to.

Once he regained a bit of strength, she helped him off the table and into the bedroom. As calmly as he could, he mentioned that it might be best if she gave him back his pistol. She brought it cupped in her hands, like a fragile object, and he stowed it under his pillow.

"I'll sleep in the living room," she said.

"The safety's on. It's not going to go off."

"You won't get any rest with me around."

When she leaned down to kiss his cheek, he said, "Don't."

Kathryn pulled back, puzzled, hurt.

"It's like broken glass," he said of his battered face.

"Will you be okay?"

"Sure. I'll look like hell for a few weeks. Then I'll just look ridiculous, which isn't unusual for me."

Left alone, Zack felt like Typhoid Mary, someone who spread disease willy-nilly wherever he went. The look Kathryn gave him—as if he, not the wild child, were an uncaged animal—cut deep. Nursing his anger, he aimed it at Anna, eager to hunt her down. It was bad enough that he hadn't found Fletcher or any credible evidence whether he was alive or dead, nothing that would save Adrienne from grieving for a husband who didn't deserve her to start with. But he'd be damned if he'd go home without his money.

On Eddie's advice, he had brought along fifty thousand bucks. "You're going to the land of *baksheesh*," Eddie said. "They don't take American Express. You'll need cash to fly Paul and this kid to the States." Now, unless Zack got those dollars back, none of them would be flying anywhere.

*I*n the bedroom he missed having the boy nearby. He would have asked Kathryn to lead him in on the leash and tie him to the bed post, but he didn't care to acknowledge to her or himself the full depth of his affinity for the kid.

Zack responded to his otherness, the coiled self-containment that implied he was asking a question and, at the same time, offering an answer, a way out.

He also missed alcohol, and this he did ask Kathryn to bring him. But she contended that it was common knowledge that patients with head injuries couldn't drink, especially when they were on antibiotics. Dr. Medvedev confirmed this on his next visit. Yet he didn't deny himself vodka and a cigarette as he checked Zack's temperature and vital signs and rambled on and on, revealing himself to be another displaced person, in some ways more marginal than the boy. Zack didn't need to know Russian to understand the old man. He could read his baffled, bloodshot eyes. Often when Kathryn translated, she told him what he had already inferred.

That he was in the care of a vet, and an unrepentant communist at that, struck Zack as comic and perfectly in keeping with the strange arc of his career. If he lived long enough, he joked with Kathryn, he'd probably wind up with a Viet Cong proctologist. But the immediate question in his mind was how far they could trust the cantankerous Dr. Medvedev. Did he have a car? Would he help them get to the capital? Did he have any idea of Anna's whereabouts?

Zack broached this obliquely. He didn't want to alarm the doctor any more than he did Kathryn. But as he discovered, even direct questions didn't prevent Dr. Medvedev from spinning off on a tangent.

"How is it conceivable," the old man railed one night, "that the Russians got suckered into Grozny? How did the inventors of urban warfare, the heirs to Stalingrad's street fighters, let a gang of Chechan criminals trap them in alleys and burn them alive in their tanks?"

In reply, Zack observed that he would have a hard time paying his bill unless he caught up with Anna. Had anyone seen her? Did Dr. Medvedev have a source inside the hotel?

The vet dismissed the subject of payment, relaying through Kathryn another in his catalogue of aphorisms. " 'Money makes slaves as whips make dogs.' I do this for solidarity." He raised his vodka tumbler and drank a toast. "You and I, my friend, are a lot alike."

Though this hit him as one of the saddest things he had ever been accused of, Zack didn't argue. He accepted that he was in the same fix as every lost soul and true believer in town.

*A*fter Dr. Medvedev left, Kathryn loitered in the bedroom, performing an absentminded pirouette. To all appearances searching for something that she had misplaced, she looked everywhere except at Zack. In the past, he had imagined he could read her moods in the minute shadings of her blue irises which radiated fire or ice. Now she was somebody he didn't know.

As though she had at last found the thing she was looking for, she tore a page out of a newspaper and blew her nose on it.

"Jesus, what are you doing? Quit that before someone throws a net over you."

"It's softer than the toilet paper," she said.

"Ever consider Kleenex?"

"I can't afford it."

"Poor waif." He held out his arms to her, but Kathryn kept her distance.

"Can we talk?" she asked.

"We're talking."

"I mean seriously. If you hadn't gotten hurt, I like to believe I would have been honest with you by now. But . . ." Her eyes resumed their hectic search for the thing, the thought, the good intention she had misplaced. ". . . but I wrote the letter."

He didn't need to ask which letter.

"I never expected you or anybody from Fletcher's family to get involved," she said. "It was such a low-ball offer, the trade for the boy, once we were in the States and people saw the situation, I hoped they'd agree I did the right thing flying him out of here."

She paused. "I wish you'd say something."

"It doesn't matter."

"It matters to me."

"I mean it's all right. It doesn't matter that you wrote the letter."

"But if I had told you before, none of this would have happened."

"Misha did it, not you."

"But if—"

"If ifs and buts were candy and nuts," he trailed off.

"We'd all have a happy Christmas," she finished for him. "Will you ever forgive me?"

"I already have."

This wasn't false bravado. At the moment, the ransom letter really didn't matter. Though Kathryn had lied to him, Zack conceded that he had done worse. He had lied to himself when he told Adrienne, then later when he gave Kathryn to understand that he had what it took to save them all. Now they would need more than money—it would require an implausible run of good luck—to get them out alive.

She laid her head on the pillow beside Zack's and let herself sink into his eyes. She surrendered to sadness and shame, then to the security of his arms. The impulse to comfort her moved Zack more than desire, and although he recognized that this was a paltry way to express what he felt, he couldn't, at the moment, imagine anything except kissing her. In spite of the electric shock to his face, he was anxious to inject everything into a single kiss—pity, absolution, apology, imperfect comprehension.

But it didn't stop at that. Their bodies fell into a familiar groove, their caresses the well-worn course. He would have pulled away were he not worried about hurting Kathryn; he might have begged off were he not afraid of humiliating himself. He had done this too many times before. Zack felt that, far from alone, the two of them were smothered by people, dead and alive, all piled together like cordwood. It was cruel to drag anybody else into that crowd. Still, he held her close, stricken with a sense that he was lying to her and himself again. He wasn't the man she thought he was or that he yearned to be.

Afterward, Kathryn urged him to lean his head on her breast, and Zack lay there listening to the beat of her heart, feeling the pulse of his bruised face against her fragrant skin. He didn't sleep. He was on guard as the room passed from black to grey to mother of pearl to gold in an alchemical process that transmuted base metals to precious ones.

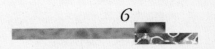

6

In the morning, Zack managed to shuffle out of bed and into the bathroom on his own. It felt good to be back on his feet—until he caught sight of himself in the mirror. His face resembled a Halloween pumpkin, with jagged hand-cut holes for a mouth, nose and eyes. Where Misha seized him by the shirt collar, he had what appeared to be rope burns around his neck, as if he had been cut down from the gallows. With time, the swelling and discoloration would fade, and after a dentist filed his splintered teeth and fitted them with caps, he might look almost human. But nothing short of plastic surgery would restore the pulverized occipital bones to their original shape.

As he studied his reflection, puzzling over mysteries of perspective and identity, his instinct was to reach out and rearrange his scrambled features in the glass. Instead, he gripped the sink. Sick to his stomach—angry to the point of illness—he regretted that he had been so quick to go for a kill shot with Misha. He should have made the son of a bitch suffer. If he found Anna and she didn't fork over his money, he wouldn't make the same mistake with her.

Suddenly there was thunder in his head. Someone pounded at the cottage door. Zack rushed to the bedroom, woke Kathryn and pulled the .38 from under his pillow.

"Don't open it," he whispered. "Just ask who it is."

She did as he said, and the two of them heard Dr. Medvedev hollering.

"Somebody murdered Anna and the priest," she translated.

Zack stepped into his blue jeans. Kathryn had washed them and they were stiff and discolored with starch. Shoving the pistol under his waistband, he let in Dr. Medvedev.

"The bastards killed them in cold blood," the old man said. "They tortured and killed them like beasts."

"Where?" Zack asked.

"The Catholic church," Kathryn told him.

He found his shoes and forced them onto his feet without socks. Blood had dried and cracked the leather.

"Where are you going?" she asked.

"To get my money."

"You're in no condition." Kathryn and the doctor were speaking in loud overlap. Maybe she was translating. Maybe not. Zack paid them no mind. She held his hand. "Please, don't."

"Without the money, we don't stand a chance of getting to the States."

"Then we'll stay."

"No. The guys that killed Anna and Father Josef, they'll come after me next. They may kill you and the kid. I've gotta go."

"At least wait until—"

"There's no time."

*T*he blinding spaciousness of the street, the sunstruck expanse of it teeming with traffic and pedestrians, yawed in front of Zack. Every step sent a stab of pain from his heels to head. He half feared that pieces of his face were flaking off. In agony anyway, he figured he might as well run. But he hadn't counted on the airborne dust and insects that slammed into him like dumdum bullets. He slowed to a walk, blinking tears from his eyes.

At the church, a gawking crowd gathered around the windows of the former gym. They couldn't make out anything inside. Father Josef had pasted up colored cellophane to create the impression of stained glass. Progressing in pinball fashion, Zack bumped through the mob. People started to push him back, but after one glance at his face they gave ground, as though the mauled bruises and cuts were a badge of authority. Even the cop at the front entrance let him pass.

Uniformed men, officers by the fastidious look of them, prowled the sanctuary, searching for evidence. A clutch of Father Josef's parishioners, shaking with age and sadness, knelt at the altar, praying the rosary. In the rectory, Tomas and the Mullah screamed at each other between two corpses tied to chairs while a man in a white gown—a medic? a coroner? a cleric?—set about the grisly task of extracting the skewers. It shouldn't have been much more difficult than pulling a fork out of meat, but the man drew the metal rod from Father Josef's ear with the delicacy of Dr. Medvedev teasing a guinea worm from a patient.

Anna was a wax effigy, a life-size voodoo doll perforated by pins that had cast a fatal spell. Her head slumped forward; her jaw hung slightly aslant so that her chin was poised at the tip of the skewer that jutted from her breast. Zack's empty money belt was buckled around her neck, and her shoulder blades flared out like clipped angel wings.

He told himself he had seen worse, a lot worse, and wasn't going to lose it now. Plenty of times in Vietnam he had smelled this sweet fleshy odor, an intimate scent like a woman bleeding after childbirth. He had never tossed his cookies then. He wasn't about to do it here. Still, a suspicion that the murderous rancor of his revenge fantasies had somehow resulted in this carnage appalled him. Regardless of what Anna had done, he wouldn't have wished this on her. As for the priest, he hadn't deserved to die at all.

Tomas and the Mullah appealed to Zack as if to a neutral arbiter, stopped speaking Russian and started in with English. Absorbed in their argument, they didn't mention the nightmare of his face.

"I warned you." The Mullah's shouting rattled the paintings of St. Agatha and St. Stephen. "Well, oh well have you deserved this doom. Too well have you deserved it."

"Show some respect for the dead," Tomas pleaded.

"What respect is due a priest who lives with a whore?"

"She wasn't living with Father Josef. She was hiding here."

"Hiding from what? You cannot hide from Allah. His angels are recording your intrigues."

The hotel manager glanced forlornly at Zack. Tucked under his arm was a cardboard box labeled tampons in four languages and three different scripts. "What God deserving of the name would do such a thing?"

"Do not blame Allah," the Mullah said. "This is the work of Satan, of the *djinn* that the American woman keeps in her house. Look and your eyes will tell all there is to know. These are signs for righteous men to read."

Zack dragged Tomas out to the courtyard, away from the Mullah. Cradling the tampon box, the hotel manager started crying.

"Stop this bullshit. I know you were in on it with Misha and Anna. I want my money back."

"I haven't seen either of them in weeks."

"You damn well knew what they were up to."

"Not until afterward. Misha's friends, they threatened me and told me to find Anna. But they found her first. You see what they did. Next they'll kill you. Then they'll kill me."

"No, I'll kill you. I'll kill you right now unless I get my money. Who was looking for Anna?"

"Four men. Three big ones and a little guy with glasses and a wig." Tomas kept on blubbering. "Either Anna didn't have the money. Or she gave it to them and they killed her anyway. There wasn't anything here except her personal belongings."

"Open the box."

He lifted the lid on the closely packed cardboard tubes. In no position to sneer at someone else's irrational choices, Zack didn't ask why Tomas would cling to two dozen tampons as keepsakes. If it was hard for him to watch Anna deliquescing into candle wax, he imagined it was horrible for Tomas.

"That's my belt around her throat," he said. "The money has to be somewhere." He dashed a hand at what felt like sweat trickling down his forehead. A cut had burst its stitches and oozed blood. Dizzy and weak, he realized he was going about this all wrong, but couldn't think of a better way.

"You're hurt," Tomas said. "You need medical attention. Go to Dr. Medvedev."

"I'm not going anywhere without my money."

"Forget that. Save your life. Go to the capital."

"How the hell do I get there without a car? How do I pay a driver with no money?"

"I don't know what to tell you. I'm in trouble too."

"Then leave town and take us with you in the Toyota."

"Us?"

"Kathryn and the kid."

"Don't tell me she's convinced you he's a wolf child."

"All I'm convinced is . . ." He snatched Tomas by the shirt . . . "you'd better take us. We'll meet you at the hotel."

"No, it's not safe. They're watching me. We'll figure out a place and time to leave. But first I have things to do."

"Look, don't fuck with me. Because if you're fucking with me . . ." He groped for words, for an ultimatum. In the end he gave up and jammed the gun barrel into Tomas's face. ". . . I'll shoot you right here. I'm not waiting for you to turn us over to Misha's pals."

Tears splashed off the chiseled planes of Tomas's cheeks. "Is this what I get for agreeing to help? I knew you had to be at Kathryn's or Dr. Medvedev's. Where else could you hide? But I didn't tell anybody."

"Lucky you didn't. I'm not Fletcher. I'm not from some cow college stamping out drugs for Uncle Sam. What I did to Misha, I'm happy to do to you." He couldn't quit threatening to shoot his way out of a corner that he feared he was backing himself into every time he opened his mouth.

"I'll drive you," Tomas promised. "But not today. I have to bury Anna and Father Josef. Then we need to make sure the road's safe."

Zack wanted to lie down and let the bell and clapper in his brain quit clanging. "We'll be at Kathryn's," he said.

Back in the rectory the bodies had been bagged and carted off, and the Mullah was haranguing the congregation. Curious passersby and throngs of his faithful had crowded in among the Catholic parishioners, and they responded to his raving in chorus. His complexion looked gangrenous in the garish light of the cellophane-covered windows, his snarled beard was a nest of snakes. When he spotted Zack and Tomas, he switched to English, shouting, "You cannot escape. Wherever you run we will catch you. If you rise, we will pull you down by your feet. If you dig underground, we will pull you up by the hair of your head."

Zack wanted to shut him up. But Tomas shepherded him down the center aisle and out of the church.

"You can trust me," Tomas swore. Then he walked off with the box of tampons under his arm.


*T*he trek to Kathryn's cottage felt like a mountain climb. The air was thin, his heartbeat and breathing were labored. The streets, frenetic an hour ago, were empty. Even the patches of shade usually busy with sidewalk vendors were deserted. From an overhead electrical wire a dead pigeon, little more than a fan of dirty feathers, dangled in the wind. It made Zack dizzy to watch it. It made him dizzier to worry whether he had played things right with Tomas.

But then nothing looked quite right to him at the moment. Kathryn's door was shut tight, yet seemed slightly out of true. Zack drew back and glanced at it again. There was the mark of a boot heel next to the doorknob. He heard voices—not Kathryn's, not Dr. Medvedev's.

His first reflex was to reach for the door. But he stopped himself and became aware of his brain racing, then idling, then racing again, as it did when he was drunk. Only in the idling spells was he capable of clear thought.

He circled around the cottage to the courtyard gate. There was a lock on it the size of a man's fist, with a keyhole large enough to accommodate a fingertip. He debated climbing the wall, but broken glass spiked the top of it, and if he got past that, the drop on the other side would knock him out. When he recalled in his haze that he had the gate key, it took some time to calm his hands and untumble the lock.

Crablike, he scuttled across the courtyard, convinced that the trip-hammer of his heart must be audible to anybody inside the cottage. At the open kitchen window, he paused. A man was speaking Russian. The boy's nails scrabbled at the floor. Zack peered over the low window ledge.

Stripped to the waist, Kathryn was tied to a chair, her arms bound behind her back. He was near enough to make out the freckles on her shoulders and the pink floret embroidered between the cups of her brassiere. Two men in leather coats and porkpie hats were trying to control the boy without being bitten. A third man clenched Kathryn by the hair. The fourth, a little fellow in tinted glasses, asked a question, and when he didn't care for the answer, he cracked her in the mouth with the purse swinging from his wrist. It was no powder puff, that purse. It split her lip. Blood sprayed her bra with a dozen new florets.

Zack braced the gun butt on the windowsill. He couldn't remember how many rounds he had left. The numbers seemed all wrong. The number of men, of bullets, of seconds he deliberated, of yards to the target—they were all out of kilter. At this range, there was every chance he'd kill Kathryn or the kid with a ricochet. And if the men rushed him, he was lost. The lightest tap on the head would lay him out. He aimed at the little guy. He couldn't afford to miss. He wasn't certain he could afford to fire. He wondered whether there was a way to do this without shooting.

The man asked Kathryn another question. He didn't like this answer either and smacked her a second time. Having seen Anna and the priest, Zack wouldn't wait and watch her be brutalized. In the next calm interval, he squeezed the trigger. The little guy's tinted glasses and toupee flew off. The fake hair hit the wall and stuck. The spectacles bounced off the cork board of family photos.

When he shot the porkpie holding Kathryn, the other two men were paralyzed by the noise and by the sight of Zack, a man with a sore for a face, clambering through the window, drawing down on them. Kathryn screamed. Maybe she thought she had been hit. There was blood, like a shawl, around her shoulders.

The bald guy rolled to a sitting position, his scalp as slick as a cue ball except for a red gouge where the shot had grazed him. He clawed at the zipper of the purse. Zack didn't wait to see what was inside it. He fired again and blew the man's brain onto the icebox door. Now he had nothing in the chambers.

Kathryn's screaming stopped in a dying strangle. She stared at Zack, struggling for air. The two men stared, too, their broad, braised Mongolian features unreadable, their eyes fathomless. They couldn't guess whether they were about to be shot point blank or ripped limb from limb by the naked creature that morphed from a kid into a shrieking beast. The boy sprung upright, flailing his arms and kicking at them.

"Tell them to turn their pockets inside out," Zack told Kathryn.

She didn't speak, couldn't speak.

"Tell them to give me what's in their pockets, then get out of the house or I'll kill them."

Kathryn writhed in the chair, fighting to wrench free.

Zack shouted the Russian word for money. He wanted his dollars back. But they dropped local currency at his feet, coins so light they barely clinked on the floor. He gestured for them to empty their pockets. They each carried a knife and a few dollars, nothing more. He motioned with the empty gun for them to go. They didn't understand. Or chose not to. They might have been challenging him to kill them where they stood. He would have been glad to oblige.

"Help me," he pleaded with Kathryn. "Tell them to get out of here."

She mumbled something in Russian and the porkpie hats sidled from the kitchen, through the living room and broke for the street. Zack bolted the front door behind them.

Kathryn was wailing, "Why? Why?" She recoiled when Zack came near her. It would have been quicker to cut her loose from the chair, but he knew that a knife in his hands would make her frantic. Murmuring phrases that she depended on to gentle the boy, he untied the knots, whispering, "It's okay."

"Why? Why?" she went on wailing.

"We've gotta go before those guys come back."

"You shot them. You shot them both."

He opened the purse and showed her the tiny nickel-plated pistol. "He'd have killed us, just like he did Anna and Father Josef."

Kathryn went over to the boy while Zack patted down the corpses. The little man had a hundred dollars, the porkpie hat about thirty. But none of these bills was crisp and new like the ones from his money belt.

"Where's the doctor?" he asked Kathryn.

"He left when you did."

"We'll go to his place. We can't stay here."

He picked up the hand-loomed prayer rug that the kid slept on and shook it out. After all that she had witnessed, Kathryn didn't know what to expect next and watched him with uncomprehending eyes. The boy watched, too. For a second the three of them were motionless in the spreading pool of blood on the parquet. Then Zack flung the carpet like a net and rolled the boy up in it as tight as a sausage in its skin.

"You're hurting him," Kathryn hollered.

Zack jabbed at his face with his shirtsleeve. His stitches were still bleeding. "Unless you've got a better idea, I'll carry him there."

"Where?"

"Dr. Medvedev's. Tomas is going to drive us to the capital soon as the road's safe. Take what you need. We won't be coming back."

Kathryn had started to tremble; a rash of goose bumps ran down her arms. Zack handed her a shirt, then hugged her, as if what she needed in that stifling room was warmth.

"I know you're only doing this for me," she said.

"No, I've got some small interest in saving my own sorry ass."

"But I don't want to see anybody else die."

"That's why we're leaving."

*K*athryn packed the attaché case that her parents had given her as a going-away present before she departed for the Peace Corps. Along with ID papers, she saved her notebooks and grant proposals and all the correspondence pertaining to the boy. Though the .38 was no good to him unless he found more ammo, Zack stuck it under his belt and slipped the PSM into his pocket. He carried the boy, cocooned in the carpet, across his shoulders. Then they set out over the boulevards of the city, beneath the baffled eyes of heroically scaled statues, in a tableau too obscure in meaning for an observer to do more than marvel at their passing.

7

*A*t his compound, Dr. Medvedev stepped out of the garage and locked its metal door behind him. He didn't appear to be pleased to see them until he heard what had happened. When he learned that Zack shot two of the goons who murdered Anna and Father Josef, the old vet said, "Good." Kathryn told him the other two got away, and he said, "Bad. They deserve to be put down like mad dogs." He let them into his house. "I trust you weren't followed."

"No," Zack assured him. The truth was that in his exhaustion he hadn't noticed. He teetered under the boy's weight.

Padding shoeless through filthy, sparsely furnished rooms, Dr. Medvedev walked them out to the courtyard. His once-white shirt was wrinkled and scorched with iron marks. Combed straight back from his forehead, his yellow-white hair heightened the startled arc of his eyebrows, the predatory beak of his nose. He didn't bother wearing shoes to cross the courtyard. His socks were little more than threads, and no amount of manure could make them more malodorous. "It's better for you here," he said.

A menagerie of animals ambled around uncaged—chickens, pigs, rabbits, a baby camel, a cow with a withered udder, an Alsatian dog that dragged its hindquarters and a pair of peacocks that had lost their tail feathers, but still preened and strutted. It was impossible to tell which ones were being treated, which ones the vet kept as pets and which ones he was fattening for the dinner pot.

Zack lugged the carpet into a pen and unrolled it. The boy lay there dazed, blinking at the largest unbroken expanse of sky he had seen in months. He must have imagined he was free. Bolting upright, he darted for the fence, hit it at full stride, and finding easy hand and toe holds, climbed up the chicken wire. Zack caught him by the harness and hauled him down. As the two of them struggled, screeching animals scattered in all directions. They crept back only after Zack had tethered him to a stake.

The kid roached his spine and his eyes rolled in their sockets. Growling, he bared his teeth until Kathryn came over and calmed him. She stroked his hair, and he leaned against her legs. Then the crippled Alsatian paddled over next to them. The dog and the boy eyed one another, nostrils quivering, and squared off as if to fight. But after a final sniff, they stretched out side by side. The sight of them at peace seemed to settle the rest of the animals who resumed milling around the compound.

Dr. Medvedev showed Kathryn and Zack to a stable at the far corner of the courtyard. Then he said he had work to do and returned to the garage. As Zack spread the carpet over straw in a horse stall, he told Kathryn, "We're safer than in the house. Anybody looking for us has to get through that brood of chickens and pigs. They're better than a burglar alarm."

He didn't mention his fear that Tomas had dispatched the killers to Kathryn's cottage and would now send them to Dr. Medvedev's. Shucking the shells out of the PSM, he couldn't believe they'd stop a man. The cartridges were the size of air rifle pellets. He might as well carry a pea shooter. He reloaded it and slipped it into his pocket.

Kathryn sagged down onto the carpet with her legs tucked under her rump, as if to limit her contact with this place. Wooden as the figurehead on the prow of a ship, her face revealed little feeling, but her voice brimmed with it. "I'm going to pay you back."

He mistook this for a threat. After what he had done or failed to do, she intended to get even. But then she added, "Once I'm in the States and on my feet financially, I'll pay you back every penny you lost."

"Don't worry about it."

"I know I haven't been any help today. And I can't promise how I'll hold up from here on."

"You wouldn't be human if you weren't upset seeing two guys get shot."

"I don't blame any of this on you. I blame myself."

"Don't." He got her to lie down beside him on the carpet and lifted her head onto his chest so that she couldn't see his face and he couldn't see hers. "It's going to be okay. Tomas'll take us to the capital and I'll talk to a woman I know at the American Consulate."

"Maybe you should get word to her right away. Dr. Medvedev might have a cell phone."

"No, she warned me not to count on her sending the U.S. Cavalry to my rescue. She said I was on my own. But once we're there, I'm sure she'll help."

Far from sure of this, Zack could picture the pert Ms. Pearson turning up her powdered nose at his problems. If she discovered he had shot three people, she might turn up more than her nose. She might turn him over to the law. Another reason not to contact the Consulate until it would do them some good.

"Before you know it," he said, "you and the kid'll be in the States at— what'd you call it?—a language center or think tank."

"Where he'll become a lab rat. That's what you think."

"Not anymore. You've educated me. I found out firsthand how good you are at teaching people to talk."

As he attempted to convince Kathryn, and through her himself, that they would pull through, he sounded to his own ears part Pollyanna, part PR flak, like some Second Looie conducting an upbeat press conference the day after the Tet offensive. In combat, Zack's rule had always been to be careful, and when caution was futile, be courageous, and when courage was beside the point, be quiet. But he couldn't quit talking now, and neither could Kathryn.

"I hate what the boy's been through today," she said. "It'll set him back six months."

"Kids are tough."

"No, they're not."

"They can take a lot."

"No, they can't. After this, I'm afraid I won't be able to reach him."

Zack wondered whether she really meant that if he did any more killing, she feared she'd lose touch with him. Still, he couldn't swear not to. He couldn't promise anything at all. He simply whispered whatever he imagined might console her and make her feel less alone. But rocking her in his arms, he felt he had uncorked a bottle that had been shelved so long that sediment had piled up at the bottom and the wine had soured to vinegar. There was a bitter taste in his mouth that no amount of sweet talk could wash away.

His brain kept spitting out questions, among them the one Kathryn had wailed over and over: Why? Why did he bother going on? Was it hope? Or habit? Of course he wanted to save her and the kid, and he wanted to see his daughter again. But the boy wasn't the only one that had been set back by this day. Zack sensed himself regressing to that period after the Punch and Judy show in Geneva when a dark fog had overwhelmed him.

In this present fix, he had no doubt what going back to the States would bring. Assuming nothing worse went wrong and the three of them survived in one piece, Kathryn and the boy would disappear from his life. He couldn't see it any other way. Then he'd start the healing process, as the shrinks put it, which, in his case, would consist of refilling his prescription. Nothing else.

*T*hat night, Dr. Medvedev invited them to the house for *plov*. He served the meal of shredded meat, vegetables and rice from a communal bowl, and they ate it at a wooden table that had done duty as a workbench. The raw planks were runed over with cigarette burns, tea stains and pencil gouges. Though Zack couldn't chew the meat, he mashed up the vegetables and rice and washed them down them with apple juice.

It was harder to swallow the old vet's non-stop hectoring. Zack interrupted and asked Kathryn to ask him whether he had any .38 caliber bullets.

"No, just shotgun shells," she translated.

"He has a shotgun?"

"No, only shotgun shells," she told him.

"Why the shells and no gun?"

"He won't say. I asked if he has a cell phone. He doesn't."

"Jesus, just tell him I need some vodka."

This prompted another of the vet's proverbs. "No. The first glass and your legs fall off. The second and your head falls off. The third and the glass flies away like a bird."

Kathryn continued translating as Dr. Medvedev segued to the murders at the church, then to other atrocities. "You know what the mujahedin does to its enemies? It packs them in container trucks, drives them into the desert and leaves them to cook alive. That's what they'll do here when the fundamentalists take over. They'll stew us like plov unless the Russians restore order."

"That's not what the Russians did in the past," Kathryn protested.

"They committed dialectical errors," he agreed. "But in world historical terms those were minor. They deserve a second chance. How many chances has capitalism had? How many chances does the church get? Why is it only Communism that must lie down and die like a vampire with a stake through its heart?"

He prophesied the rebirth of fascism, the imposition of martial law and an uprising of the masses against repression. The prospect appeared to delight him. "The worse things get, the better they'll be."

Kathryn lapsed into silence, then into tears, and Zack uttered one of his few Russian words. "*Pazhalusta!* Please," he implored the old man to stop.

· · ·

*A*fter Kathryn and Zack left to sleep in the courtyard, Dr. Medvedev remained at the table, smoking and surveying the dirty dishes. He saw no reason to clean up the mess. Usually he drank in the evening, but he had to be clear-headed and steady-handed tonight. After a long day of work, he couldn't lose his wits now. There was a balance to be maintained and vodka could tip it to the wrong side.

He needed to remember and he needed to forget. In nations, as in people, it was unproductive to suppress all recollection of the past, but it was worse to reopen wounds too deeply. That risked infection, the loss of limbs and vital organs from the body politic. Between amnesty and amnesia, he believed in a third path—action. The one effective antidote to terrorism—indiscriminate, ideologically indefensible, ultimately self-defeating—was a calibrated response, a carefully planned campaign of counterterrorism. But the current context didn't allow for conventional methods. In military terms, the town scarcely existed anymore. There were no strategic spots worth seizing and few targets that had symbolic value. Still, there was one.

His dented Moskvich had traveled over 300,000 kilometers. All he asked was that it cover a few dozen city blocks tonight. On the back seat, two oil drums were nestled in cardboard boxes packed with nails and bolts. The drums contained ammonium nitrate, a basic component of fertilizer, a common commodity in this cotton-growing region. Dr. Medvedev had had no problem buying it. But black powder had been difficult to obtain. Determined not to deal with criminal elements that he reviled, he bartered for boxes of shotgun shells in the bazaar. Then he had spent tense hours tweezing them apart and tapping the explosive powder into canisters attached to the oil drums.

Though it had been decades since he constructed a bomb, he remembered enough about chemistry and physics to produce roughly what he wanted. And that was all he required—a rough approximation, an improvised formula and crude equation for a crude device.

Raising the garage door, he rolled the Moskvich onto the unlighted street. He didn't dare start it in an enclosed space and risk leveling the house, all its outbuildings, his animals, the two Americans and the defective boy. Having fouled up one blast in his life, he wouldn't let that happen again.

He switched the key in the ignition and the engine kicked over with a catarrhal fit of sputtering and spitting. To a patient who sounded that bad, Dr. Medvedev would have recommended lung X-rays and a long rest. Coasting past rows of dilapidated buildings that bore the blueprint of collapsed rooms on their freestanding walls, he encountered no soldiers, no roadblocks. Not that he had any intention of stopping. If that meant running them down, so much the worse, so much the better.

As he drove by the Christian cemetery, crosses and winged angels propped up a vast net of vines. They reminded him of camouflage cloths tented over artillery emplacements. Next to the river, whores tended their fires like mourners at funeral pyres along the Ganges. Beyond the bridge, Dr. Medvedev entered the park that surrounded the thousand-year-old mosque. Dark within and lit without by moon and stars, the façade had flattened to two-dimensionality. The filigree brick looked no thicker than a screen of palm fronds. Opposite it, around the former caretaker's quarters, music boomed from jeeps and vans and four-wheel vehicles.

He debated where to position the Moskvich—not as an ordnance officer would, but as a political strategist. If the blast destroyed the mosque, Moslem fundamentalists would revenge the sacrilege. If it damaged the cars and the caretaker's house, the mafia would retaliate. Either way, he counted on the Russians to return and take control.

Somebody shouted. One of the delinquents blinded by Dr. Medvedev's high beams hollered an obscenity and ordered the vet to dim his lights. Instead, Dr. Medvedev accelerated in that direction, picturing himself as a projectile, a torch, a fuse and blasting cap combined. He had considered triggering the bomb from a distance, but didn't trust himself not to make the same mistake. Striking a match, he was atomized in an instant, whirled off amid lethal fragments of shrapnel. Nails and bolts and blades of metal from the oil drums slashed through the park, shearing limbs and peeling bark from trees. Men in the doorway to the caretaker's quarters blew back into the building and smudged the far wall. The mosque's weftwork shattered into brick shards. Vehicles turned turtle and burst into flame. Gas tanks erupted. The music stopped and the moaning started. Figures fringed in fire crawled out of the ashes. Ululating and rolling in the dust, they beat their breasts like penitents, while the heavens rained dead embers, live sparks and cindered scraps of flesh down on them all.

8

*H*igh on the hotel roof, at a table under a striped umbrella, Tomas sipped a glass of sweet tea. Sunlight filtered through the umbrella, then through the glass and left a lemony shadow swirling with mica glints on the tabletop. Tomas stared alternately at the mica flecks and off at the woven tapestry of the city slowly unraveling. Dressed in summer-weight slacks and a polo shirt, he affected the demeanor of a man remote from the fray, a detached observer of events. A journalist, perhaps. A UN advisor or businessman stoically tarrying until he was evacuated by helicopter. An expert hired to file a report. The scalloped planes of his face, the false smile, his dead eyes disclosed nothing of what he had witnessed in the last few days or what he felt now.

After the car bomb leveled the mosque and killed dozens, the town's population had divided along deeply drawn battle lines. The shooting didn't figure to stop until the ammunition and the combatants were exhausted. Fundamentalists fired on Christians. Uzbeks and Tajiks fought skirmishes with Russians and Poles. Armenians defended themselves against Mongols. And everybody vented their hatred of the Chalas, a sub-sect of Jews who had opportunistically converted to Islam and were universally loathed. Soldiers attempted to subdue them, but were outgunned by warlords, ethnic clans and religious zealots.

From where Tomas sat, he saw the Mullah's apartment tower come under attack. Explosions reached him as claps no louder than books falling from a shelf in a carpeted library. He noticed the unmistakable parabolas of rocket-propelled grenades. Bursting from a trumpet of smoke, a flame spurted, and something like an ostrich egg arced lazily across the sky. On impact it hemor-rhaged a fiery orange yolk that runneled down the building's facade.

In every window there were muzzle flashes as the Mullah's defenders fired back. Down on the ground nobody was anxious to rush the issue. Rather than risk hand-to-hand combat, they were content to spend days at this distance, softening the opposition to bloody mush.

Tomas had a clearer view of the bombardment around the Grand Mosque. Calligraphy from its walls and dome riveleted away in elegant lines of *sul*, *neskhi* and *divani* script—a slithering alphabet river. Along with the disintegrat-ing architecture and vanishing Koranic verses, people were dying. He heard them scream. When the wind changed, he smelled corpses. Yet their suffering lacked for him the searing reality, the same deep loss, of Anna's death. She had, he decided, been the love of his life, and the current disaster touched him as no more than a continuation of the calamity she had set in motion by leaving him.

To his regret, he hadn't been able to give her a proper funeral, just a per-functory burial in the Christian cemetery along with Father Josef. Apart from the gravediggers, the handicapped flower seller and her palsied dog, nobody had been present except Tomas, and there were no prayers for the repose of the lost souls except those that he whispered.

Yet even then, in the throes of his fervent muttering, he had been aware of a large measure of relief and gratitude. By dying and leaving behind McClin-tock's money, Anna had restored his life. In his room each day he ran the bills through his fingers like rosary beads. Then he rerolled the forty-eight thou-sand dollars and stuffed them back into the tampon tubes.

Rich enough to buy his way out of the country and travel anyplace in the world, Tomas delayed his departure, weighing where to go—Prague or Rome? He longed for a countryside of modest dimensions and unmenacing views, relief from the annihilating sky and devouring sunsets here. He recalled evenings in Prague when swans glided off the river into the canal between Malastrana and Kampe Island, swimming among reeds that jutted out of the water like quivers of arrows.

But the image of arrows reminded him of Anna speared with shashlik skewers, and Tomas couldn't bear to think about that. He forced himself to picture that quirky bell tower in Prague that had a clock with Hebraic numerals and backward-moving hands. As they juddered from one digit to the next, they appeared to recapture lost time.

Zack and Kathryn had been waiting for days. Tomas knew this, and that they had to be at Dr. Medvedev's. But he couldn't make up his mind about a question every bit as vexing as the debate about his destination: Should he leave them or take them along? If McClintock found out that he had his money, Tomas was bound to lose it. Worse, McClintock was likely to kill him. And yet, as much as anything, it was all those dollars that inclined Tomas to abide by his promise. As long as he laid his life on the line to save theirs, he thought he was justified in stealing the money.

Postponing a decision, he peered beyond the town to the mountains. They looked close, though the distance was deceptive. Foothills broke the horizon thirty miles away. The highest snowcapped peaks were a hard day's drive in an off-track vehicle. His Land Cruiser could easily climb into alpine valleys lush with spring water, wildflowers and cedar forests, and for a second, he let himself flirt with the idea of fleeing in that direction. Once up there, however, what then? On the other side every road ran downhill to someplace dreadful.

His thoughts zigzagged back to Kathryn and Zack. It might be advantageous to have them along. At roadblocks they'd come in handy. If things fell apart, Tomas could always use the Americans as bargaining chips. Even the stupidest thugs would understand that it was smarter to hold foreign hostages and send him ahead with the ransom demands.

A deafening blast shook the roof terrace under his feet. An RPG had hit the hotel, and splashed a drop of tea on his tan pants. Stepping out from under the umbrella, Tomas started for the staircase, intent on maintaining the vital illusion that he was in control and capable of rational planning. But then a second explosion toppled the table, and he dashed downstairs.

The halls were hazed over with dust. Bits of plaster and debris blew in through broken windows. The door to a room on the fifth floor had been ripped off its hinges. He glanced through it and a hole in the outer wall at a flock of pigeons beating their wings as if fanning smoke into flames.

Tomas collected the suitcase he had packed days ago and a vinyl shoulder bag that contained the tampons in their original box. In a city bristling with weapons, he may have been the only person who had never owned a gun. But he wasn't unarmed. Misha had left behind a couple of grenades. Tomas shoved one in each of his pants pockets. He liked the feeling of ballast they gave him as he hurried down the hall.

The doors to the elevator yawned wide. He knew better than to chance it and get stuck between floors. He took the stairs, pausing at each landing to press a hand to the door before opening it. He had been in burning buildings before and had seen flaming backdrafts get sucked up stairwells, incinerating bodies and spouting putrid ashes.

He shouted as he went along, warning everyone to get out. But people had fled at the first salvo. In the lobby, the abandoned bar, restaurant and front desk roiled in smoke. Splintered glass sparkled on the tile floor. As Tomas skated across it, he had the sensation of a novice skier hurtling downhill on a black diamond slope. He was an inch away from losing his equilibrium.

In the underground garage, he tossed his suitcase into the Toyota Land Cruiser and raised the reinforced door to the side street by remote control. He kept the vinyl bag on the front seat beside him and the grenades in his lap. At the crest of the ramp he glanced left and right. With a stricken plunge of his stomach, he realized he had made a mistake, maybe a fatal one. Gunmen patrolled the street. Boy soldiers, scarcely bigger than their weapons, amused themselves by firing off rounds at the pigeons flapping in and out of the hotel windows. Before Tomas had a chance to roll back into the garage, a kid drew a bead on him with an RPG. He felt very tired, but reacted as he had on the roof, as if it were crucial to remain calm and serve as the necessary witness of this scene.

And what he saw was the boy cant the RPG at an acute angle against his shoulder, tilting it much too far. The instant he pulled the trigger, the back-blast blew him away. His body sailed down the street like a rag doll shot from a rocket.

Ears ringing, Tomas accelerated over monumental boulevards that had been designed to showcase Communism as inevitable, invincible. Now the right-angled horror that Russia had imposed on the city was being revised by gangs who had different notions of urban planning. He passed a bakery that had been burgled. Men, women and children, all powdered ghostly white with flour, mis-took the Toyota for an army vehicle and surrounded it. Stuffing bread into their mouths, stuffing loaves into their pockets, they pounded the door panels and rocked the Land Cruiser on its chassis, straining to flip it over. Somebody with a crowbar bashed in the rear window. Tomas heaved one of the grenades. Shock waves slammed into the crowd, and he roared off to Dr. Medvedev's.

On the whitewashed wall of the compound, there was the blurred outline of a body in motion. This blood splatter was all that remained of a looter who had been hit by a recoilless rifle. Tomas beat his fist at the vet's door. He thumped it for a full minute before an eyehole slid back. Then Zack opened up.

"Where were you?" Tomas asked.

"Where the hell have you been?" Zack yanked him into the house. "Kathryn and the kid are half nuts." McClintock didn't look entirely sane himself. His cuts had become infected, and their lurid colors distorted his face into a Japanese lantern.

"Where's Dr. Medvedev?" Tomas asked.

"Beats the shit out of me. He drove off one night and never came back. All that noise, what's happening out there?"

"The fighting's getting worse. It's time to leave."

"We're ready. Lemme get Kathryn and the kid."

"The kid? No, that's crazy."

"If he doesn't go, we don't go."

"Suit yourself." Tomas turned for the door.

"And you don't go." Zack caught him by the shirt collar and crushed the tiny PSM against the side of his jaw.

"The drive's going to be hard enough without—"

"There isn't going to be a drive without the boy."

"You can't believe he's what Kathryn claims."

"Whatever he is, he's coming. You don't like it, you stay."

"Is this how you treat me when I help you?"

"Yeah, this is how I treat you. I keep a gun at your head."

McClintock marched him through the house out to where Kathryn was in a wire-fenced pen with the boy. Filthy and frazzled with static electricity, her reddish hair flared around her head. Spooked by gunshots outside the compound, the kid had dropped down on all fours and was trembling. Small arms fire sent the rest of the animals into a yipping frenzy. The crippled dog fumbled around, but couldn't run. The peacocks flapped about, but couldn't fly.

The sight of them all—beasts and humans both—had the urgent quality of a parable whose point eluded Tomas. Was it the myth of Noah and the Ark he remembered? The last living creatures on earth ready to set sail with no clue when, where or whether they would land on solid ground again?

"We can't leave without Dr. Medvedev," Kathryn said. "We owe him that much."

"He may have left on his own," Tomas suggested.

"He wouldn't do that. Not without telling us."

"He may be dead," Tomas said. "I almost got killed on the drive here."

"We don't have time," Zack said. "Get the prayer rug."

While she went to the stall, he gathered the leash and lashed it around the boy's ankles. Then when Kathryn returned, they rolled the boy up in the carpet like a papoose.

Tomas was beginning to grasp the full gravity of his mistake. The Americans were as clinically disturbed as the child. It was dangerous to travel anywhere with those two. But how could he ditch them now?

The animals stampeded them into the house, barking and howling, a phantasmagorical zoo in migration. McClintock wouldn't hear of leaving them behind. He insisted on setting the whole menagerie free. Otherwise, he said, they would starve to death.

While Zack helped the baby camel, the crippled dog and tail-less peacocks out into the maelstrom of the street, Tomas jogged to the Toyota, desperate to escape. But Kathryn and Zack caught up to him, she lugging a leather attaché case, he staggering with the boy across his shoulders. They arranged the rolled carpet on the floor in the rear. Kathryn stayed there with the boy, whispering idiocies to him. Zack sat up front, the tiny pistol in the palm of his hand.

Dense clouds of tear gas foamed along the boulevards and mingled with the darker smoke of burning tires that barricaded intersections. With his vision at ground level limited to less than a block, Tomas took his bearings from the Grand Mosque and the grainy scintillations given off by its gold-leaf dome. Crowds careened out of alleys on either side of him. Rocks clattered against the Land Cruiser. He heard the rapid stutter of automatic weapons. He couldn't tell whether snipers in the mob were firing at him or soldiers were shooting at rioters.

A woman in a *burqa* fluttered into his front bumper, seemingly as insubstantial as a butterfly. She hit with a solid wallop and bounced off, but Tomas didn't swerve or slow down. A clutch of school kids snaked into the street trailing a banner daubed with Cyrillic script. The streamer of cloth snagged on his radio antenna, and as it flattened across the windshield, Tomas drove blind, running over what may have been potholes or people. Then the banner slipped from the glass and swam away in the Toyota's turbulent wake.

At the far end of town, traffic converged at a checkpoint manned by helmeted and heavily armed soldiers. There wasn't an officer in sight. This was a random smash and grab by greedy low-level grunts. They rousted drivers out of their cars and pistol-whipped them until they paid up. Then depending on their whim, they waved them through or turned them back into the chaos of the city.

As they shook down the motorists, some of the soldiers fought to hold the mob at bay. Without bothering to aim, they squeezed off clips from AKMs, funneling their fire down narrow alleys. The crowd's natural instinct was to hug the walls. But shells and shell fragments skipped along the buildings, chewing up people who mistakenly believed themselves safe.

"Are you carrying a weapon?" Zack asked Tomas. "I can't hold off an army with this pop gun."

"One grenade."

"Gimme it. Stop and keep the motor running. Stay in the car. When I say go, go." He glanced at what Tomas had handed him. "This isn't a grenade. It's a flashbang, just a big fucking firecracker to scare people."

Soldiers rapped their gun barrels against the windows. When Zack didn't roll his down, one of them opened the door to drag him into the street. Zack fed him a mouthful of the PSM and was astounded by what the toy pistol did to the back of the man's head. Pulling the pin on the concussion grenade, he flung it at the other soldiers and barely had time to scream, "Go!" An earsplitting detonation cleared a path, and the Land Cruiser rumbled out into the countryside.

On a road that swerved through cotton fields, Tomas muscled the Toyota into four wheel drive, bucking up and down gullies, then onto a straightaway. A stone flew up and cracked the windshield, spreading a spiderweb in front of his eyes. Kathryn was crying, the kid whimpering, McClintock screaming. Still, Tomas didn't slow down until Zack rammed the PSM into his ribcage.

"You asshole. First you hand me a flashbang. Then you drive like a maniac. Are you trying to kill us?"

Tomas let up on the gas. "Quit yelling and take that gun off me." The equanimity of his voice surprised him. Dead calm though he sounded and stone-faced as he appeared, he was terrified. Minutes ago, he had made up his mind to do whatever the situation demanded, turn the two Americans over to the soldiers if that meant saving himself. Now with McClintock holding the only gun, he recognized that there was nothing to prevent them from dumping him and stealing the car.

As long as he had the money, he'd gladly get out and walk. Planting an elbow on the vinyl bag, he glanced at McClintock's butchered face. It made Tomas's eyes water. How could he let himself be bullied by somebody who held his head up only by sheer willpower? It shouldn't be beyond him, he thought, to outsmart a man in such sad shape.

He gazed at the fields where women in harlequin scarves and vermilion leggings were rooted like flashy scarecrows amid a miniature forest of cotton. The planted furrows resembled surgical incisions with thorny stitches down the center. Beyond the arable land, tin hovels huddled in the shade of birch trees. After that, the desert rippled with heat mirages.

In the other direction, grassy steppes stretched to the base of the mountain, and the snowcapped ranges that had seemed so inviting from the hotel rooftop disclosed their true starkness. Shark-toothed ridges of ice opened immense gullets to swallow anyone unwise enough to seek salvation there.

Checking the rearview mirror, he willed himself to find warmth and kindness in Kathryn's eyes. Her fair, freckled complexion appeared to have been scoured by steel wool; her hair streamed in the hot air that swirled through the busted rear window. Her concern for the boy, moronic as it was, indicated a tender nature, a nurturing heart that Tomas hoped he could exploit. If he spoke to her alone, he was sure he could connect with a responsive chord. But how could he separate her from McClintock?

As the sun sank, the windbreaks of trees went from copper green to milky blue. Then night closed over them, and Tomas punched on the low beams which wavered on the cratered road as tentatively as an insect's feelers. There were no cars, just trundling oxcarts. Any other time, grateful that there were no roadblocks, he would have counted off each mile, relieved as they sped toward the capital. But tonight he had no sense of approaching safety. He considered telling McClintock that he refused to go on. They could take the Toyota and he'd hike back to town. Quoting the Mullah, he would declare that a man should remain in the spot where Allah placed him. To do otherwise was to step outside of Allah's plan, and at the moment Tomas wished to be inside some plan, any plan, that let him keep the money and stay alive.

"What the hell are you doing?" McClintock shouted.

Lost in thought, Tomas looked up and saw too late that they were plowing at impossible speed toward the rear-end of an oxcart. On its flatbed, workmen were heaped up like burlap sacks. Tomas hit the horn and the brakes at the same time. Heads swiveled around; eyes glittered crazily. The Land Cruiser skidded to a halt without colliding with the oxcart. But then there was a flash of lightning, a loud clangor of metal, and an aftershock that swept him into darkness.

Tomas revived with what felt like the steering column impaled in his chest. The horn blared. Oxen bellowed. Reluctant to look down, he groped for the thing that had speared him. It was a wooden stake. Grabbing it in both hands, he pried it free, but still felt splinters in his rib cage. They stabbed him as he breathed, they crackled when he moved.

He observed through the oblong where the windshield had been a jumble of broken bodies swaddled in winding cloths. Catapulted off the oxcart in all directions, cadavers sprawled on the hood of the Land Cruiser. Others had flown far out into the cotton fields, where they lay like dead paratroopers in their chutes.

Astonishingly, the oxen stood yoked in the road, trailing a trace chain and singletree, chewing their cud, oblivious to everything, including their own gruesome wounds. Staves of wood twitched in their shoulders. Some, the size of lances, skewered their flanks so that they looked like carcasses freshly spitted and ready to be roasted.

He heard gunfire—far away at first, then gradually nearer. As he gaped through the glassless frame of the windshield, a sharp smell of gasoline fumes sifted through his fog. McClintock called his name, and it came to Tomas that he needed to get out of the car. This was his chance to escape.

Kicking open the door, he floundered out onto the road dragging the vinyl bag. He stumbled over bodies and body parts, bloody caftans and sandals. Zack called to him a second time, but Tomas didn't answer, just crashed on through the thorny cotton plants. Over his shoulder, he watched armed men with torches closing in on the wreck. They must have fired at the Land Cruiser—a mortar? a rocket?—and hit the cart by mistake. Now they were swooping down to pick over the corpses.

He skidded into an irrigation ditch, waded hip deep through a canal as thick and warm as soup, but couldn't crawl up the other side. The vinyl bag filled with water and weighed on him like an anchor. When he refused to let go, the dollars pulled him under, and the taste of salt and chemical fertilizer burned his nose and mouth. He would rather drown than release his grip on the money.

Then miraculously the bag lightened, became buoyant and seemed to float Tomas to the surface. An instant later, without realizing how he got there, he was beside the ditch, studying the horizon for firelight from some farmer's hut or the safety of trees. As he set off into the nothingness of night, swarms of stinging mosquitoes drove him out onto a salt pan that had hardened to a white crystalline crust. Luminous in the moonlight, the saltscape suggested snow, and he shivered and sweated and thought how curious it was that heat and cold were the same. When the crust broke under his feet, he fell through its surface as if through the top of an hourglass, tumbling into the timeless sands on the other side.

By dawn he wandered past stumps and sticks poking up through cracks in the baked earth. He staggered through a city reduced to dust by some disaster of weather or war, its knee-high walls the lone remnants of a forgotten mud metropolis. As sunlight cascaded over the eastern horizon, the desert seethed around him in crescendos of bronze dunes, volcanic slag and scorched magma, yellow undulant scum in irrigation canals and rank iridescent pools of oil seeping from underground deposits. As the heat increased at midday, it trapped him in a fluorescent tube ten miles long, and he walked hunched over through the glass holding his breath.

By afternoon, he glimpsed in the distance the glinting disk of the Aral Sea and raced toward its receding shores. Over a stone floor stenciled by blowing sand, he followed the bed of a river that once ran from the mountains to the sea. Now it had disappeared into the desert, and dead trees lined its desiccated banks. Peeled of bark and polished silver grey, they were wind-sculpted into human shapes and reposed there like giant arms and legs of beautifully grained marble.

By evening Tomas's shadow was as elongated as the primitive pictograph of a giraffe. Ambling over alluvial soil, he kicked up oyster shells, seaweed and kelp. The skeleton of an aquatic creature—a pike or sturgeon—curved out of the dirt like the stiletto teeth of a monster.

Just before dark, he spotted the first ship, a fishing vessel stranded on dry ground, and knew that he didn't have much farther to go. Marooned between him and the water was a ghost fleet of skiffs, rowboats, barges and freighters. Some still bore the hammer and sickle insignia on their bows and "CCCP" on their sterns. Nets swinging from davits trapped a putrefying reliquary of fish and of birds that had gotten snarled in the string as they feasted on the fish.

When he reached the shoreline, Tomas dropped face forward and lapped at the water as eagerly as an animal. It wasn't until he had gorged himself that he understood he was losing his grip on the vinyl bag. He made a futile stab, but the money floated beyond his fingertips. Then he remembered a fact he had forgotten—something everybody in the nation knew. The Aral Sea was dead, and so was he.

9

*B*elted into the back seat, Kathryn watched the oxcart fly to pieces and passengers pinwheel through the night. It looked as if somebody on the wagon
had set off a bomb. But in recent years she had heard enough incoming rounds
to recognize the sound of a Katyusha rocket. The blast demolished the cart,
and shot scraps of metal and wood through the Land Cruiser's windshield.
Fortunately Zack had fallen under the dashboard and missed the shrapnel.
Tomas caught the brunt of it, but tumbled out from behind the wheel and
staggered into the fields.

Kathryn smelled gasoline and was fumbling with the boy, still rolled tight
in the carpet, when Zack moved around to give her a hand. Men with torches
were loping down the road. She believed help was on the way. Zack thought
otherwise. "We gotta go. Quick, into the fields."

"Wait," she said. "What are you doing?"

"Finding out who they are before we say hello."

Hugging the carpet to his chest, he ran on ahead. She followed him, toting
the attaché case like a commuter sprinting to catch a train. Spiny, sprigged
plants raked at her legs. Cotton boles eddied like snow around her shoes.

Over her own hoarse breathing, she heard Zack fighting for air. Halfway down the first irrigation ditch he bent at the waist and dropped his burden onto the muddy embankment. As he stretched out beside the boy, squinting back at the wrecked Land Cruiser and oxcart, Kathryn slid in between them, the attaché case tucked under one arm, the kid under the other.

The boy's shaking set her trembling. She started to speak. Zack pressed a finger to his lips and pulled the PSM from his pocket. The men with torches fanned out through the fields. Capricious as fireflies, they flashed along the cotton rows, casting an orange glow and calling to one another. A single gunshot resounded, then died in the empty landscape. For miles around there was nothing for it to echo off. Kathryn felt the boy flinch. There was a second shot, then a third, and she guessed that they weren't putting people out of their misery. They were executing survivors.

One of the torches advanced in the direction of the irrigation ditch. Zack leaned his mouth to her ear. "Don't move. Keep him quiet."

He crawled up out of the ditch, over the tilled earth for ten yards, and flopped onto his back in the disjointed posture of the dead. The hand that concealed the pistol was clamped to his belly as if he had been gut shot. His mangled face and blood-streaked clothes made him such a convincing corpse, it caused a sick commotion in Kathryn's belly.

Preceded by a pool of torchlight, a pair of legs in camouflage pants approached the spot where she and the boy had molded themselves to the embankment. Zack coughed and groaned, and the legs veered toward him. Zack let him get close, so close that, from Kathryn's perspective, the man appeared to be straddling him, drawing down on his chest with a rifle. Zack fired straight up into the man's crotch, sprang to his knees and shot him again, this time behind the ear. None of the other men took any notice. They assumed it was one more execution.

A second later Zack was back in the ditch, carrying an AK-74, a new, smaller caliber version of a Kalashnikov. The boy had stopped shaking, but

Kathryn couldn't. As the torches withdrew to the road, Zack nuzzled his mouth to her ear again, like a lover murmuring endearments. "Let's go before they count off and find a man's missing."

"Go where?"

"Wherever. Just outta here."

"I can't do this."

"You have to. They'll hunt us down."

"Why?"

"They're looking for whoever was in the Land Cruiser. They know it wasn't those fellas in caftans. Somebody probably called ahead from the roadblock to have us stopped."

"What about Tomas?"

"He went the other way. He'll have to take care of himself."

Below the rim of the irrigation ditch, he hauled her to a standing position. When she tried to sit down, he held her up. "Look, you want to save the kid, don't you?"

She nodded that she did.

"Then do what I tell you." He gathered the rolled carpet in his arms. Though whippet-thin, the boy weighed eighty pounds, Kathryn knew.

"You can't carry him," she said.

"Yeah, I can. Just gimme a hand with this." He passed her the AK-74.

She slung it over her shoulder and picked up the attaché case. It was far too heavy. Popping open its clasps, she removed her passport and notebooks and tucked them under her belt as she had seen Zack do with the pistol. She dropped the leather case and the rest of its contents into the canal.


*O*n the road, the men milled around the wreck. A torch must have touched the leaking gas. A fireball limned the scene in orange, highlighting a frieze of stunned figures that faded to ink. Zack didn't bother to glance back. Fixing his course by the crenellated silhouette of the mountains, he shoved one foot in front of the other, setting a dogged pace. Soon Kathryn was winded and wheezing. Still, he didn't let her slow down.

Once they were beyond the cultivated fields, out on the steppes, walking became more difficult. Hidden gullies, boulders and anthills marred what appeared to be a smooth grassy plain. She thought it was time to stop, but Zack pushed on.

Slope-shouldered and swaybacked, he leaned into each stride the way a workhorse would, hauling his weight and the boy's and seemingly the weight of all that had gone wrong. The bandage on his head flapped loose from his shaved scalp, and blood purled down his neck. Through the furious static of her fear, she heard him counting to himself, mindlessly repeating numbers, cadenced mumble after mumble. She suspected that a final blow had scrambled his brain and he believed he was back in the Marines.

"Zack, Zack." She tugged at a belt loop on his jeans. "Let's stop."

"A little further."

"No." She tightened her grip on the belt loop and sank into the grass as if into eddying surf.

His momentum carried him another step or two. Then he said, "I'm coming." His voice sounded far, far away, and when he gazed down at her, his jack-o'-lantern face looked far off too.

"I need to rest," she said.

"Okay. A minute."

In excruciating stages, like an ungainly animal whose legs had to be folded in sections, Zack bent his knees, knelt, leaned forward, lowered the rolled carpet to the ground and yanked his arms out from under it. His joints popped. For an instant his upper body froze. Then feeling returned in a rush of pain that reduced him to moans.

"Lie down beside me," Kathryn said.

"No, I'm afraid I'll never get up."

The boy had wet himself and was fighting to kick off the carpet. Zack wouldn't let him. He did uncover his face, however, and the kid's deep-socketed eyes burned at the stars. As Zack stood up, his ankles and hips snapped like kindling. "Time to shove off."

"Why not stay here?" Kathryn asked.

"We have to find shelter before daybreak."

She looked back and could see neither the road nor any torches. "You really think they're following us?"

"It's not just them. In a couple of hours we'll need to get out of the sun."

He stooped to accept the kid around his neck in a fireman's carry. Reminded of the yoked oxen in the road, she watched him stolidly going through the motions and wondered whether it mattered. What was the point in pretending? The dimensionless steppes defeated all of Kathryn's efforts to envision a goal or purpose. Still, wielding the assault rifle as a crutch, she climbed to her feet. Then she marched into the shadows after him like one of the many soldiers he had led off to war.

Bugs dive-bombed her, insects so small she dredged them in as she panted for breath. She glued her eyes to the back of his head, on the gory bandage, the gaping wound. Zack began counting cadence again.

At dawn, an oyster-shell iridescence erupted from behind the mountains, and as the sun rose over the highest ridge, huge as a helium-filled balloon, Zack hurried as if hoping it would lift them out of this place, this predicament. But daylight found them in waist-deep weeds, with mice and lizards skittering in front of them. Everything out here was trivial, terror stricken, and Kathryn didn't exclude herself. Zack had been right about sheltering from the sun. Heat was only half of it. She couldn't bear what the indifferent light revealed of them.

They arrived at an unfinished irrigation project. The canal had filled in with sediment except for a trickle of murky water at its bottom. Beside it lay a single section of concrete pipe big enough to accommodate several crouching people.

"We won't find a better spot," Zack said.

She couldn't conceive they had walked all this way only to stop at what might have been a sewer. But she followed him, side-slipping down the embankment to the sluggish stream. There, in a series of awkward maneuvers, he shrugged the carpet from his shoulders. Plastered together by sweat and blood, he and the boy had become one, and Zack had to peel him off like a layer of flesh. Then he unrolled the carpet.

The boy smelled the water, shied away and sniffed it again before lowering his face and swigging. In between sips, he lifted his head and listened, like a deer at a pond. The sight of him lapping at his reflection, then warily regarding it, sent a pang through Kathryn. She hated to think that he was being reclaimed by his previous self.

She shut her eyes, and out of a clutch of wriggling thoughts, struggled to grasp a comforting one. But her brain kept unspooling catastrophic possibilities. It seemed to her that Zack was in shock, flashing back to an old battle, a different dizzying trauma. Much as it had distressed her to hear him counting cadence, when he began to babble the names of diseases, she almost panicked. Bilharzia. Schisto-something-or-other, he said. The water was foul, and full of bacteria.

Kathryn didn't care. She was so thirsty. Crouching on her hands and knees, she scraped the scum off the stream and sucked at what was underneath. Like the boy, she dipped her head up and down, gulping mouthfuls. When her face was in the water, she went blind and listened intently. When she swallowed and went deaf, she glanced around wildly. Lying on his belly beside her, Zack drank the water, too, and cursed himself after each swallow.

Then the three of them clambered hand over hand up the embankment and into the pipe. Zack knotted the boy's leash to his belt loop and slumped against the concrete. "'Nam," he mumbled, and again Kathryn didn't know what he meant. Not unless he was referring to those old photographs of Hanoi with families cowering in pipes during air raids.

With the morning light on his face, she got a full frightening look at Zack. Slamming into the dashboard had left him with a dimpled knot the size of a golf ball on his forehead. More of his stitches had burst, and new cuts had spines of glass embedded in them. They glinted like the steel splinters that pop out of a girder, the first danger signal of metal fatigue and the imminent un-making of a bridge. She was convinced that he had suffered a concussion. She worried about a skull fracture. When she tried to tweeze out the glass frag-ments, he shoved her hand aside.

Flies followed them up from the water and landed on his lips and eyelids. Zack didn't bother swatting them away. As Kathryn shooed them off him, he cringed. The slightest breeze was an abrasive to his skin. Drunk on blood, the flies buzzed back where they had been.

"We'll start after dark," he said.

"Start what? Start where?" She stared down the length of the pipe. It was like looking down a cannon barrel.

"We'll start after dark," he repeated, cut off from reality, it seemed to Kathryn, by an agony so profound that nothing, especially not her feeble ef-forts, could ease it.

The kid watched her watching Zack. As she rubbed the rough warmth of the boy's skin, his stringy muscles shuddered under her hand. He licked her fingers, and the sorrow that surged through her was so strong it stung her eyes. She glanced away toward the mountains. That end of the pipe captured an improbable alpine scene as if in an oval frame.

The force of this desolate moment threatened to undo her. She felt she couldn't fight it any longer. She gave herself over to the question: What are we waiting for? She phrased it in the plural, but knew that it came down to her. Zack wasn't going to recover in a day. Maybe never. They were all going to die unless she did something.

As Zack babbled in his sleep, his tongue was a dry leaf rasping his ruined teeth. Kathryn watched his heart beat, the pulse at his throat and temple. His eyelids, ribbed with red and blue spider veins, fluttered. He seemed to be hav-ing a bad dream, but there was no point in waking him to a reality that was worse. His nostrils bled, giving him a ghoulish moustache. It may have been the corrosively dry air. Or was it a hemorrhage? She didn't attempt to stop the bleeding, didn't dare touch him for fear of causing more pain.

Instead she removed the notebooks from under her belt. Perspiration had sealed the pages shut. As they dried, the wind riffled them in reverse order so that the words appeared to be unwritten, the summary of her months with the boy streaming away.

*T*hat afternoon Zack revived in a fit of gagging and vomiting. Rushing to the end of the pipe, he retched until he had nothing more in his stomach. Then he cleaned his mouth with a clump of grass and crawled back. "I'm not going to make it," he said.

"We don't have to leave tonight. By tomorrow morning—"

"I won't be any better."

"Yes, you will," she lied to him. "It's the ditch water that made you sick."

"No. It's worse than that."

He waited for her to say something. The boy seemed to wait too. Chin resting on his crossed wrists, he cut his eyes back and forth between them.

"I know it and you know it," Zack broke the silence. "You're going to have to go on without me. Maybe you could lead the kid on the leash?"

"No. He'd jerk me off my feet and get away. And where am I supposed to go anyhow?"

"Back to the road to bring help."

"I'll never find it."

"Sure you will. It's dead west of here, downhill all the way."

"What if nobody comes?"

"They'll come."

"What if it's the wrong person?"

"You'll have the gun."

"Oh Zack, don't you see, I can't force somebody to help me at gunpoint."

"The gun's just to keep anyone from messing with you. You'll get a lift, and once you're in the capital, go to the consulate and talk to Ms. Pearson. She'll know what to do."

"That'll take a long time."

"It's the only chance we have."

"You'll die." She suspected that he planned to shoot himself as soon as she left.

"We'll all die if you don't go."

"But what about the boy?"

He didn't answer, didn't need to. Kathryn knew. She should have known since Zack set the animals loose from Dr. Medvedev's compound. For a second she was tempted to accuse him of arranging things this way—leading them through the night to nowhere, counting on her to go back, knowing that she'd realize if he died with the boy tied to his belt, the kid was as good as dead too.

"You're saying I should set him free. You've said that from the start."

"I changed my mind there in the middle," Zack said. "I did everything I could to get you two to the States. But we're at the end now, and there's no point letting the boy cook in this pipe. If we wait much longer, he'll be too weak to make it to the mountains."

"He won't last up there."

"He did before. He will now—if he is what you claim. Don't you believe he's wild?"

To avoid the question and Zack's eyes, Kathryn turned west to where the cotton fields were invisible under a veil of haze. "Give me a minute to get myself together," she said at last.

"I can do it after you leave."

"No, I'm the one who took him in. I'm the one who'll let him go."

She skinned back her hair, twisting it into a knot at the nape of her neck. She shut the notebooks and tucked them under her belt. Their pressure was uncomfortable against her spine. She took them out and tossed them aside. She found nothing else to do, nothing to say.

Untying the leash from Zack, she led the boy to the end of the pipe. He didn't strain at the harness as she unbuckled it and didn't realize he was free once she removed it. The leather straps had left crisscross lines on his chest and back. He flexed his shoulders, unkinking them after months of captivity. Then he rubbed his face against her knee.

Still, he didn't leave. Kathryn had to push him out. He reacted like a pup or yearling reluctant to abandon the pack. She feared that she had ruined him for the wild, reduced him to defenselessness. But she gave him a last push, and he scrambled down the bank, crouched and drank his fill, then slipped into the water as if melting and crossed it, barely causing a ripple. After scampering up the far side, he cocked an ear, indexing wind-borne information, perhaps expecting Kathryn to call him back. When he finally took off, his limbs bunched and stretched and bunched again in a parable of pure running. It was impossible for her to believe that he had ever been housebound or broken. If anywhere, he belonged out here.

Long after he vanished into the mercury pool of a heat mirage, she couldn't quit looking after him. Before she gave up, she wanted to know that he was on his way. Too tired and despairing to hold much hope for herself, she longed to believe he would make it, bearing with him some deep-down recollection of having been cared for and loved.

*I*n the time that remained, Kathryn and Zack spoke like a heartsick couple at an airport plotting where and when they would meet next. She insisted that they discuss every contingency, except the matters that worried Zack most. He wanted to teach her how to fire the PSM. She didn't care about that. He pressed her to take his last dollars and made her repeat Ms. Pearson's name. When she broke down and begged to stay with him, he told her, "Go now and give us both a chance."

"I'll be back," she promised. She pocketed the pistol and her passport, but left the notebooks as a guarantee of her return. Selecting a spot on his cheek that wasn't infected or bleeding, she kissed him and started off, fearing that at any instant she would hear the AK-74 reverberate in the pipe. Anxious though she was to get out of earshot, she fought the urge to run back and remind him—remind herself—that she loved him no less than she did the boy and didn't want him to die feeling he had thrown away everything for her.

10

*I*lluminated by stars, the land appeared to slope at a gentle gradient toward the road. But it was steeper than it looked, and Kathryn's thighs ached and her knees buckled from the difficulty of plodding downhill. Insects rustled from under her feet, then settled a short distance ahead so that she had the impression that she was traveling in a capsule of silence preceded by a hissing drizzle.

Where the steppes ended and the arable land commenced, she slid on her rump down the bank of an irrigation ditch. She had splashed through the canal and up the other side before it dawned on her how thirsty she was. She doubled back and drank the chemical-tainted water. It was like licking the soapy residue from the bottom of a dishwasher. She set off again, sick to her stomach, belching greasy bubbles of bile.

In the cotton fields, walking was easier for awhile. The rows guided her toward the road, and whenever she strayed from the plowed furrow, she bumped into a spiny plant that nudged her back on track. But then in the hours before dawn, the stars dimmed and the darkness and her exhaustion deepened.

She tripped and fell, staggered to her feet and stumbled on with tufts of cotton carded in her hair.

The second time she fell, she stayed down and thought she would shut her eyes for an instant. She woke an hour later to a loud whirring sound and feared she had been overrun by bugs. The noise was her own ragged breathing.

As she made herself get up, she remembered the Russian proverb: "Life is not a stroll across an open field." No, it was more like this—a forced march through a terrain of distorted perceptions where moving forward or turning around each felt wrong.

By sunrise she was at the road and flopped beside it, uncertain whether to wait here or keep walking. Already heat radiated from the macadam; blisters of tar bubbled up between the cracks. Her tongue foul-tasting from the ditch water, she peered north along the line of the wavering pavement and spotted what seemed to be black scraps of asphalt that had been sucked up into the vortex of several distinct dust devils. Kathryn attempted to blink them away like eye floaters or some figment of the imagination. It took her a few seconds to recognize the birds of prey.

Pushing to her feet, she floundered toward them. Somehow the vultures reminded her of ashes swirling from the chimney flue of her grandparents' farm in Wisconsin. The memory—or was it just the sight of the swarming birds?—brought tears to her eyes. Then she got close enough to catch the smell and understood why she was crying.

Bodies that had been blown off the oxcart littered the harrowed land. Bloody caftans luffed in the wind marking each cadaver's location. What was left could barely be seen beneath the hunched shapes of birds. Shouldering and squawking and pecking at one another, they tore the last flesh from the bones.

In front of the shell of Tomas's Land Cruiser, the oxen had collapsed. Legs stiff with rigor mortis, bellies swollen with gas, they resembled cumbersome pieces of upholstered furniture that had been upended off their casters. Here, the vultures went about their business more cautiously, burying their beaks between the studs of wood that bristled in the animals.

A little farther along, a Lada sedan was parked in the middle of the road. As Kathryn neared it, she heard above the shriek of birds a human voice hollering. Out in the fields, a woman in a blue burqa was tugging at a man face down in an irrigation canal. She didn't notice Kathryn edging toward her. Tall and stout, she gripped both legs and hauled the body out of the water. Kathryn was about to rush over and help when she saw the dead man's beige pants.

The woman rolled him onto his back. Bloated, his face had lost its sculpted contours and was almost the same shade of blue as the *burqa*. He bled from a chest wound that spread a bib of red down the front of his polo shirt. In his weakened state, Tomas had fallen into the ditch and drowned, his head held underwater by the sodden weight of the shoulder bag.

The woman unzipped the bag, fished around in the soup of cardboard and glue, and plucked out a handful of tampons. The paper cylinders unraveled, revealing the dollars rolled inside them.

"That's not your money," Kathryn cried out in English.

The woman whirled around. Concealed behind a mesh screen, she resembled a beekeeper, invulnerable under a complicated bonnet.

"Put down the bag," Kathryn switched to Russian. Convinced the money was Zack's, she pulled the tiny gun from her pocket.

"Don't shoot," the woman shouted in English. Without dropping the bag, she shoved the mesh hood away from her face. Kathryn didn't know whether to trust her senses. A man with close-cropped hair and pale, freshly shaved cheeks said, "It's me."

Only then did Kathryn recognize the Mullah. "That money doesn't belong to you," she told him.

"But Tomas is dead and—"

"It wasn't his either. Give it to me."

Sidling forward, the Mullah made no move to hand over the bag. "It is bad to talk now. Somebody may see. Better in the car."

"Stand still." She felt a wobbliness in her legs and heard it in her voice. The Mullah had to have heard it too.

"There is not the time to argue," he said. "I have run away as a woman. But enemies are after me. On the ride, I explain."

He was right. They didn't have time to talk. Leveling the gun at his back, she gestured for him to lead the way to the road. As they negotiated the path between cotton rows, the Mullah ripped off the *burqa* with his free hand and let it float off behind them. Bellying with air like a wind sock, it sailed a great distance. Under it, he wore the tunic that had been his bellboy uniform at the hotel.

"With this money, I rebuild the mosque," he said. "Then peace returns."

"It's Zack's. He's hurt. He needs help."

But as they reached the Mullah's car, Kathryn knew the Lada couldn't cross the cotton fields, much less the canals and the steppes that lay between here and the irrigation pipe. And it was futile to spend hours hiking there. The Mullah and she together couldn't carry Zack. Even empty-handed, Kathryn doubted she had it in her to cover the distance again. "We have to hurry," she said.

"Where?" the Mullah wanted to know.

"To the capital. The U.S. consulate."

Gladly, he scrambled behind the wheel and she got in on the passenger's side, still pointing the PSM. The bag rested on the seat between them, leaking water. When he switched the key in the ignition, the engine backfired and the buzzards took wing. Then as he drove away the birds dived back onto the bodies.

The Mullah talked. Kathryn scarcely listened. He quoted the Koran. She didn't answer or react. Her stomach cramped, her eyelids were heavy, her grip on the feather-light pistol weakened. She nodded off and woke with a start.

The Mullah had tipped over the bag, and the tampons washed out onto the plastic upholstery with the last of the water.

"I save you," he said. "You save your friend. We both have half."

She didn't argue. No matter how much he stole, she wouldn't shoot him—not as long as he drove her to the consulate.

Steering with his left hand, he scraped the damp dollar bills free of the cardboard mulch and flattened them to the seat. Then he counted them. Or tried to. He lost track in English and resumed in Russian. But flabbergasted by the amount, he dropped into dialect. Even then he had a hard time computing the numbers and repeated himself, like Zack counting cadence.

"So many dollars," he said. "It gives me joy—the good I will do."

Despite herself, Kathryn dozed again. Her chin fell to her chest and she jerked upright. The Mullah rattled on talking and, at the same time, sorted the money into roughly equal stacks. Kathryn didn't watch his hands. She focused on his face. Without the beard he looked less intimidating, but no more dependable. At any second she feared he would push her out onto the pavement.

He asked what had become of the *djinn*, the satanic child who had caused all the trouble in the town. Since she didn't trust him not to hunt the boy down, Kathryn claimed that he had been killed, his body burned beyond recognition in the Land Cruiser.

"Praise be to Allah," he exclaimed. "This is why we are saved."


*R*ocketing past cotton fields whose rows at this speed flowed backward like the fletches of an arrow, they spied at the horizon the smudge of industrial grime and smoke that hovered above the capital. They passed factories, rusting military vehicles, deflated storage tanks. Men hunkered beside the road, stationary as toadstools, only their eyes shifting to track the passage of traffic. Where the road turned into a two-lane highway, boys tended goats and cattle grazing on the median strip.

The Mullah stuffed one stack of cash into his tunic. He encouraged

Kathryn to conceal her share. "In this city they see money, they smell it, and they are crazy with greed."

Never lowering the pistol, she folded the damp bills into her pockets, down the front of her shirt and into her bra. For the first time she allowed herself to believe that there was a chance the Mullah would keep his word and Zack would be saved. They came to a lane of low-slung stucco cottages and stopped in front of the steel gate at the U.S. Consulate. The Mullah raced the engine in neutral, anxious to be gone. But he permitted himself the courtesy of wishing her good-bye and good luck. Then she climbed out and he sped off in a spray of gravel.

Thinking the worst of the ordeal was over, Kathryn slipped the tiny pistol into one pocket and took her passport out of the other. The gate resounded under her knuckles. An eyehole shot open. She flashed her ID, shouted that she was an American citizen and needed to speak to Ms. Pearson.

An instant later, she was inside the compound, under the wire canopy tented over the courtyard. Two Marines frisked her, and as dollars in various denominations fell in confetti around her feet, a third man barked questions. He demanded that she state her business, account for the thousands in cash, explain where she was from and why she was covered in blood. When they patted her down and found the PSM, they flung her to the ground.

"Someone's dying," she sobbed. "You have to help him."

They flex-cuffed her, cinching a plastic band around her wrists, and escorted her into a cell where the furniture was bolted to the floor. The Marines left and two women wearing latex gloves showed up with a jar of KY Jelly. While they strip-searched her and probed her body cavities, Kathryn begged them to listen. She had to speak to Ms. Pearson. She kept saying that until she felt a sharp jab in her buttock and the sedative knocked her out.

She dreamed that she was back on the steppes, down in the dirt, studying the matted roots of grass. Insects scuttled over her, inside her. They landed on her arms and laid eggs that burrowed into her skin. She scratched at the eggs until larvae wriggled from her flesh, sprouted wings and flew away.

A prim, well-groomed woman disrupted the dream. Was it her mother? No, this woman was younger, dressed in a stylish pantsuit, her tinted hair neatly parted down the middle. Her expression suggested that Kathryn smelled bad, and that Ms. Pearson—that's who it had to be—didn't relish being cooped up in the same small cell with her. Still, she was persistent in her questioning and patient in listening.

Kathryn's tongue felt too large for her mouth. She had difficulty controlling it and speaking coherently as she implored Ms. Pearson to send a rescue team for Zack. If they retraced the road to the wrecked Land Cruiser, she said, then pushed on through the fields past the remains of the dead and into the steppes toward the mountains, they'd come to the concrete pipe.

Again a sharp jab ended her frenzied babble, and Kathryn slipped in and out of sleep. Semiconscious, she felt a team of medics insert an IV in her wrist and a feeding tube up her nose. Before she blacked out the last words she was aware of were "dehydration" and "hysteria."


*P*eriodically Ms. Pearson provided updated reports. She punctuated them by asking, Are you awake? Do you understand? Eventually—it must have been days later—she informed Kathryn, "You're lucky to be alive. Do you understand?"

Kathryn didn't.

"Our people found the pipe. But there was nobody in it, just a rifle and some notebooks. Are you awake?"

She wished that she weren't.

"Are the notebooks yours?"

She nodded and noticed that the feeding tube had been removed from her nose.

"You're welcome to them, but there could be a problem about the money. We'll need to know where you got it."

"It's not mine. It's Zack's," Kathryn managed to say.

"And where did he get it?" Ms. Pearson wanted to know.

"He brought it with him."

"He didn't declare it to customs."

Kathryn fell quiet.

"If he doesn't show up, what do we do with it?" Ms. Pearson asked.

"He'll show up. Keep looking for him."

"Hey, don't fade on me. You can sleep on the plane. We're medevacking you."

"I'd rather stay until you find him."

"No, you wouldn't. It's better for you to be in the States. Reports are filtering in from up-country. People there are searching for you."

Kathryn shut her eyes and said she was tired.

"A lot of locals died in a very short time," Ms. Pearson said, "and questions are being asked about McClintock. You understand?"

Kathryn didn't answer.

"Do you know anything about the killings? Are you awake?"

Kathryn pretended that she wasn't. Whether Zack was alive or dead she knew of no better way to repay him than to keep her mouth shut. It was the last lesson in the arduous process of language acquisition—learning when words were worthless and silence invaluable.

*L*ate the night that Kathryn had left for the road, the pipe rocked and swayed, pitching Zack out of sleep. It felt as though tectonic plates were colliding in a seismic storm at the high end of the Richter scale. But it wasn't an earthquake that woke him. The pipe was motionless and he was shuddering like a drunk with terminal d.t.'s and a gut-wrenching hangover.

He wrapped himself in the carpet, which smelled of the boy and retained some of his body heat. Burrowing into it, he sought comfort and oblivion. But while his violent shakes eventually gave way to shivering, his mind drifted amid rattling chains of strange associations. As he squinted from the pipe toward the mountains, he imagined himself loaded down the barrel of a cannon, about to be shot through space, like one of those circus clowns that torpedo into a safety net at the far end of the Big Top. Somewhere miles away, the kid was running, and Zack attempted to calculate how much gunpowder would be required to propel him that far and reunite them. And what would it take for him to catch up with Kathryn?

Yet as he reckoned the distance, the thrown weight and theoretical trajectory, he didn't doubt for a moment that he had made the right decision. He had done everything in his power to allow Kathryn, the kid and himself a shot at surviving. If he died now, it would be with the conviction that he wasn't one of those men who claim to be rescuers, but end up ruining everything.

As his shivering subsided, he became aware of something popping out of his skin. He touched his fingertips to his face and felt spines of glass in his cuts. One by one, he tweezed them out. The task was painful, but obsessed with the idea of dying clean, Zack was determined to rid himself of the last shreds of a septic identity.

Afterward, he crawled from the pipe down the embankment and dipped his face forward. The irrigation canal opened a seam in the earth that had sucked in long beaded strings of stars. A breeze combed across the scum and mosquito larvae, scrawling a sentence Zack couldn't decipher. Then the wind died and the stream cleared, and what he couldn't accept as his own reflection rose up, horrible as the hatchling of some creature breaking out of its egg.

His mind recoiled, an octopus squirting ink in self-defense, and he ducked his head under the water and held it there a long time. That cooled the cuts and brought some clarity to his thoughts. Then he pulled back and drank. Storing up as much liquid as his belly could carry, he lumbered back to the pipe fat as a camel.

With the assault rifle on one side of him and Kathryn's notebooks on the other, Zack rolled up in the carpet but couldn't sleep. In the first light of false dawn, he flipped through one of the journals. The pages of handwriting made less sense to him than the wind-scrawl on the water had. Every line seemed to be in shorthand or a secret code reserved for scholars. He couldn't understand Kathryn's observations about him any better than he could her comments about the boy's learning curve.

It dawned on him that he must be delirious. This wasn't the time or place for wool gathering anyway. He should have depended on the set drill he had been trained to follow. Locked in the drone-zone, letting muscle memory to compensate for his fragile mind, he should have broken down the AK-74, analyzed how it differed from the original Kalashnikov, and counted the rounds in the clip. He needed to devise a frank, no-shit assessment of his situation, prepare to defend himself, and just as crucial, prepare to be evacuated when the consulate sent a combat search and rescue team.

But Zack couldn't bring himself to do it. He didn't believe a CSAR team was on the way, and now that Kathryn and the kid were gone, he saw no point in plans, no point in defending himself. The notion of going down fighting, taking as many people with him as possible, had no appeal. He had done more killing than he cared to recall and had no patience with acting like a soldier any longer.

He let his mind roam. He slept and in due course dreamed. The boy and he were in Kathryn's kitchen staring at each other. As always, he wished they could talk. He had questions to ask, and there were things he longed to tell the kid. He'd like to say he was sorry and that he knew how it felt to be half-human, to fall somewhere in between, to be eager to find solace on either side of an invisible divide.

But it occurred to him that the boy would have questions of his own and might ask how Zack came to be as he was. He couldn't imagine how to account for his blemishes to a blameless child. He had had the same difficulty with Adrienne—explaining, or rather avoiding any explanation of, his absences, his moods, his failings as a father.

The idea that he still faced the problem of telling her what had happened to Fletcher popped Zack's eyes open, and he confronted his sorry reflection in convex mirrors that were almond shaped and agate colored. He sat up, disbelieving. But after a blinding head rush, he realized this was real. Joy poured through him, a drug so powerful that his pain disappeared. The boy had returned.

Apart from the crisscross of the harness straps on his shoulders, all outward evidence of his time with Kathryn had vanished overnight. Mud caked his legs to the knees and his arms to the elbows, and there was straw matted in a ruff down his spine. Brambles had scored his brown skin, and the soles of his feet, soft from captivity, bled a little.

In his cupped hands, the kid carried fat white grubs, legless crickets and grasshoppers, speckled bird's eggs, and a porridge of weeds chewed to pulp. Proud of himself, he picked a single grub out of the wriggling mass and put it to Zack's mouth as he had watched Kathryn do with mashed vegetables as Zack recuperated on the kitchen table. When Zack turned away, the boy dropped the grub into his own mouth, demonstrating. Then he bit into a cricket with a loud crunch.

From Marine Corps training, Zack knew the nutritional value of bugs and roots and berries. He wasn't surprised to see the kid eat them. What startled him was how uncannily he imitated Kathryn, her murmuring reassurances, the maternal show and tell. Sticking a straw into an egg, the boy sucked up the yolk, then urged him to do the same. He gave him crickets and grasshoppers, and made chewing gestures. Zack bit into them gingerly with his cracked teeth. They tasted acidic, like citrus juice that had curdled.

The effort of eating tired him. He lay back on the folded carpet and expressed his gratitude to the boy in sign language. Soon benign dreams were transporting Zack to a time so remote that Stefanie was still alive. She was in a bathing suit, a one-piece Jansen with the diving-girl logo on the hip. She stood in calm, clear water with shoals of silvery minnows around her ankles. Then Zack was in the warm, healing water with her, and the minnows nibbled at him in a kind of kissing caress.

When he woke, it was dark, and he sensed the boy, smelled him. He had brought fistfuls of mud up from the canal and was rubbing it on Zack's face, covering his cuts. Afterward he applied a poultice to his head. Awful as the muck smelled, it was better than the coppery stink of blood, and it kept the flies and mosquitoes off him. Zack let the boy lave it over every inch of his skin.

By morning, he felt stronger. The wind bore intimations of mountain air and ice melt and the faint suggestion of cedar trees and cedar smoke. Breathing it in, he remembered the first time he had smelled that intoxicating odor, the aroma of home, of kitchen fires in winter and breakfast cooking. He believed he had smelled it even before he was born. Maybe men entered the world with memories, Zack thought, and that was what brought the boy back, some lasting recollection of blood kin.

But he recognized that it was dangerous for the kid to keep coming and going from the pipe. The wrong people might follow him here. Even the right ones—Kathryn or somebody from the U.S. Consulate—would want to re-capture him, while Zack wanted him up in the cedar-scented mountains.

Later that day, when the boy showed up with a banquet of berries and bugs, tuberous roots and a melon the size of a baseball, Zack wolfed the food down. Though he couldn't distinguish the sour berries from the sweet beetles, he devoured them all. Taking time to savor the melon, he gnawed its thirst-quenching pulp, and licked and scraped out the rind.

Then seeing no alternative, he was ready to chase him away. The kid viewed this as play, a rough and tumble game. When Zack shoved him, he seized his hand, pulling him out of the pipe toward the ocean of grass. Zack let himself go a short distance before he dug in his heels and pushed the boy again. He made a shooing motion, signaling that he had had enough. Recess was over. The pupil should trot along. But the boy wouldn't leave without him.

Retreating to the shade of the pipe, Zack turned the matter in his mind, slow and thorough as a stone milling grain. The solution seemed clear. He considered scribbling Kathryn a note. He didn't want her thinking he had run out on her or that she had failed him. He wasn't acting in disappointment or despair. He had seldom felt such a sure sense of mission, and if he couldn't spell it out in words, that was only because he had nothing to write with.

But he arranged the rifle as a paperweight atop her notebooks and aimed it in the direction he intended to take. To his thinking, the discarded AK-74 read like a road sign that Kathryn should have no trouble comprehending. It meant that he hadn't been killed or captured. He had departed under his own steam without firing a shot and had no need of a weapon where he was going. He planned to walk the boy to the mountains, put him on the right path, then re-trace his steps to the pipe and wait for her.

Light-headed, lighthearted, they waded across the canal just after dark and advanced into a hip-deep swale of wind-tossed grass. It beat at their legs, parting and closing in smooth waves behind them. The boy plunged ahead, frisking and diving, surfacing with a shout and sometimes with a thing he had caught—a locust, a moth or lizard. After they ate it, they set out again, always toward the mountains.

Zack soon lost any sense that he was leading. He followed the boy, floating in his wake, scarcely aware of effort or pain. He picked up his feet and put them down. He ate what the kid gave him and wondered whether some of the weeds he chewed on might have had narcotic properties. The scent of crushed grass reminded him of summers in Virginia, of baseball diamonds, damp lawns, picnic grounds and his high school prom forty years ago.

At daybreak, the steppes were starred with flowers. Poppies, buttercups and lupin grew wild, as did pistachio bushes with silvery limbs and reddening nuts. He saw the sun rise in the boy's eyes. Flames rimmed the edge of his own irises. He inhaled the odor of camel-thorn, a shrub that exuded the fragrance of fire, and he passed saksaul trees that had been tortured by wind into grotesque shapes. They grew almost horizontal, their gnarled trunks sprawling along the ground like roots nourished by air rather than earth. All aspects of the upside-down world Zack was becoming accustomed to.

The kid hazed him along as a collie would shepherd a lamb. When they needed sleep, he brought them to a patch of shade beneath one of the saksauls. Bedding down in the warm sand, Zack thought he was hallucinating, but the tree's leaves did, in fact, resemble pinkish-grey feathers.

By nightfall, he had no knowledge of where the day had disappeared to or when they had resumed walking. The tightness in his calves told him they were climbing and had been for a long time. That was all that mattered. The air was sharper, the stars brighter, and the snowcapped mountains leaned close. As they emerged from the grass, moving from the steppes up into the foothills, they followed a fan of gravel and flints. But the footing turned treacherous as they entered a defile where no moonlight penetrated. Zack and the boy both barked their shins and stumbled blindly into boulders.

Sheltering under an overhanging ridge, they might have been at the bottom of a quarry, resting on rock tailings. But that didn't prevent Zack from plummeting into beatific dreams. In Kathryn's kitchen, he watched her through an ether of sunlight. She had just washed her hair and stood at the window drying it. Eyes shut, face serene, she shook her head from side to side, whipping her auburn tresses back and forth. She seemed to be dancing, inviting Zack to join in. The image was so vivid, his desire so keen, it drew him toward her.

The clatter of hooves woke him. Horses were pounding up the canyon in dawn light, chasing the boy. A dozen of them. Only as an afterthought did it register with Zack that the animals had riders. Sun-blackened figures clung on with their knees and sawed their arms in the air, shouting commands at the horses and at each other. A slurry of shale flew out from the shod hooves as they harried the kid toward the ridge. They thought they had him cornered and closed in. But at the last second he skimmed up the cliff face and vanished.

Then the riders spotted Zack, and their shouts died, their arms dropped. The horses went motionless and monolithic as charcoal sketches on a cave wall. Animals and men peered at him as if at an apparition that the wild child had changed into—the naked boy supplanted by this fantasm in clothes stiff with blood, an effigy molded out of mud that had melted in places. His bare arms and hands bore a brown crust, but around his eyes, nostrils and lips it had crumbled, and at the crown of his skull, the poultice formed a dull point, like a horn that had broken off.

The men called to him, and he responded. What he said sounded like no human tongue, and they muttered among themselves that he and the boy might be father and son, if such links existed between beings so extraordinary. Having watched the little one escape, they were determined not to let the big one get away. The riders dismounted and spread out, intent on taking him alive. They cut off every avenue of flight except the cliff face. If he could scale that, they were willing to concede that there was no catching him.

But Zack didn't make a move to flee, nor did he give any menacing gesture or growl. Swaying unsteadily, he held out his hands, as though he wouldn't mind being manacled. Then he jabbed a thumb at the dry hole of his mouth. He wanted water.

They grabbed and tied him to a saddle, securing his legs at the ankle with a rope they passed under the horse's belly. Then, unplugging the hoof of a goatskin bag, they squirted warm, tar-tasting water between his swollen lips. He drank, to their astonishment, like any other man.

Soon he sat up and seemed ready to ride. As they set off at a canter out of the canyon and along the scree at the bottom of the hill, they noticed that despite his docility in allowing himself to be captured and his failure to escape by assuming a different shape, he had started to change after all. With each hoof-fall of the horse, Zack's outer shell cracked and the mud flaked off, then the scabs and splinters of glass.

Later, some would describe him as like a snake shedding its skin. Others said he was more like an insect in the chrysalis stage just before it sprouts wings and flies away. But as they rode on, they witnessed a metamorphosis far more remarkable and sent word ahead of them so that others might see him. By the time they reached their village and were awaiting word from the capital as to what they should do next, this man of full growth, well along in life, much nearer the end than the beginning, had turned pink and tender as a newborn baby.